Burying Steele

H. B. Tyler

BURKWOOD
Media Group

Burkwood Media Group
P O Box 29448
Charlotte, NC 28229
www.burkwoodmedia.com

Printed in the United States of America

ISBN:978-0-578-62538-6

Dedication

For Cindy, my person.

Acknowledgements

I would like to start by thanking Cris Steele and Jeff Bolton for the use of their names, as the fictitious characters share some of their wonderful qualities. They are both strong, good hearted, caring people; who are willing to sacrifice, go out of their way to help others and put them before themselves. I am thankful to have met them both.

There are also many people I would like to thank for their expertise and help in the writing of this book.

First and foremost, a special thanks to Debra Funderburk for her endless patience and putting up with me throughout the publishing process.

Thank you, to Cindy, Georgia, Gwen, Marla, Stephanie and all my Breaking Steele fans pushing me to hurry up with the sequel.

Last, but certainly not least, my family who continues to stand by and enthusiastically support me as I have locked myself away to write or walked around musing about another world that was entirely in my head.

As with the previous book, Breaking Steele, if I have missed anyone, with my sleep deprived brain, please accept my sincerest apologies.

No doubt, there are some errors in the book, and they are all mine.

"If I must die, I will encounter darkness as a bride, and hug it in mine arms."
~William Shakespeare

A Note from HB Tyler

This is Book 2 in the Steele series. You really need to read Breaking Steele first to better understand the background of the story and characters. I suggest you get Breaking Steele immediately and read this one right after. If you're too stubborn to wait, here is the last chapter of Breaking Steele. It will, however, ruin much of Breaking Steele when you read it and already know the end, but it is right where Burying Steele picks up.

Prelude

Chief had just finished getting the last of the bags out of the back when Pete pulled in. Stormy sitting in the passenger seat of his truck, her whole body moving with excitement as she saw her mommy and her home. Pete came rushing over to the side of the SUV where Cris and Chief were standing.

"Go ahead, Chief, get back to the station. I'll help Cris with her bags."

"Thanks, Bryan. I appreciate it." Chief looked over at her. "Steele, I'll catch up with you later."

Cris mumbled under her breath, "Yes, you certainly will."

Pete started walking to his truck as Chief pulled out, he yelled back to Cris, "Hang on, I'm going to grab Stormy. You can love on her while I gather your bags."

Before she could even respond about the bag carrying, Stormy came bounding over and jumped up on her. Her heart immediately melted and the bizarre conversation she had just been having with Chief faded away. She sat on her front lawn so Stormy didn't knock her down. She felt so much lighter with Stormy by her side. This dog was their baby, and she still couldn't help but feel a part of Luke was living on through her.

Pete came over and joined them on the lawn, looked at them and smiled. "Aw, the simple joys a dog can bring. I know I've enjoyed spending these last few days with her. She's so happy to see you."

He spoke a little quieter. "And so am I. Although, I have to say, between your arm and your head you look the worse for wear. I thought you were kidding when you said you got a little scratch on your arm. Damn, Cris."

Cris tried to speak through Stormy twirling around her, sniffing and licking her.

"They're both a long way from my heart, I'll survive. Thank you for taking care of her for me Pete; it was really nice to know I didn't have to worry about her." Cris decided to ignore the other part he said about her arm and being happy to see her.

As Stormy started to calm down slightly, she focused on sniffing Cris' bandaged head, suddenly seeming concerned. "It's okay, Storm. Momma's okay. Things are gonna start calming down now girl, I'm gonna stop coming home smelling like blood."

Pete chuckled. "That would be nice, sounds like a good goal after this past week! Campbell filled me in, whether I wanted her to or not. It sounds like it was a pretty eventful couple of days."

"Yeah, sorry, I have no control over that girl. I should probably send the Jasper PD a sympathy card for having to put up with us."

Pete smirked. "I'm sure the two of you spiced things up a bit up there for those country boys."

"I was actually pleasantly surprised and quite impressed with a lot of their technology and equipment. It was kinda like a hidden gem or something."

"Well, we are all certainly glad to have you back. I'm not sure about Campbell, but you for sure." Pete gave a little laugh.

Cris didn't respond to his comment and again looked up to the empty house. "Speaking of which, I guess it's time to get back to reality."

Pete stood up. "You okay to handle Stormy? If so, I'll grab your bags."

Cris kept a hold of Stormy's leash as she stood. She saw stars and things swirled briefly, but she tried not to let on.

"Yes, I can handle this wild beast, huh, girl?!" She gave Stormy a pet on the head and moved on to scratch her ears.

They walked up the porch steps together. Upon reaching the door, Cris remembered her house keys were in the hospital bag.

"Oh, you actually have my house keys in one of those bags."

"That's okay, I'll just use mine, it's easier than digging yours out." Pete quickly pulled out his key ring, unlocked and held the door open for Cris and Stormy.

Cris took Stormy's leash off, and she took off tearing through the house. "Guess she's glad to be home."

Pete set the bags down just inside the door. "I'm sure she is. She was very content at my place, but there's no place like home."

Pete gently placed his hand on Cris' shoulder. "I'm going to go grab her stuff from the truck. I'll be right back."

Cris picked up the bags from the floor and carried them to the couch and began unpacking them. Once she set the supply bags for the Vets aside, she was only left with her backpack and hospital bag. She walked to the bedroom with her backpack. Going into the closet, she placed her dirty clothes in the basket, and only gave a quick glance at Luke's dirty clothes still laying there that she refused to move. She heard the front door shut and knew Pete had come back in. She shook her head as she shut off the light and left the closet, closing the door, and Luke's clothes, behind her.

She finished emptying the bag in the bathroom where she quickly put away her toiletries. Going out to hang the empty backpack in the coat closet, she noticed Pete putting Stormy's things back in place and was staring at the closed door to the office as he passed it.

Shit, I forgot about the office! I hope he didn't go in while I was away and see my own war room I've got going on for Luke. Nothing I can do about it now if he did. She wondered if he caught her staring at him, staring at the door. She straightened her shoulders as best as she could muster and kept walking.

She turned just slightly and yelled back to Pete. "I'm going to go check the mail quick, I'll be right back."

"Okay."

Cris took the short walk out to her mailbox and wondered why she told Pete she was coming out to check the mail. It wasn't like it was his business, he wasn't Luke. Then, she realized it was a habit she had with Luke that she wasn't even aware of. She grabbed the stack of mail from the mailbox alongside the road. She was hoping none of her neighbors were out as she tried to hurry back in. With all the police activity last weekend, her outburst, and now being all bandaged up, they must really wonder what the hell was going on.

She walked back in to see Stormy playing and jumping all over Pete. Hearing Stormy's bark and Pete's laugh automatically made Cris smile, whether she wanted it to or not. Pete must have heard her come back in even through Stormy's antics because he looked over at her.

"Hey, Cris, what did you have planned for dinner? All that food you have is frozen. I've got nothing going on. If you're up for some company, I thought maybe we could order in?"

Cris hadn't thought about dinner, she really didn't have much of an appetite. Even more, she didn't know how she felt about Pete staying for dinner. She was torn with her emotions with him right now. She couldn't help but still be suspicious of him, even if she had no solid evidence; other than a gut feeling. The fact that he hadn't found Luke's murderer in her book also made it logical to further warrant her suspicion. At the same time, he was still Pete who was always so nice to her and always so good with Stormy. Luke's death had definitely come between them, at least to her, and she really didn't know if she was being logical or not.

She noticed Pete had come to the entryway of the dining room. Trying to avoid eye contact and answer the question right away, she looked over at the breakfast bar. She saw a piece of paper laying there and grabbed it. No matter how much she didn't want to, she couldn't hold back the smile as she read Pete's bill for his cleaning services. She glanced at Pete as she shook her head and snickered.

Setting the "bill" back down, Cris picked up the mail again and turned to set it on the table. *I'll deal with this later, right now I guess I have to see how I'm going to deal with Pete.* When she set the mail down, she saw a piece of paper folded in half sitting in the middle of it. She knew she left the table completely clear before she left.

She turned to look at Pete as she pointed to the paper. "Is this yours too? Did you leave that there?"

Pete walked over towards the table, looking as he shook his head no. "Nothing I brought in. It was probably something you left there when you left."

"No. I know I have a head injury, but I am positive the table was clear."

Cris picked up the plain white paper and opened it, reading it to herself. The message inside was typed on a computer in a large font:

You are a sick coward bitch! You throw your husband in front of you to take the bullet instead of yourself. I will make sure I get you alone next time and I will not miss! Sweet dreams bitch!

In her peripheral vision, Cris vaguely saw Pete come rushing over as she gave a whimper, put her right hand over her mouth and slowly dropped to her knees.

CHAPTER 1

Detective Pete Bryan was lost internalizing his thoughts as he walked into the dining room with Stormy tight to his side. He could tell Detective Cris Steele was avoiding answering his question about ordering in for dinner. Typical Cris. But damn her, he did momentarily forget about her avoidance when she looked on the bar and smiled after seeing his "bill" for the cleaning services. His world stopped for a fraction of a second. The twisting, turning, emotional roller coaster ride of Cris quickly resumed when she sarcastically chastised him about her head being injured, indicating she knew exactly how she had left things. *Of course, she does!*

Still being tossed on her roller coaster, Pete wasn't ready for the sudden plummet into hell that ensued. Opening the questionable piece of paper, Pete watched Cris' pale face transform to albino. He stared helplessly as she covered her mouth with her right hand and whimpered as she dropped to her knees by the dining room table. The note that brought her there now fell from her left hand, fluttering to the floor like a feather slowly, cunningly, stealing a ride on a breeze.

Pete ran over to Cris, half tripping over Stormy en route. He grabbed her around the torso, trying to lift Cris to her feet though she was still doubled over. Pete stole a glance at the typed note that landed face up to see what could have possibly given this tough woman this reaction. *What the hell?!*

His thoughts started spinning and racing like a squirrel on speed. *Who wrote this? How did they get in? When did they get in?* Pete didn't remember seeing it when he cleaned the kitchen a few days ago. Cris was right, the table had been clear.

Instinctively, Pete went into detective mode. He knew enough not to touch it without gloves on his hands. It would now be evidence. Pete had been the lead on this case and had just concluded it an accident. Even though he really looked incompetent now, Pete knew this would still be landing right back in his lap.

He squeezed her a little tighter. "Shit, Cris, I'm sorry! Don't touch it again though. I've gotta call this in and have forensics come dust and look for prints."

Hearing Pete's voice obviously cleared her head as Cris came out of a trance. Her crystal blue eyes looked up and a shiver slithered up Pete's spine. The look Cris gave him was colder than a brass toilet seat in the Arctic. He tried to steady himself. Pete swore he could see the switch flip in her cold, narrowed eyes. Cris didn't disappoint Pete's ability to read her. The sharp tongue she was known for sliced through his veins as she rose the rest of the way to her feet, ramrod straight, never breaking her accusatory eye contact.

"*You*, are the only other *living* person who has my house key."

Cris was pointing her finger in Pete's face now, backing him up towards the wall. "How convenient for *you* that you were

Stormy's sitter while I was away on the case, so your fingerprints *should* be in the house?"

Pete didn't think it was possible, but while still pushing him backward, her eyes got even more narrow as Cris continued the attack. "You knew how to murder my husband to make it look like an accident, you also knew you would be assigned to the case. Again, how convenient for *you*? The perfect opportunity to rule it as a hunting accident. You knew just how to plan that too. Make sure there was minimal evidence on the scene. It would be the only logical explanation, not much convincing would be needed."

When Cris inhaled to begin the next barrage of evidence in her head against him, Pete knew enough to steal the opportunity. He grabbed her. All 5'2" of her was fighting him, but Pete stood his ground and pulled Cris in and held her. Hard.

Trying his best to both restrain and soothe Cris, Pete spoke softly and calmly. "It's okay, let it out. I'm not letting you go. Cry, yell at me, blame me, curse at me, beat me, do whatever you gotta do. I don't care, just get it out. Stop keeping shit bottled up. I'm going to be here for you no matter what. I promise you; I'll find this sick bastard and prove my innocence. Right now, just get it out."

Pete began caressing the back of her head as Cris slowly eased up on resisting him and began to hesitantly calm down. As Cris loosened up, Pete gingerly pulled her head tighter to his shoulder, careful to avoid her injured side while trying to console her. Gradually, although there was an almost imperceptible tremor, Pete could feel her tension slightly release. He rested his head on top of hers, slowly and inconspicuously inhaling the scent of her hair and squeezing a little tighter.

His temporary utopia was quickly wrenched away. Pete felt the separation coming in the flexing of her muscles even before she physically began pulling away. Cris was back. He could see the hardness in her eyes, her wheels turning. With a faint shake the slight emotion Cris almost showed was gone. She was suddenly like a tornado in a trailer park.

"Where's my phone? I have to call Chief. I'm going to find this asshole myself, prove his guilt and watch him fry."

Pete did not miss the fact that Cris turned to look at him while she accentuated the last part. He shook his head as he pulled his cell phone from the holster on his belt.

"I'll call Chief. You might want to calm Stormy. She can tell you're upset, look at her."

Cris looked over to where Pete pointed. Stormy had backed herself into a wall with her tail between her legs and ears pinned back. The saddest big brown eyes were looking between Cris and Pete.

Scurrying over, Cris was full of sorrow and love. "Aw, Storm. I'm sorry girl, it's okay."

Leaving them in the dining room, Pete walked into the living room to call Chief. He stood in front of the window looking past the empty swing on the front porch and into the yard. He was dawdling again. This was the second time in the past few days. Pete was not a procrastinator at all, this case had changed him in ways he couldn't have imagined. The realization of this flaw irritated him, and he quickly pulled up Chief's name in his contacts and hit the call button a little too hard.

Chief Jeff Bolton answered on the second ring. "Bryan, what's up?"

"Hey, Chief. I'm sorry to bother you. I know you got called in for a shit storm there, but do you have a minute?"

"Yes. I actually got this under control quickly. Knowing I was here dealing with this, you wouldn't be calling me unless it was important. What's wrong?"

Pete could hear the genuine concern in Chief's voice and couldn't hold back his annoyance. Anything that had to do with Cris seemed more important or worrisome. Like Chief was protective of her. Pete hadn't noticed it up until this past week, little things here and there. He found it increasingly difficult not to notice, ignore it, or let it go. It was really getting under his skin now.

"Bryan, what's going on there?" Impatience was in Chief Bolton's voice now.

Snapping out of his hostility, Pete came back to the situation. "Sorry, sir. We have a storm here now too. Steele found a note on the table. It's from Luke's killer. Apparently, she was the intended target. I think it would be best if you could come back."

Atypically, it took Chief a second before answering. "Are you sure it's from the killer? Never mind, of course you are, or you wouldn't have called me. Is forensics already on their way?"

"No. I'll call them next; you were the first call on my list."

"Thanks, I appreciate that. Don't worry about the calls, I'll make them now. I'm heading out the door. You go take care of Steele. How's she taking it?"

Pete wanted to tell him, *"Like the grown ass woman that she is,"* but thankfully thought better of it by the time he opened his mouth. Knowing Cris was in the other room and could hear, Pete also wanted to be careful with what he said. He softly responded, "The usual stubborn, hardheaded, wall up, bury emotions way."

"Mm-hmm, no surprise there. Try to be with her as much as she will let you. I'll be right there to help out along with the crime scene techs."

"Thanks, see you soon."

The call was disconnected, and Pete took one final look at the lonely porch swing. He could almost see Cris sitting with her legs straight out along the length of the painted white wood, her back resting against a pillow. Her infectious smile as she was laughing at something Luke had said while he was sitting next to her in the matching white rocking chair. Cris' throat exposed as she throws her head back laughing, then stealthily rolls on her side to reach over and hit Luke in the arm. Pete wondered if the chair and swing would stay empty and lonely now, or if maybe someday he could get her to sit out there again. Forced out of his daze, Pete's thoughts were tersely abandoned as Stormy came bounding into him.

Unable to resist, Pete kneeled to pet her. "Hey there girl, what are you doing? Did you not see me standing here or were you that desperate to get my attention?"

Stormy's tail thwacked against the grey beach wood floor and she pushed her head harder into Pete's hands as he was petting her. Cris appeared over them, holding Stormy's red ball. Her face and body language indecipherable. Not happy, sad or mad. Just serious, all business Cris.

"She was trying to play with her ball and evidently lost control of where her body was in comparison to the space around her. I was trying to keep her out of the kitchen and dining room area, so it doesn't get any more screwed up than it already is."

Pete stood up. "I called Chief. He's on his way and is also reaching out to forensics. They should all be here soon. In the meantime, it might be a good idea to get out of the house. We wouldn't want to disturb any other potential evidence."

Narrowing her eyes again, Cris looked at Pete accusingly. "They will be here soon. I'm sure they won't find anything that didn't have some reason to be here anyway. If there was, we probably already messed it up." Cris took a deep breath and lost a little of the bite in her words. "Plus, I'm really not up for sitting outside all bandaged up for the neighbors to gawk at. I would probably open my mouth and I think we both know how that would go."

"Why make it any easier on this asshole? Let's not take a chance. C'mon. I'll pull my truck up further into the driveway and we can sit on the tailgate. Stormy will be safe up there with us and nobody will see. You're right, we don't need you going after the neighbors. We are going to have to be questioning some of them now."

Cris cut her eyes. "Screw it, whatever. Let's go."

She grabbed Stormy's leash and clasped it on her collar. The sound of the snap echoed through the silent house before Cris opened the door and briskly walked out.

Looking back, Pete spoke to the empty house. "Okay, I guess we're going outside then."

Pete swiftly walked out behind them, hauling his keys from his jeans pocket as he went. Cris and Stormy went around the corner of the house and up the driveway. Pete hopped into his truck, bringing the engine and exhaust roaring to life. He pulled forward about 15 feet to where Cris was waiting and stopped the pistons from pumping.

Quickly going to the back of the truck, Pete put the tailgate down while Stormy was pulling Cris to come over. Stormy mistakenly thought she was going to get another ride.

Effortlessly, Pete picked Stormy up and put her in the bed of the truck. "Sorry girl, not this time. This is probably a tease for you to just be sitting here." Pete turned to look at Cris. "I wouldn't normally ask you because I know better, but with your injuries I'd be remiss if I didn't. Do you need help getting up on the tailgate?"

Cris responded by cutting her eyes again and squaring her shoulders. "No. Thanks for the offer but I can manage. It's only a few bandages, I'm not a friggin' invalid."

Pete watched as Cris put her palms on the tailgate and wince as she lifted herself up. Not for the first time, he had to wonder why she was so damn stubborn and independent. Cris was a good and caring person when she thought no one was looking. But the wall she had was impenetrable. Even more so now with him since he hadn't solved her husband's murder. Cris was completely alone, albeit she wouldn't let anyone past her shield, nevertheless, Pete couldn't blame her for the confusion and feeling the way she did.

Jumping up to the other side of the tailgate, Pete thought back to the phone call about the blood on the kitchen baseboards and the concocted story Cris had given him. Pete was so thankful Cris was okay that he cleaned it up for her and made the bill as a joke to get a laugh out of her. Pete hadn't known about her bandaged arm then. He wondered what really happened and questioned if he should've cleaned up the blood. And now, the note.

"Listen Cris, this changes things. You need to get an alarm installed now. I'll give you back your house key. If you need me to watch Stormy, you'll have to let me in with the alarm. This will also remove future suspicion of me."

He figured Cris would probably agree with the key returning but disagree with the alarm. In her mind that would probably be saying she couldn't handle the killer on her own, she needed some form of help. A defamation to her character.

Cris looked at him, her face unreadable again. Pete was thankful to hear the county vehicles pulling up.

"Saved by the Cavalry."

CHAPTER 2

Cris never thought she would feel so relieved at the sight of crime scene tech vehicles at her own house. She was relieved to have other people around and not have to be alone with Pete anymore. Cris was always decisive about everything, especially her emotions. Luke's murder had shaken up her feelings about Pete and left her conflicted, unsettled and downright pissed off with herself. He was still good ol' Pete and Cris knew it, but she just couldn't deny the nagging feeling in the pit of her stomach. There were too many coincidences for her to dismiss so quickly and they kept growing instead of being reduced or going away.

Trying not to wince along the way, Cris hopped down from the tailgate. Her sneakers barely making a sound as they landed on the concrete driveway. Following suit, Pete slid forward slightly and firmly planted his feet. They both turned to face Stormy who was already creeping her way towards them, her tail doing an air assault.

Pete leaned in and reached for her leash. "C'mon girl, I'll help you down."

Cris tried to keep the venom out of her voice, but even she noticed her slightly clenched teeth and terse voice. "I can take her. You can head home if you need to. I'm sure Chief will contact you if he has any questions for you."

"I'll stay out here and watch Stormy while they do what they need to do inside. That way, you can stay focused on this. Tell them exactly how you found the note and anything else they may need to know. I'll be right here if Chief wants to question me. Since this is technically my case, if I wasn't here, he would be calling me to come investigate anyway." Pete looked calm as he wrapped the leash around his hand.

She wanted to disagree. Cris considered him on the suspect side instead of the investigative side now. Pete shouldn't be allowed to continue with the case. Before she could open her mouth and protest, which most likely would not have a good result as history had proved over and over, Cris heard a vehicle pulling into her driveway. She was thankful to see Chief Jeff Bolton pulling in alongside Pete's truck. His SUV lurched forward as he hit the brakes and slammed it into park.

Deciding not to respond to Pete and having to worry about what came out of her mouth, Cris left him standing there and curtly made her way over to Chief as he was lumbering out.

"Hey, Chief. Long time no see."

"Yea, no shit. This wasn't exactly what I had in mind for our next meeting."

"Pft, you and me both. So, what was the fire you had to go put out? Did Campbell crack a fingernail?"

"You always manage to keep your sense of humor, don't you? It was another department and it's all handled."

"Well, fantastic timing for you to get thrown into this shit show."

They started walking towards Pete, who was still standing near the back of his truck with Stormy. Cris wanted to keep going to the house but apparently Chief wanted to include him because they stopped there.

"Hey, Bryan. It sounds like we'll be reassessing this case again."

Cris was about ready to crawl out of her skin. She wanted to interject, to refuse to let him be involved in the case in any way. She clamped her jaw and squeezed her hands into fists, inadvertently cracking her knuckles and joints.

Pete looked at her from the corner of his eyes. "Yes, sir."

Bolton looked between Pete and Cris. "Steele, I know you have Stormy here, but you really need to have a security system installed."

"I just told her the same thing. She's obviously in danger."

Cris cocked a hip and crossed her arms over her chest. Chief was looking directly in her eyes, even though he was clearly talking to Pete.

"I agree. Bryan, can you stay here for a couple of nights if need be?" Chief must have seen a look on her face because he put his hand up to stop her. "Steele, you should not be here alone."

"I don't need someone to stay with me, I can handle myself."

"It looks like it with your bandaged head and arm."

Cris could feel a tick in her eye, her patience was stretched as far as it was going to be. There was no way she was going to let anyone spend the night with her, especially "Suspect Pete." Not only was she suspicious of him, but the couch was where she slept and Cris couldn't admit that to them. They couldn't know she wasn't strong enough to sleep in their bed. Fortunately, Cris caught a glimpse of movement in her peripheral vision. She turned to see forensics had all their paraphernalia out and were ready. *Perfect timing!*

"It looks like they're ready to get to work. Chief, if you would like to join me inside, I'll show them the note and where I found it." Cris blatantly looked at Pete as she continued speaking to Chief. "Then, we can also speak privately."

Without waiting for Chief to answer Cris turned on her heel and began walking away knowing he would follow. The techs were halfway through her front yard. She walked to the bottom of her porch steps and waited for them. Chief reached the porch about the same time.

"Hey, guys. Thanks for coming out. I don't expect you'll find anything that doesn't belong, so this should be quick for you. Come on in, I'll show you where I found the note."

They all followed Cris into the house and to the dining room table. "This is where the note was, folded in half at the center of the table. Thinking it was something Bryan left, I didn't have a second thought about grabbing it to read it. This is where it landed after I dropped it. Nothing else seems out of place or has been touched."

Cris knew the drill. She watched as they were scanning the kitchen and dining room with their eyes, already looking at possible entry and exit points. No doubt everyone in the room already knew the French doors were the most likely access point.

She turned to Chief. "Can we go talk in private, please?"

"As long as it's about this right here, then yes."

Cris knew exactly what he wasn't saying. They weren't going to talk about the bizarre conversation they had been having a short time ago when Chief was dropping her off. He had to run back to the office abruptly, leaving their very important discussion unfinished.

Trudging into the living room, they stopped next to the mantle. Blue candles and pictures of Luke and Cris were interspersed across it, beckoning her to look at them. Needing to focus and remain strong, or at least continue to pretend to, Cris put her back to the fireplace. She noticed Chief turned slightly so he wasn't looking directly at it either. His 6-foot frame loomed over her.

"Here's the deal. I'm willing to meet you halfway. I'll agree to the security system, but someone staying here with me, not happening."

Chief subtly shifted his weight, but Cris noticed. "I don't recall saying this was going to be an option up for debate."

"I don't recall seeing in my employment contract that you would be my surrogate father and tell me what I'm going to do in my personal life. Besides that fact, I am a grown, independent woman who can handle herself and don't need anyone, I'm not going to let my potential murderer sleep in the damn house with me!"

From the corner of her eye, Cris saw turned heads and quickly averted eyes from the forensics team. Cris knew they should probably take this elsewhere, but it was too late now.

Bolton sighed. "We are not going down this road again. We've had this dance before. I have no problem reminding you of your last outburst. I was clear that you wouldn't throw those accusations around unless you had some form of real, solid, evidence to back it up. Beyond a suspicion because he is too nice."

"He is too nice! Real evidence? What's his real agenda? Bryan had no alibis for the time of Luke's murder. He would know how to commit one and leave no evidence, as was the case. Bryan knew he would get assigned to the case. What more convenient way to rule it a hunting accident by an amateur? We're looking for involuntary manslaughter now. Finding this person is like finding a strip club with no poles. It's understandable if it goes unsolved. Bryan's off the hook, how convenient? And to top it all off, he has a key to my house; his prints are expected to be in here. What better way to jump on the opportunity?"

Bolton patiently cut her off, "Are you done? Think about it. Why would Bryan want to kill you that day with Luke there? Why would he want to kill you at all is the real question, but I'll play your little game here. He could have so many other opportunities to do it and make it look like an accident. Going after a suspect that went wrong would be a much more effective way."

"I can't answer that one. Yet."

Chief rambled on, "Also, why even leave the note? Bryan concluded Luke's case as a hunting accident. Like you said yourself, he's as good as off the hook, leaving more time to plot your murder so he wouldn't get caught. You're not thinking logically. He wouldn't be giving you a heads up and call more attention."

"Maybe this was his plan as a way to stay with me since he didn't get it right the first time. It would be too obvious if I ended up "accidently" shot too. Bryan could have an elaborate story and set up of someone breaking in. Conveniently, he doesn't hear any of it and the perp is gone when he wakes up and finds me dead. Chief, if I'm right and he's guilty, it's leading the lion right in my den. Let's just roll out the red carpet for him."

"First off, Bryan staying here was my idea, not his."

Cris cut him off, "He's smart and he knows you. Bryan knows the note would make you insist on this decision."

"Damn it, Cris! I don't know why you have a bee in your bonnet about this, but you're wrong. For the last time, I am telling you unless you have solid evidence, we are not having this discussion again."

"Speaking of discussions, I will remind you that we have another one to finish sooner than later. This distraction is only a temporary diversion from the insane chat we were having just a short time ago."

"Yes, we'll finish it, but this is not the time. We need to figure this mess out and secure your safety first."

Cris glared and exhaled loudly. "So, what if I refuse to have Bryan stay?"

"Either I will myself or I'll ask Campbell to."

"You need to be home with your wife. And, seriously? Campbell? You really think she's going to keep me safer than I'm going to keep myself? Plus, I've had enough of her this past week."

Bolton tilted his head slightly and held his hands out, as if to say, *well then?* "Sounds like Bryan it is."

Not responding for a moment, Cris went into an internal zone, her problem-solving ability in overdrive. She had to covertly come up with sleeping arrangements for herself. Also, the office had to remain closed and inaccessible. Nobody could see the war room she had set up. Logically, Cris knew she'd have to furtively set up camp in there somehow, while keeping the door always locked. It wouldn't be easy, but she would have to do it. Taking no chances and being prepared, her Smith & Wesson wouldn't leave her side.

"I'll get the alarm and let Bryan stay, but listen; I know you like I know myself, this would be a very big deal, a part of you would probably die. I'm warning you to remember this; this is your choice, not mine. If something happens to me while under Bryan's watch, it will be on your hands and conscience for the rest of your life."

CHAPTER 3

Pete was left standing in the driveway with Stormy, which was just fine with him. He watched as Chief followed Cris around like a little lost puppy dog. It caused a nerve to pulse in his temple, but he pushed it aside. Pete had enough other headaches to stew over, he didn't need to dwell on what Chief's "deal" with was Cris right now. That thought brought him back to the first time Cris accused him of being involved in Luke's murder. It was during her interview. After asking her about any accusations or uneasy feelings from parents or anyone about Luke with his students, Cris let loose and turned on him and even Bolton a little. She asked them both what their "deal" was; why were they both so nice? To Pete, it was a ludicrous question, but he took it with a grain of salt since he understood her state of mind. Even though she couldn't explain what Chief's "deal" was, Cris quickly excluded him because he was in the office at the time and therefore had an alibi. That's when she first unleashed on him.

Realizing he was starting to fixate on negative things he couldn't change, Pete walked away with Stormy hoping to clear his mind. There was nothing productive about rehashing what was said. Instead, Pete tried to focus on the different birds he heard chirping and singing. The squirrels were running and playing while chattering in their language. Pete realized how loud they were in the otherwise quiet environment. After a minute, he also heard an owl hooting somewhere nearby. He was pleasantly surprised to hear them during the day. Stormy seemed content no matter where they were, so Pete started towards the house. Stormy stopped at the back of his truck again, which happened to be where Cris' living room was located.

Through the windows, Pete could see Cris and Bolton talking on the other side of the living room. He knew this must be the "private conversation" Cris had asked him for. No doubt it was about him being the killer. It hurt, but screw it, he had broad shoulders. Pete loved Cris and knew he couldn't fathom what she was going through, much less what she may have gone through to make her the way she was now. Even so, Pete wondered what they were talking about and if it involved him. Did Bolton agree with her conspiracy theory? It wouldn't necessarily surprise him the way Chief seemed to treat her compared to everyone else. Pete knew that wasn't really true and had to rescind it. Chief was a fair and great leader, and Cris was held to the same standards. It wasn't that. It almost felt like Chief coddled her or was overprotective or more worrisome of her. It wasn't because she was a woman either, because he didn't treat the other women that way. It was like they knew each other, but that didn't seem right either since Cris was questioning what his "deal" was too. Pete couldn't put his finger on it, but the bottom line was, there was something with those two and it probably would not bode well for him in this case.

Beyond them, Pete could see the team moving around in the kitchen and dining room area. Yet again, he remembered the blood he had just cleaned off the baseboards for her, convincing himself he was not covering anything up. All he needed was to inadvertently become an accessory to something. Glancing back through the living room window,

Cris' body movements and "talking arms" made it clear she was not happy about something. It must have been the end of their conversation because they turned and were heading to the front door, probably coming his way.

Kneeling, Pete began scratching Stormy behind the ears. "Well, here we go. Let's see what they have to say now."

Bolton was conspicuously trying to lighten the mood as they approached. "Aw, Stormy! Are you getting your fill of lovin's or what?"

Pete smiled wide. "I think she's been slightly spoiled this past week and has thoroughly played it to the hilt."

He could see irritation in Cris' eyes. Thankful for his awareness and quick thinking, Pete added, "Of course, there's nothing like Mommy. I couldn't even hold a candle in that regard."

Chief, who was even more perceptive, chimed in to break the current tension, while no doubt adding a whole new level of it. "So, Bryan, are you sure you'll be able to stay here until we can ensure her safety otherwise?"

Pete was shocked Cris actually agreed to letting him stay after everything she had said. They had been down this road before when she accused him the first time. Afterwards, Cris told him she wasn't thinking straight and felt horrible about what she said. She promised to never say anything like that again, yet, here they were. Pete understood Cris just had yet another shock. This was too many in just one week alone. Although it hurt, Pete was trying to not take offense. He did have to admit, he was secretly elated to be staying with her. Pete inwardly hoped they could work on patching up their relationship. If nothing else, he would be here for her, no matter what her needs were. Now, Pete thought he had a pretty good idea what those hand gestures had been about right before they came out.

Standing up, Pete tried to lighten the mood. "Oh, well it won't be that long then. Stormy always keeps herself safe with her blankets."

Apparently, Cris wasn't in a humorous mood. "I can keep myself safe with my Smith & Wesson too, so no need to stay at all."

Bolton glared at her. "Steele, don't even start. We've discussed this, and we agree that Bryan will stay until your safety is secured."

Never one to disappoint, Cris had a comeback. "I could get hit by a bus tomorrow while checking my mail or walking Stormy. My safety can never be secured."

Chief countered, "Stand down and put your pride aside for the moment. Don't worry, we won't tell anyone."

Pete couldn't hold back a smirk. "Yea, no worries, I won't tell anyone. In fact, if anyone finds out I'm staying here, I'll be sure to tell them how brutal you are."

Cris waved her hand at them both. "Fuck all y'all."

Chief chuckled. "There she is."

"And the jackass you rode in on too."

Pete felt like Cris had loosened up much more since Bolton got there, which was certainly a good thing. He was still facing the windows and had enough experience to know it looked like they were wrapping things up inside, which was ridiculously quick. Pete didn't know in this case if it was a good or bad sign, but his gut told him it was the latter, at least as far as evidence was concerned.

He wondered how thorough they were. More specifically, did they use black lights and see the blood spatters that had been on the baseboards he had cleaned with the bleach solution? Since Cris headed them off at the pass, Pete didn't see what they were bringing in. It didn't matter, what was done was done. He couldn't change it and he had to try to let it go. Now Pete really wished he had gotten the true story before he cleaned it. He was so focused on helping Cris and hopefully making her smile with the "bill" he would leave, he didn't put much real thought into it. Any other time, it wouldn't have been a consideration, Pete would've known better. That whole hindsight being 20/20 thing. *Damn it and damn her!*

Trying to return to the present reality, Pete looked from the windows back to Cris. "Seriously, I'm happy to stay and keep you safe as much as humanly possible. I won't let anything happen."

Cris gave her characteristic eye roll. "Whatever. I don't have an air mattress. You'll have to sleep on the couch. Consider yourself warned, you may have to fight Stormy for it. She likes to sleep on it when someone is there."

Stormy's tail thumped on the concrete at the mention of her name. Pete rubbed behind her ears. "I can assure you; I don't mind. I've been sleeping with her most of the week. I'm happy to get a few more days."

Cris looked like she wanted to say something in response but was interrupted by the techs coming out with all their equipment and evidence in hand. Seeing Chief, Cris and himself gathered just to the side of the front yard, they began walking towards them.

Cris marched over to the head of forensics. "You're done already? Did you find anything?"

"Well, the only thing we found were some prints. We will run them through the lab and see if there are any that don't belong to yourself, Luke, Bryan or Chief Bolton. There was nothing on the letter itself, not that we were expecting there would be. We bagged it though and will check it more in depth at the lab. Maybe we'll get lucky with something."

Cris leaned in closer to the tech and tried to lower her voice but Pete could still hear them. "I'm sure you won't find anything unexpected. Could you do me a favor though? Please give Chief Bolton the results and not Bryan."

"I'll be happy to help if Bolton's okay with it. I'll let Bolton know of any findings first and then ask him who else I should inform. This way, I'm not getting in trouble, but also, he'll have the information you need before anyone else. If something comes up "missing," Bolton will know about it. I understand your concern and I'll stretch my parameters to help you the best I can."

"Thank you, I really appreciate it!" Cris moved her head back to a more reasonable and normal distance.

He responded at an ordinary volume, "Yes, ma'am. I truly hope things start turning around for you, Steele."

Pete was pissed. The grain of salt he was taking this with was almost dissolved now. He reminded himself to stay calm and bide his time. It would all work out in the end.

CHAPTER 4

J eff removed his glasses and mopped his brow with his forearm. Dealing with Cris and Bryan felt like a father trying to keep the peace between his two kids. This was all new since Luke's death, and Jeff didn't like it one bit. They used to be good friends and great colleagues. Now, from Cris, it was suspicion and struggling to keep her sharp, seething tongue contained. Bryan, well, in all honesty Jeff didn't know what to think. His gut told him Bryan was the same great person he always knew he was. Jeff believed very strongly in listening to his intuition, it had never steered him wrong in the past. Cris had, however, put a twinge of doubt there, and he didn't like that either.

Acid tried to fight its way up his esophagus as he listened to Cris talk to forensics about not giving Bryan any information. Jeff desperately wanted to get to his vehicle to chew down a few antacids, but he wasn't leaving this situation for anything. The thought made him realize how it felt like he had eaten more antacids in this past week than he had in the past 18 years. His thoughts started flashing back to the time when he consumed antacids as his meals. *Oh, hell no, you are* not *going back there, not now!* Jeff inconspicuously shook his head, put his glasses back on and stood at attention next to Bryan, all the while looking at Cris. He saw Bryan noticeably shift his weight and could tell by the look on his face he heard what Cris was saying and he was pissed. Jeff couldn't blame him. Thinking about it though, he couldn't blame Cris either. What she did was very smart. *That's my girl!* Jeff tried not to make a facial expression either way, which given his past wasn't too difficult. He was well trained.

Cris turned briskly back towards them but didn't bother to acknowledge either of them. Instead, she went straight to Stormy, knelt and began petting her head and scratching her ears.

"Are you ready to go back inside girl?"

Bryan was still holding Stormy by her leash and Jeff could see him tighten his grip on it as Stormy was getting excited and began wiggling around. Jeff was impressed and surprised to hear Bryan play dumb about the exchange which had just taken place. He sounded so nonchalant.

"So, I guess we're all clear to reenter then? Did they say if they found anything?"

Cris responded coldly, "Nothing that looked like it didn't belong."

Jeff was done with the tension between these two. "C'mon, let's go in and make our game plan."

He began walking towards the house purposefully, making it clear he knew what was going on and it was over, at least on his watch. On the short jaunt to the front porch, his thoughts kept coming back to Bryan. His body language indicated he had heard the conversation and he was riled. Jeff was concerned with how quickly and easily Bryan was able to suppress and hide those feelings while talking to Cris. Could his gut be wrong this time? Was Bryan actually a master manipulator? *Damn it, no! Bryan is a great guy, Cris' unfounded accusations are getting to me. I need to stop!*

Trying to get out of his own head, Jeff went up the stairs first and opened the front door, holding it open so he could watch them walk in. Cris looked straight ahead, her body rigid. Bryan walked right behind her, his body relaxed, but his eyes boring through the back of Cris' head. Jeff didn't bother to gently hold the door to make it close quietly, he wanted to make noise. Unfortunately, it was hinged to shut slowly on its own, but it still made a loud enough noise as he pulled, catching the latch. They both turned around to look at him. Jeff stood straight and tall; his words were concise while his tone was normal. His presence and message were abundantly clear.

"Now that we're inside and I have the attention of both of you, I am going to say this once and only once. I expect you to listen and comply. This bullshit between the two of you stops now. I don't want to have restless nights worrying about you two and your ridiculous shenanigans. If I keep my wife awake with tossing and turning, she will have me neutered, which I will in turn take directly out on the two of you. I don't want this. Do I make myself clear?"

Neither one broke eye contact with him as they shook their heads and gave a harmonious, "Yes, sir."

"Good. Since we agree, let's move on to what's important and get a game plan in action."

They were all still standing in the living room and Jeff noticed they both looked sheepish, like they just got scolded by the principal. *Good. Hopefully, it worked, at least until this is over.* He started making his way towards the kitchen. As Jeff walked past, Bryan released the clasp of the leash from Stormy's collar to let her roam free. He hung the leash on the hook by the door and promptly brought up the rear, joining them in the kitchen area. Jeff strode over to the bar to sit and start strategizing their plan of attack. He turned his body in the chair, so he was able to face them both. Cris and Bryan stood across from each other on opposite sides. Bryan started to rest his arms on the top of the bar, then slyly grabbed a piece of paper sitting in the center of it.

Jeff noticed Bryan's face appeared edgy as he stealthily handed the note to Cris. "You might want to throw this away."

Cris gave what Jeff could only describe as an evil smirk in response as she folded it up and put it in her pocket. "Thanks, I think I'll hang onto it though."

Bryan's face turned slightly ashen as he looked over at him. "So, what's the plan, Chief?"

Jeff looked between the two of them with a slight scowl, making it clear he was aware of the curious interaction that occurred. "Well, first, Bryan you need to go get the belongings you'll need for a few days and Steele, you need to get a security system scheduled. I want it installed within the next 24 hours."

Cris inhaled, having something to say. Jeff held his hand up to stop, cutting her off and Cris rolled her eyes in response.

"Second, we're going to discuss this before you go, Bryan. I want you to have your own code, so you're not sharing one with Steele."

Bryan interrupted. "Sir, I don't want a code at all. I prefer to rely on her to let me come and go. If I have no access to the house, there should be less opportunity for accusations."

"I understand your thought process, but I disagree. Having your own code means she could know when you come and go, which should help ease minds and suspicions. You are supposed to be here for safety purposes. Not having access to the house and relying on Steele to let you come and go isn't practical or necessary. You'll have your own code that only you know, allowing you to be tracked by it in case of future questions, which I know there won't be any."

Jeff glared over at Cris, then noticed Bryan giving him a sideways glance. He wondered if Bryan thought he was also suspicious of him after talking to Cris a little while ago.

"Let me change my wording. This is not a discussion; this is a directive to you both. Bryan, this is for your own good and it will help appease Steele's overactive mind. Think about what you want your code to be, so you're prepared for tomorrow. Now, cut out of here and go get your stuff. I'll stay until you get back."

Bryan stopped leaning on the bar and stood up, fishing his keys from the pocket of his jeans. "It won't take me long. I'll be back within the hour."

"Alright. Steele, get your computer fired up. We're going to start researching and schedule the security install."

Cris' eyes got a little wide. Jeff could see a sense of panic even though she was trying to hide it. What he couldn't understand, was why.

"You can stay there. I'll grab my laptop and bring it out right quick."

Jeff turned in his chair so he was facing forward now, where the laptop would presumably be going. The office was the first room off the hallway. Jeff noticed Bryan paused to watch her go into the office. Cris looked back furtively before entering and Bryan continued to the front door. They were both very swift and covert in their movements and motions, but Jeff picked up on them. *First the note, now the office. What the hell is going on with these two?*

He heard the front door softly click shut, momentarily followed by Cris walking out with her laptop. She closed the office door just as the exhaust of Pete's truck thundered to life. Sitting down next to him, Cris opened her laptop.

Jeff watched the screen circle as it was booting up. "One advantage of being in this business is we already know which security companies are top of the line, which will save us lots of time."

Cris pulled up the two sites and they began comparing them side by side. They were both similar, but one was slightly better in its technological aspect. Jeff knew with her circumstances these advancements would be important to Cris.

"Look at these specs, Cris. The features on this one includes an app for your phone to arm or disarm remotely and access the reports for the codes that have been entered. I think these would be great features for you. It also says they have prompt installation appointments."

"Yea. I also like that it allows for an authorized user in case of emergency or you can't be located. See here, this authorized user can have access to the logs and any information in writing or over the phone with protected passwords. I've been thinking about it and I really feel this is something I should have. So, I guess you need to start thinking about your codes and passwords too." Cris looked at him and swiftly turned her attention back to the computer screen scrolling to the scheduling tab, undoubtedly, to cover the emotion she was close to showing.

Jeff knew all too well Cris was completely alone now. He also knew that even though she wouldn't mention it out loud, Cris realized it too. Jeff was grateful she trusted him and let her shield down enough to do this. It was unusual for Cris and no doubt she didn't make this decision lightly. Jeff felt the responsibility for her even stronger than it already was.

He responded softly, "Yes, ma'am. I'll get right on it."

"Good. While you're getting on that, don't forget the enigmatic chat we still need to finish up, because I certainly won't."

"I promise we will, Cris. But your safety is top priority right now. The conversation can hold off a little longer, and the timing really needs to be right. Certainly not in the middle of this nightmare."

Cris looked up from the laptop. "Well, the install is scheduled for tomorrow morning, so with my safety in place I expect we should be able to finish the conversation with the utmost urgency."

Jeff was relieved to hear Bryan's truck returning, ending any further discussion for now. "It sounds like Bryan's back. You have my word we will finish it. When the timing is right this time."

Standing up, Cris cocked her hip and crossed her arms over her chest. "I know we will. Sooner than later."

Bryan walked through the front door with his backpack. "Hey guys, I'm back."

Cris characteristically rolled her eyes and mumbled something inaudible under her breath. Jeff set his hand on her shoulder before walking away.

"I'll have the passwords ready before the install tomorrow. You know my phone will be on me if you need anything tonight."

He removed his hand and turned to walk away. Bryan had walked in and furrowed his eyebrows. Apparently, he heard what Jeff had said and didn't like it.

"Don't worry Chief, I got this."

"I know you do, Bryan. I'm heading home. Call me if anything comes up."

Jeff gave Stormy a quick pet on his way to the door. He mounted up in his SUV, grabbed a few antacids and began to chew them up. Jeff hoped his leaving those two alone wasn't going to be the biggest mistake of his life.

CHAPTER 5

The door softly closed behind Chief and Cris realized she didn't know what to do with herself, particularly since Pete was there. She felt alone, confused, confined and extremely uncomfortable. Cris couldn't endure being in her room and couldn't go into the office. This only left the workout room, of which you can only spend so much time, and the kitchen, dining and living room, where Pete would be. Adding to her anxiety, Cris' growling stomach reminded her she hadn't eaten since this morning. Remembering the offer from Pete she had been trying to avoid before all hell broke loose, Cris knew she couldn't avoid it anymore. She would have to order in that dinner with Pete now. *My, how quickly things change!*

The two of them were standing in the kitchen. Cris wondered if Pete felt as awkward as she did. It was time to break the ice and figure out how to get through these next few days.

"Well, since all the excitement is over, I guess it's time to think about dinner. I know before the shit hit the fan you asked if I wanted to order in. I'm not sure if you still want to eat with me. We could always adjourn to separate rooms I suppose."

Cris realized she was rambling. She knew their relationship was unsteady at best right now, all due to her mouth. Cris didn't know what to say or how to say it, especially since it ran so close to the emotions she insisted on keeping stuffed in.

She was grateful to see Pete soften as his shoulders lowered and jaw unclenched. The stiffness was visibly leaving his body.

"Aw, Cris. I told you I would be here for you, to beat, yell, accuse me, to just get it out. What you have said is hurtful, and sometimes it's easier for me to swallow than others. I can't even imagine going through what you are right now though. I at least semi-understand and 100 percent stand by your side. Shit, I think you must be the only woman or person in the world who can say the things you do to me and I still want to join you for dinner." Pete shrugged his shoulders and chuckled.

"I'm sorry Pete. We've been over this before, I know I have a hard time controlling my mouth."

That was more emotion than Cris was comfortable showing. Time to move the conversation in a safer direction.

"So, was there a specific place you had in mind a few hours ago, or something you're craving?"

"No, I hadn't thought any farther ahead than seeing if you wanted to order in and have company," Pete chortled. "I guess you got both whether you wanted them or not."

Choosing to ignore the latter part and seeing no humor, Cris opened her laptop again. "Well, now I'm starving. Here, let's pick a place and order online."

Cris was slowly scrolling through the list of local restaurants. Pete was now looking over her shoulder. He pointed to one.

"How about this one? They have a good variety, from sandwiches to steak and seafood, and the best part is they're a local mom and pop place."

Trying very hard to keep her mouth shut, Cris clenched her teeth. On the rare occasion when they ate out, she and Luke always preferred local places over franchises or large group restaurants. This happened to be one of Luke's favorites. They had gone there a few times, Cris felt like it was their place. The commonality with Pete pissed her off.

She tried to respond without the annoyance in her words. "Works for me."

Already knowing what she was going to order, Cris stood up. "Here. You go ahead and put in what you want."

"Oh, no, you can look first."

"I know what I'm going to get. You put yours in, I'll add mine after right quick."

Sliding to the other side of the bar, Cris made it clear she was not going to look right now. Pete must've taken the hint because he started scrolling and clicking.

"So, you've eaten from there before then?!"

Cris thought her teeth might break from clenching so hard. "Yes. It's good."

Pete either didn't hear the tension in her voice or was polite enough to ignore it, which was more likely the case. "I've been there a few times myself. I've never been disappointed."

He stepped aside. It was Cris' turn to put her order in. She put in a cup of she-crab soup and seafood pasta, both hers and Luke's favorite. Clicking on the button to place the order, a confirmation screen came up. It was all she could do to hold it together. Pete had ordered the same damn thing! Most people would be thrilled with parallels, but Cris was seething. She had put up a front when she made it look like they were both going to decide. She let him choose and shouldn't be mad about his decision. Yet, Cris couldn't help herself, she was. She felt her cheeks get hot and didn't trust herself to speak as she finished the process. Pete set his credit card down next to the laptop, making matters worse.

"Here, put it on this."

Cris was about ready to explode. She knew her cracked gasket was about to blow and couldn't take any more. "It says to pay at pick up."

This was a semi-lie. There was a choice to enter a card now or pay at pick up. Cris chose the latter just to get his card out of her face. She would figure it out after the order was placed, she just had to get through this without going off right now. Cris pushed his card back at him as gently as she could at the moment and closed the laptop.

"All set."

She saw Pete scowl as he took his card but did not put it back in his wallet. Cris knew he must've ordered online before and therefore knew her pretexts were bullshit. It seemed like life was a game of chess between them now. Cris wasn't sure which one should've just called "checkmate."

"There's some time before it needs to be picked up. I'll make sure there's room for your stuff in the guest bathroom so you can get settled."

Cris already knew there was space for Pete's stuff. She needed an excuse to walk away and come up with a plan for her own sleeping arrangements. Earlier she told Pete that Stormy would sleep with him on the couch because Cris needed her to. Otherwise, Stormy would give away her sleeping quarters and Cris couldn't have that. This way, Stormy would also give Cris a warning whenever Pete was up and walking around because she would be right at his heels. Most importantly, Cris knew Stormy really wouldn't mind. Stormy got used to sleeping on the couch with her the few days after Luke was murdered. Then she stayed with Pete while Cris and Detective Kim Campbell were up in Jasper helping with a case. Stormy would be happy with both Pete and the couch. In turn, Cris would be happy keeping her sleeping place a secret and always knowing where Pete was.

Coming back out, Cris saw Pete going into the living room with his backpack, playing and frolicking with Stormy as he went. She couldn't resist the smile tugging at her lips as she watched. He threw his backpack on the couch and got down on the floor on all fours, talking in a higher pitch and pushing his head against Stormy as she tackled him. His shirt rode up a few times, uncovering the butt of his pistol from his jeans.

"I hate to break up your little love fest, but the bathroom is all set if you want to start putting your things away. There's clean linen and empty shelves."

Pete stopped his mischief and looked at Stormy. "Aw, she busted us. To be resumed again later girl."

Standing up, Pete gave Stormy a few pats and one final rub behind her ears. Grabbing his backpack, Pete began heading to the guest bathroom to unpack. Cris was waiting for some kind of opportunity to grab her pillow and blankets and get them into the office without him seeing. Not knowing if she would get any better chance, Cris hurried down the hall to grab them. She ran into her office with them as quickly and quietly as she could, set them off to the side and rushed back out the door. Hearing Pete coming, Cris sat down next to Stormy and pet her, acting like she had been there all along.

"The shelving space worked out perfectly. Thanks."

"Oh, good." Cris looked up at her laptop still sitting on the bar and stood up walking over to it. "I better go get this plugged in before the battery dies."

Grabbing the laptop, she noticed Pete watching her as she walked towards the office with it. She opened the door just wide enough for her to fit through, trying to act nonchalant to Stormy who was right by her side.

"I don't need any help, Storm. I'll be right out." Cris quickly shut the door.

Setting her laptop on the desk, just below her murder board, the sight of her dad's glass pulled her attention. This was the last glass he drank out of 18 years ago as she sat on his lap for the final time. The memories of that fateful day came rushing back, like the waves of the ocean crashing down on her. The sights, sounds and smells as fresh now as they were then. Cris steadied herself on her desk. She knew Pete was right outside the door and she had to get a grip and get back out there. Cris decided she wanted to get some Sailor Jerry. Feel the feeling her dad used to feel, maybe get out of her own head. It felt right. Her mind was made up. Now she had to figure out how to get out of the house without Pete. Divinely, her email chimed. It was an automated message from the restaurant, the food was ready for pick up. *There's my excuse.*

Walking out, Cris barely cracked the door as she came through. As expected, Pete was nearby in the kitchen area. Cris tried to cover her extended absence for simply plugging in a computer.

"The restaurant emailed. The food is ready. I'll go grab it quickly and be right back."

Cris turned and started walking towards her room, hoping to avoid an argument. No such luck.

"I'm supposed to be keeping you safe, no way are you going to get the food."

Cris slowed but didn't stop walking. "Damn it, Bryan, stop friggin' arguing with me. I'm going to my bathroom to take this bandage off and attempt to be presentable. I'll be out in a minute."

Still chasing her down, Pete gently yelled after her. "Are you supposed to take the bandage off?"

Cris responded by shutting the bedroom door. Trying not to look around the room, specifically the bed and Luke's nightstand, she went straight to their master bathroom. Now, trying to get her mind off her dad and not look at Luke's toiletries, Cris hurriedly started ripping at the bandage wrapped around her head like a bandana. She felt the pain first from her hair pulling, followed by the stapled area. It was exactly what Cris needed to refocus her thoughts. She jerked even harder. Hair, blood, and pus stuck to the gauze.

Cris smiled as she finished ripping it off harshly, then tried to adjust her hair to cover the staples and shaved area as best she could. She knew by the throbbing she was sufficiently focused and ready now.

Thinking about her plan, Cris knew Pete couldn't know where else she was really going. This pitstop and corresponding drinking would show the growing cracks in her sanity. Cris was not a drinker. Occasionally a glass of wine or a beer with Luke, nothing more. He had always balanced her, she never felt that pull for alcohol. Now that he was gone, she was ready to see how her dad always felt with his companion, Sailor Jerry. Cris assured herself she wouldn't be like her dad with drinking. Her mind was made up and she wasn't going to change it. Tonight, she was going to meet and make friends with the Sailor.

Standing tall and squaring her shoulders, her head burning, yet simultaneously numb from the pain, Cris was ready to battle with Pete. Strutting out, her 5'2" frame feeling like it was at least 5'8", she made a beeline for her car keys. Pete shattered her fantasy when he grabbed her left arm and yanked her around.

"We were having a discussion before you shut the door in my face."

"Oh, is that what you called it? I thought it was a one-sided conversation. Mine. I'm going to get our food. I'm a starving female and I would highly advise you to stand down right now."

"I'm sure you would. I'll reuse Chief's phrase earlier about his wife. If something happens to you, Chief would have *me* neutered. I'm not okay with that." Pete released her arm and leaned his right side against the wall, cocking his left hip, placing one foot over the other as he crossed his arms in front of him.

"Stop being so damn dramatic. Think about it like me; logically. The note was left here, in my house, on my table. Do you really think I'd be better off here alone while you go get the food? No, I'd be safer going to make the pickup myself. I can assure you; nobody will catch me in my car."

"My logical thought was we both go together."

Trying to make a point, as much as stand her ground, "No matter where I am, my weapon is not leaving my side. There's only so much babysitting I'm going to allow here, Bryan. I'll cut you some slack though. You choose, which one of us goes to get the food?"

Cris was fine either way. If she went, she would make a pit stop on her way. If Pete went, she would run out while he was gone. Cris knew she would beat him back. She had him by the balls and the poor bastard didn't even know it. No matter what, she won.

Pete stood there silent, his bright blue eyes unblinking, glaring at her. Cris could tell he was brooding. After what seemed like an eternity, Pete finally shifted and broke his stance as he exhaled excessively and rubbed his buzzed black hair. He pulled his wallet out of his pocket as he began to curse, more to himself than Cris, "Son of a bitch."

Looking back at her, Pete's face was atypically inimical and his jaw tense. "Damn it… you stubborn, hardheaded, pain in the ass. Given the choice, I do feel you're safer by yourself out of the house than in it. You had better have your weapon on you and you had better keep yourself safe, or what Bolton will do to me will be nothing in comparison to what I will do to myself." He ran his right hand over his head again. "Ugh, shit Cris, I could strangle you right now! I'm going to go take a cold shower, you had better be back by the time I get out!"

Pete pulled his credit card from his wallet and roughly thrust it in her hand before storming away towards the bathroom, not allowing a response. Even though his words were hostile, his tone was not. Cris was conflicted about him, but she didn't feel threatened by what he'd just said. She knew it was mere frustration. She turned briskly, grabbed her keys and rushed out the door.

Sliding into the driver seat, she threw his credit card in the cup holder. No matter what suspicions she had, she couldn't prove anything. One thing Cris knew for a fact was that she owed him. Pete watched Stormy while she was up in Jasper, and not having to worry about her was priceless. Now, he was spending more of his own personal time to help her out. Nevertheless, if he did have malicious plans, Cris, along with Smith & Wesson were ready.

Cris meticulously slammed the gears and the clutch, tires squealing trying to catch some grip as the ass end swung around. Her head and neck cracked in unison as the rear snapped back straight. The nearest liquor store and the restaurant were both close by. Cris wheeled into the package store first. Since she wasn't a drinker, she had no idea where Sailor Jerry was located. Frantically looking at the signs and layout though, common sense helped her find it swiftly. Cris rushed to pick up the food and charged back through her front door in just under 15 minutes. She knew she had to beat Pete out of the shower to get the contraband in the house unnoticed.

Setting the food on the counter, Cris heard the shower shut off. She made a dash for the office to store the liquid purchase. Coming out and closing the door, her heart was pounding. Cris wasn't used to having to sneak around, and she didn't like it one bit. She was known for her brutal honesty. This deceit was already killing her, but Cris knew it was necessary.

Not planning to use the more formal table, she hurriedly set up the bar area. She had just finished up as Pete walked out of the bathroom in athletic shorts and a fitted t-shirt. Drops of water still lingered on his skin. He looked at the bar with everything prepared, his surprise was evident.

"Looks like you'll get to keep your manhood a little while longer. You're welcome."

Pete flashed his bright smile as he sauntered over. "Well, thank you, I do appreciate that."

She didn't respond to him, but sat down, blessed herself, said a grace in her head, then blessed herself again. Cris noticed he was watching from the corner of his eye, but she didn't care.

There were some attempts at small talk during dinner. Cris mostly crammed food in her mouth so she couldn't respond much. It was late, and she was ready and anxious to adjourn for the day. Cris finished eating then quickly cleaned up, stretched and told Pete she was exhausted and ready to call it a day. He followed suit with cleaning and agreed.

Inconspicuously, she had Stormy join him on the couch, then went back into the kitchen and put two ice cubes in a glass. She initially went towards her bedroom, pretending to be going in. After waiting a few minutes and hearing Pete and

Stormy settle onto the couch, Cris noiselessly made her way into the office, locking the door behind herself. Not wanting light to show under the crack of the door, she turned on her cell phone's flashlight, walked over to her desk at the other side of the room and turned on the reading light. Then Cris grabbed a towel she had set in there earlier with her supplies and placed it at the bottom of the door. This allowed her to turn on the light to make her sleeping quarters on the floor, then pour the amber liquid in her glass.

Cris couldn't stop thinking about her dad, even more so now that she saw and smelled the Sailor Jerry. She made it just like he did, on the rocks. She winced at the first drink, felt the burn slowly traveling down, then at once realized it wasn't as bad as the first initial taste seemed. Downing her glass, she poured herself a little more as she already started to feel the numbness beginning to take over.

CHAPTER 6

*C*ris watched what looked like a train racing through with images playing in each window. It was like a movie slide over two-years, when she was between the ages of 8 and 10.

Cris was on the floor, crying from laughter because her dad was tickling her so hard. The two of them together, cutting and measuring wood to make improvements on the house. He laughs deep from his belly as he flicks paint on her. Cooking breakfast together on Sunday mornings, washing, cutting and cooking all the food together while singing, dancing and tickling. Out back having target practice with dad's Glock, his pride beaming through each time Cris handled the recoil and made the shot. The first time Cris fired it and it came back and cracked her in the forehead, cutting it open. Dad was right there to quickly patch her up. Competing in fitness tests together and him letting her win by a second. Dad's sarcastic, salty, Sailor mouth that Cris loved. When he met shy Luke for the first time. Playing hide and go seek and Dad didn't come a few times; her not knowing if he was pretending not to be able to find her or he just gave up. Dad breaking various forms of glass and screaming at unseen apparitions at the walls. Sitting home on the fourth of July, praying for quiet, instead of out watching the fireworks. Quickly cleaning blood off the back of her scraped legs and burying the towels deep in the trash can so he wouldn't see them. Thunder booming while doing dishes together and she had to be quick on her feet with the tuck and roll to avoid the plate in his hand that he instinctively threw. Cleaning the aftermath of his episodes before mom got home from work so she wouldn't have to do it. Always traveling with his glass of ice and amber liquid. Getting a ride home from the bar from a friend after the bartender called him. Mom having to go pick up dad's truck the next day while he slept it off. Dad sitting at the table that fateful morning with his fellow traveler and companion Sailor Jerry, seducing, consoling and conspiring. His words as dark as a moonless night.

The last image that appeared in the train window was always the worst. Dad's blood spattered all over the room. His Glock loosely in his right hand. The picture of the three of them on his chest, covered by his cold left hand. The blood-spattered envelope with the letter and dog tags left on the nightstand with Cris' name. Cris screaming for her daddy before she called 911. Collapsing just under their picture across his torso crying and convulsing, until the police came in and dragged her away. Physically fighting them, swearing, punching, kicking, scratching and biting. Then sitting against the wall in his room, catatonic, refusing to leave him. Not moving until well after he was bagged up and taken out. Cris continued to sit in there more times than she could remember over the next several weeks. She couldn't find a darker place to hide.

Cris only went in his room when mom was working, which was most of the time. She had to be strong in front of her mom, so she wouldn't worry about her. She had enough to worry about as it was. Cris sat in his room, reliving every moment of their life together, the good and the bad. Like stalking the mailman in hopes of receiving letters from him. Dad always sent three. One for Cris, one for her mom and one for them both. Cris could still see him in his dress whites or blues, depending on the season, standing at the rail as the ship came into port. Cris was always ready to burst with the excitement she felt at getting to see him again. Life as Cris knew it when he was active duty and life as she knew it after he became a civilian. It all ebbed and flowed, skulking through her cranial cavities.

Cris would light their endless supply of blue candles incessantly. Whenever mom wasn't home Cris would leave the lights off, preferring the darkness, and light the blue candles throughout the house. Lighting blue candles was what you did for Sailors or their families. Especially those who needed prayer or had fallen. Cris knew they fell into both categories. There was a poem written by an unknown author that most Sailor's families knew. Cris would try to say it each time she lit the candles. Somedays she would get more lines out than others, but never could she get the whole poem out anymore without breaking down and having to stop. The most she could get through now was the first five lines.

She remembered the day her mom picked up Dad's empty glass. She stared at it for a moment then grimaced and pulled her arm back, ready to pitch it across the room. Cris jumped in front of her and almost took it to the head. Her mom stopped at the last second and yelled at her.

"What the hell is wrong with you? Do you want to get hit with this?" She never yelled at Cris before; never needed to.

Cris' eyes got glassy. "Mom, please don't break it! It was his glass and the one he drank out of that morning when I was sitting on his lap for the last time."

Placing it roughly in Cris' hand, she turned her back and walked away, practically running. Cris saw her go around the corner into her room and lean against the wall next to the door. She slid down the wall, her hand over her mouth to hide the noise trying to escape before quietly shutting the door.

Cris went out in the back yard to the cabin she and Luke had been in the process of building when it all happened. The blood that dripped from her thumb, which she had struck with the hammer when she heard the crack from within the house, had all been washed away. Everything had stopped since then. Remembering that day and moment, Cris started throwing the lumber across the yard. She blamed herself for what happened. She should've stayed inside with him. She should've known what the real reason was for the sudden clearness in his eyes after his dark talk. She could've saved him. She should've stayed inside.

Anger, sadness, desperation, and longing all overtook her. Cris stopped throwing the pieces of wood. She dropped to her knees, looked up as she reached towards the sky, calling to her father. If only she could bring him back. She wanted him here more than anything, wanted to fix him. Cris felt lost and had no clue how she was going to move on with her life. She received no divine intervention or answers. Cris covered her eyes, doubled over, put her head to the ground and wept wildly.

Hearing her mom leave for work, Cris knew it was time. Nothing was getting better or easier, time was not healing anything. Life sucked more every day. Now Cris was left alone with the letter and his dog tags that she had been unable to open or look at for a few weeks. She fleetingly thought of Luke. He tried to be supportive. He was one of the few who could semi-understand since he recently lost his parents in a car accident. He had been in the car and had to see their lifeless bodies. It was sudden, unexpected. He couldn't possibly understand the psychological roller coaster of ups and downs that had come before this. Not that one was any easier or harder than the other, they both sucked, but they were slightly different. This mutual heartbreak had further strengthened their already indestructible bond.

Luke kept telling her he would be there to support her while she read the letter if she wanted. Cris always thanked him and told him how much she appreciated it, but never went beyond that. She knew this was something she had to do on her own. Cris had already formed her iron shield years ago and had not cried in front of Luke, or anyone else for that matter. Knowing the letter would break her, Cris knew she would have to be alone when she finally opened it up. She headed into the house, and more specifically, her bedroom; to the letter and dog tags she had tucked away.

Before grabbing them, she lit the candles and started the poem, like a prayer, as soon as she flicked the lighter: "I will burn my blue candle and hold my head high. I will burn my blue candle and try my best not to cry. I will burn my blue candle because he wasn't afraid to take on the world. I will burn my blue candle, in honor of all those who fight. I will burn my blue candle, for all those who may or may not be there at dawns early light..."

Cris couldn't hold back and make it any further than that. She was weeping hard enough and the lump in her throat was so big, she could no longer speak. Cris tried with every fiber in her body to compose herself and gain some strength.

She finally went over to her dresser and pulled the bottom drawer completely out, revealing the letter and dog tags. Cris removed them and wrapped the blood-spattered dog tags around her right hand as she removed the letter from the equally blood-spattered envelope. She sat on the floor and leaned back against the wall for extra support. Tears were silently pouring down Cris' red, blotchy face. Her chest and shoulders were a matching spectacle of red and blotchy patches. Her nose was simultaneously stuffy and runny, swollen and snotty. Cris didn't care and wiped it on her shoulder as she began to read:

"Cris,

I love you and your mom more than anything in this world. The burden I put on you is not fair. I'm not going to get better, baby. Please don't see this as a sign of weakness, but instead as a sign of strength. To lose what I love most in life so they can have the chance of a better life. Don't waste this life, you fight every chance you get for the best and you run with it. You are so smart and wise beyond your years; I couldn't be prouder of you. You are my spit and image and a Sailor's daughter through and through. Always remember what I told you (besides one of these days you're gonna cut those eyes at the wrong person), when times get tough, you're tougher, you're my girl! And don't forget, you take care of Luke. I have good instincts, and I know he's going to be a great man. I don't think you could make me any prouder, but I want you to get out there and try every damn day! Each day try harder than you did the day before. You, my daughter, are destined for greatness. I love you so much, baby! Now you can stop worrying about me and go kick ass in life! I'm going to join some of my shipmates, so you will have many angels watching over you as we once again stand side by side. I left you my dog tags for courage, strength, inspiration and to feel close to me. Hold or wear them when you need me. It's time for me to be getting underway for the last time. Anchors Aweigh baby. I love you more than life, Daddy"

Barely able to catch a breath, Cris broke down into uncontrollable sobs. Doubled over, squeezing his dog tags so hard she thought her own hands would bleed. Somehow, Cris managed to sit up and reply to him as she looked out her window towards the sky.

"Fair winds and following seas, Daddy."

CHAPTER 7

Cris opened her eyes and felt wet cheeks. She flexed her hand feeling for the dog tags that were wrapped around it. Not feeling the sting and sharpness pressing back, she brought her right hand towards her face. The room was pitch black. Cris had to bring her hand inches from her eyes, squinting to try to adapt as much as possible to the external darkness, only to find her hand was empty.

She gently whispered, "Daddy?"

Her eyes began to adjust. Cris looked around the room disoriented and became cognizant to the present. She was a grown woman, not the 10-year-old girl anymore. She had been in too many different places in the past week. Last Saturday night it was her bed, with her husband. That would be the last time she could sleep there. After that, it was two nights on the couch, then two nights at the Jasper Inn, a night in a hospital bed and now… *Where the hell am I?* Cris abruptly recalled she was on the floor of her office, which was confirmed by feeling cricks in her neck and back from the hard floor. The cricks were accompanied by a pounding in her head. After glancing next to her pillow, Cris realized that was thanks to Sailor Jerry. Her father's glass next to it, empty except a trace amount of liquid latent at the bottom as the last of the ice had melted.

The reality of sleeping in the office slammed into her like that train sailing through with the images, derailing to hit her on its way through. Cris knew she had to lock up her demons and pull herself together. She had to figure out how to sneak back out of there, or at least make it look like she had only gone in for something. Hitting the light on her watch, Cris realized she should have no problem. It was only 5:00. Knowing that after her dream she couldn't go back to sleep if she wanted to, Cris got up. Getting up and moving before Pete awoke, made it easier to cover up the slumber party in the office. Grabbing at the small of her back as she cracked it, Cris picked up her sleeping stuff and took it to the closet. She placed the Sailor Jerry bottle and glass next to it and covered it with her blanket, knowing the security company would have to go in there today and it would all need to be hidden. Cris would be sure to keep Pete away from this room. He should be going to work anyway, as Luke's case was now red hot again, and Pete best get working on it.

Cris decided to get moving to the shower. She wanted to work out in her gym room or go for a run since that was her form of stress relief, but the doctors said she couldn't work out for 48 hours. She had to allow the spot where the bullet grazed her head to heal a little more. Cris wasn't exactly known for being a rule follower, but instead more of a stubborn and hardheaded creature. She was focused on solving Luke's case, finding the murderer herself and bringing him to justice. Cris knew she had to heal a little more to be able to do that. Conceding for today, Cris skipped the exercise and quietly shut the office door as she tiptoed out and down the hall to her actual room.

Opening her bedroom door, Cris saw the hospital bag she still hadn't unpacked from yesterday. Knowing the shower cap she needed was in there, Cris decided it was the best place to start. Looking into the plastic bag, her eyes were drawn to the rosary at the bottom, broken.

"Really?!" Cris rolled her eyes as she roughly grabbed the shower cap and placed the bag aside, trying to forget about the rosary for now.

Going to the closet, Cris grabbed a pair of jeans and a t-shirt, trying to stay focused and not look at Luke's side. Proud of her effort, despite her broken spirit between her dad and Luke, she headed to the master bathroom to shower. Not looking at Luke's toiletries all around, Cris placed the shower cap over her open head which was supposed to still be bandaged. She turned the shower head to massage and stood letting the hot water beat down until her body and mind were numb. Hoping that was enough of a pounding to replace the workout and get her redirected on her present reality instead of her past, Cris got out.

The steam covered mirror dredged up the memory of that day so many years ago. It started the same way; clearing the fog off the mirror. Cris had been so excited for a great day building a cabin in her backyard with Luke. Coming out of the bathroom, her father hunched at the table, his promise of trying to make things better for Cris and her mom, then the sound of that fatal shot just a short time later while she was building in the back yard. What started as an exciting day ended up being the worst day of her life. Cris wondered if the memory came so easily because of the dream she just had, or if it would've happened anyway. A tear threatened to spill. Cris shook her head as she lifted her chin to stop the thoughts, forcing herself to think about the present instead. Oh yes, which reminded her, that day was now tied with last Sunday as the worst day of her life. Cursing herself under her breath to stop it, Cris ripped the shower cap off extra hard to feel the sting of it and pull her back to her new reality and fight. The sharp and lingering pain along with the strands of red hair, pus and bloody skin that came off in the shower cap confirmed she had done a good job.

Feeling she had composed herself enough, Cris went into the kitchen to officially start her day. Walking past the living room, Stormy came bounding out to greet her, tail whacking the wall along the way. Cris looked towards her and inadvertently saw Pete sit up on the couch and reach for his shirt. She quickly looked away from his chiseled chest and abs. She had no interest there and didn't want Pete to notice that she saw him. He might think she was trying to look at him instead of looking at Stormy when the movement in the background drew her attention.

Pete came into the kitchen not long after, rubbing the stubble of his buzzed black hair, blue eyes shining brightly. "You're up early."

Cris glanced habitually at the clock on the stove, 5:45. "Yea, I don't normally sleep late. This is usually my workout time. So, you look like you slept well."

She hoped Pete didn't read more into that than what she meant. Cris quickly chastised herself for the thought. Pete was not like that, he was not conceited in any way, or of grandeur delusions. Pete was the same good ol' Pete. Cris hated how torn she felt with him because of all this. They used to be friends and her nagging suspicion was really getting in the way and clouding her judgment, but she still couldn't back off.

"I did. The couch is actually very comfortable and Stormy kept my feet warm all night, which I have gotten kind of used to in the past week."

"That's good. Feel free to help yourself to whatever you can find before you head out. I don't even know what I have for food aside from all those casseroles in the freezer." More small talk, Cris was so over it.

"I could always go grab us something when the security company gets here. Apparently, we have the same taste in food, as we discovered last night." Pete smiled wide and genuine, his perfect, white teeth brighter than his blue eyes.

Cris could feel her blood pressure kick up a few notches. She managed to ignore Pete's comments about it last night and get through the meal quickly. Trying hard to bite her tongue for once and not to let her ignited fuse blow, Cris thought of Luke. So many times on the playground he would try to do deep breaths with her before she pummeled that bitch, Raquel. It usually didn't work, as she always stood up for herself, Luke and her family. Cris was never one to back down. She obviously couldn't stand here and do deep breaths in front of Pete, for what would seem like no reason to him. Feeling like she had nowhere to go in her own house again, Cris fought to keep her composure. Taking one deep breath in and exhaling it out, she tried her best to respond as evenly as possible through clenched teeth.

"I'm fine for breakfast. The security company is scheduled to be here at 8:00, so you're good to leave for work at your normal time, I'll be all set. The company said they would send you a link to enter your code that's all encrypted and layered in security."

No doubt Pete picked up on her tone, but he was gracious and ignored it, sounding sincere. "Well, Bolton told me to stay here and work from the house today while everything was getting installed."

Cris mumbled under her breath as she turned her back to Pete to start making her caffeine concoction. "You have got to be friggin' kidding me."

Cris had to find a way to keep him from seeing her murder board and the makeshift war room in the office when the security company had to go in there.

Maybe Pete realized she felt trapped in her own house or maybe he wanted to stop the small talk and start his day. Cris wasn't sure of anything with Pete anymore.

"If you don't mind, I think I'll hop in the shower and get ready for the day."

"I don't care, do whatever you want. I'll get your work area set up while you're in there."

Cris turned her back and walked away, smacking her hand against her hip and making a kissing sound with her lips indicating to Stormy to follow her. Snapping the leash to Stormy's collar, Cris decided she would set Pete up with a little work area in the living room, knowing he couldn't see into the office from there. Cris was pleased with her quick thinking and of turning a negative into a positive. She looked up towards the sky as she walked down her porch steps.

"Let's keep this positivity flowing, huh?!"

CHAPTER 8

Cris had barely finished setting up Pete's mock office area in the living room when he came out of the shower and swaggered in. Stormy was sitting next to Cris and started thumping her tail on the floor as he came in.

He looked over at Cris. "Oh, hey! I didn't realize you were tucked in the corner over there."

"I'm just finishing up your office area. I hope it's sufficient enough for you."

Pete looked impressed with raised eyebrows and wide blue eyes. "Um, it's great. I could've sat at the table with my laptop, or even here on the couch with it on my lap." He gave a slight grunt. "This little station you set up here just might be better than my office at work."

Pete turned to start folding the blankets and picking up the couch. Bending down to put them away, Pete's shirt rode up just enough to see the grip of his weapon sticking out of his jeans and constricting against his muscles. Cris quickly looked away.

"Well, I don't know about that, but you should have what you need for the day at least."

Needing to get away from Pete and being satisfied with the location and set up serving its purpose of keeping him from seeing the office, Cris turned and walked into the kitchen. Seeing Pete still kneeling, Stormy took it as an invitation to play and opted to go tackle Pete instead of following her.

A combination of hearing Stormy's claws scrape the floor with excitement and Pete laughing while rough housing back and forth with her, made Cris want to punch something. The two of them couldn't be happier and she was dying inside. Trapped, not only in her own house but imprisoned to solitary confinement in her own head. Cris looked out the French doors beyond the back yard and up to the sky. She placed her hand on the glass pane as her vision blurred, her mind a deep stupor. *Luke, Daddy. I need you guys. I can't get through this alone. The only reason I survived after you, Dad, was because Luke was there for me. I have nobody now. The darkness has a firm grasp on both of my ankles, pulling me further down each day. I'm so close to drowning. I don't know if I can fight it much longer, I have become too weak after this capsize. There's no one to throw me a life preserver anymore.* Cris' unfocused and unblinking eyes suddenly snapped into focus as two cardinals swooped past the door, right in front of her face. Simultaneously, she felt a hand gently touch her shoulder.

"Cris, are you okay?"

She snapped around, face to face with Pete. The irony and message were not lost on her. Luke always said everything happened for a reason. It was something they both firmly believed, and it helped them get through the tough times and keep their sanity.

Really? You guys have got to be kidding me right now! Apparently, you still have your sense of humor up there, huh? You're telling me Pete is my life preserver? Your possible murderer, Luke? Hell no! Oh wait, I get it now, you were just trying to piss me off. You guys are still saving me, in the way that works best for me, determination. Thanks, guys, I love you!

Pulling back from Pete and squaring her shoulders, Cris looked him in the eyes. "Of course, I am."

"You worried me. You were just standing there, not moving. It didn't even look like you were breathing."

Cris didn't know how long she'd stood there lost in her thoughts. "I was enjoying the morning wildlife and looking for deer. It can be very peaceful and relaxing."

Pete furrowed his brows; she could tell he wasn't buying it. "Sorry I disturbed you, but I told you, I'm here for you Cris. You can blame me, hit me, cry to me or ignore me. I don't care. I'm here for whatever you, Stormy, or your house needs."

"What I need is some fucking space!" Cris turned, stormed out the door and sat in a chair on the deck.

She pulled her phone from her pocket and held it up. Cris had nobody to call or text, no social media or emails to check. What she did have was a meager reflection on the screen. She could see the figure of Pete sitting at the breakfast bar looking out the window, right in the direction she was sitting.

Deciding she had to keep up her hard façade while refusing to go back inside with Pete, Cris pulled her legs up into the chair and did exactly what she had said she was doing before. She looked out into the yard and watched the wildlife wake up and do their own morning routines. The squirrels chased each other, leaping from branch to branch or racing on the ground below, while the birds sang and looked for their breakfast, hopping and pecking at the ground. Over the songs of the birds, she heard the owl hooting loudly and the rooster crowing off in the distance somewhere. Cris put her head back on the chair and closed her eyes, trying to be present in the moment and bring some peace into her constantly over aroused central nervous system. Cris knew it wasn't possible in its entirety, but she would be content with whatever she was able to gain.

The day was already starting to heat up. The humidity getting as thick as a cluster of flies on a dead whore's body. Cris could envision it slithering up her legs like she was being felt up and violated by its suffocating enclosure. The sweat began stinging her wound. Cris grabbed her sticky hair and pulled it up in her hand. She looked around at the Spanish moss dangling from many of the surrounding trees. The magnolias in full bloom emitted their fragrant scent. Cris tried to concentrate on breathing in the perfume of the flowers instead of inhaling the heavy liquid air. The emergence of sweat also brought the onslaught of gnats.

"Well, there goes my outdoor escape."

Cris put her phone in her pocket as she stood up and stretched. Turning to go inside, she saw Pete was still sitting there, calmly watching her. Turning the doorknob, Cris tried to grab a centering breath, while hailing a silent prayer for patience before opening the door.

"Do you feel more relaxed and at peace now?"

"Not exactly. Why were you sitting there staring at me the whole time? It's more than a little creepy."

"I didn't mean to seem like a stalker. It's the only way to be sure you are safe."

"Really? I'm on my deck, in my own back yard!"

"You were in the semi-private preserve next to your property last week, it doesn't seem to matter. I'm not willing to take a chance Cris, sorry."

Pete raised his eyebrows as he tilted his head and lifted his hands before leisurely dropping them back down on the counter. It was clear he was not really sorry.

She did have to give him that one though, damn him. They had felt completely safe in there last Sunday before the fatal shot. Even so, Cris would not admit defeat. She was thankful when she saw the security company pull in from the side kitchen window.

"Well, I'm back inside now and the security company is here, so you are relieved from your duty."

"Hmm, this one at least. I have a lot of work to go do now. You know where to find me if you need me."

Cris ignored him and walked to the front door to meet the security crew. She confirmed with them they were to secure every exterior door as well as the windows, but not to include a camera at the exterior or perimeter at this time. Even though Cris knew it might help catch Pete, it would definitely get in the way of her own plans and the sneaking around she knew she was going to have to do. Cris also confirmed she would have the app on her phone to arm and disarm, along with viewing the codes entered and would be the only one allowed to have this remote access.

She showed them around the house, and they discussed each area. They agreed on the location for the physical keypad and told her they would set up all the access codes at the end of the installation. They had everything they needed from her at that point, so Cris left them to work in peace. Pete had settled into his office area and was working on his laptop, with papers scattered all around.

Constricted, Cris again felt like she had nowhere to go in her own house. This was beginning to feel like her lot in life and was already getting old. Feeling satisfied Pete was settled into his area, Cris decided to grab her laptop and go back out on the deck to sit. After dousing herself with enough bug spray to kill any bug or colony within 100 miles, Cris filled a glass with ice water and went out to reclaim her parcel on the soupy air deck.

Cris brought her laptop, initially thinking she would have work she could get done. Checking her emails, there wasn't much to be done. There were a few reports left which needed writing and wrapping up from the case they assisted with up in Jasper county, but it looked like Detective Kim Campbell had already completed them. Kim did a very accurate and thorough job in the reports. Cris was impressed as she read them over and signed electronically on the required lines.

A short time had passed when Cris heard Pete's voice nearby. She had intentionally left Stormy inside. Not only due to the heat and humidity, but also to not give away her privacy, and instead alert her to Pete's presence. Even without Stormy, Cris had no problem hearing Pete and knew he was next to the house. She was glad Stormy wasn't with her, or Pete certainly would've known she was there, and she wouldn't have heard him.

"Yes, sir. The security company is here and working on the installation." Pete paused, obviously listening to who, Cris knew, must be Chief Bolton.

"I've been going through all my notes and rethinking everything." It sounded like Pete was shuffling his feet slightly, pacing.

"I keep coming back to the church service. Nobody was a suspect because they were all mourners. If they had shot Luke by mistake, it's logical they would've been truly mourning. The murderer probably was there as we initially expected." Another pause, listening.

"I feel like I'm starting at ground zero again in many ways since nobody really did want to hurt Luke. But I'm going to try to use that to my advantage, look at things with new eyes. Everything is different now. I need to relook at all the church attendees and interviews. Since I know Cris is the target, I need to investigate her past now. See if there's any connections in her history."

Cris about jumped up from her chair and was thankful to hear Chief's voice. She couldn't make out what he was saying, but it was audible now. She knew he must somehow be putting the kibosh to that idea. Cris didn't know just how much Bolton knew about her past since they still had their inexplicable conversation to finish. That aside, she was pretty confident he would stand up for her, knowing she wanted to keep her past hidden. Pete's voice began to sound farther away. She assumed he must be heading back in.

"Okay, sir. I have other places to start in the meantime, no problem. We'll discuss that at a later time if needed."

With that, she knew for sure Chief had her back. She also knew they needed to finish their talk sooner than later. Cris' thoughts were interrupted by the back door opening.

"I didn't realize you were out here. I was coming to ask if you would like something for lunch. I thought you were inside to help guide or answer questions for the security crew." The look on Pete's face said he knew he was probably busted on his call with Bolton.

"Nope, I figured I'd be better off out of their way. They could find me if they needed me. And, I'm competent enough to feed myself."

"Thanks for that earth-shattering testimony. I thought we discussed this already. You shouldn't be out here alone right now."

"I'm not alone. I have my weapon with me at all times."

"Stop being so damn hardheaded and stubborn. You really think that's going to do you any good after the other shot has already gone off?"

Pete's voice was raised. Cris couldn't remember ever hearing him raise his voice before. He was always so even tempered. She could tell he was trying to regain his composure. Sitting down in the chair next to her and leaning forward slightly, he rested his arms on his thighs and folded his hands. He was breathing evenly and staring out into the back yard.

He took a deep, seemingly centering, breath before he spoke. "The grass looks like it needs to be cut. I can do that for you if you would like or let me. I remember Luke saying once that was his job. It would be one less thing for you to worry about and I'd really like to help you around the house, or with whatever else you need. It's not like I have anything to do outside of work anyway."

That finished off her already short fuse. "You have a case to be working on and you shouldn't have much free time until you solve it this time."

She closed her laptop and stood, getting up before she said anymore. Cris always had a problem with saying what she was thinking, and it didn't typically end well. She was thankful to see the head security technician walking towards her. Cris opened the door and walked in to meet him with Pete right up her ass. They were at the end of their installation and needed to get the codes programmed.

They all walked over to the keypad where they would enter their codes. "Mrs. Steele, we will install and do your code through the app at the end. We have already emailed Mr. Bolton to be the authorized user through our secured and encrypted site. His data goes directly to our home office. It's been confirmed that he has already entered his information and is all set."

Cris saw Pete look at her with raised eyebrows from the corner of his eyes. Must be he didn't like her having remote access or having Chief as an extra layer of security. *Tough shit!*

Despondently, Cris reluctantly agreed to let Pete have access and enter his code. At least that way she'd know when he entered or left and could catch him if he was the murderer. Cris made a point of having her whole body turned when he put in his code. She didn't want any accusations that she knew his code and entered it to frame him.

If there was a need to take him down, Cris wanted it done cleanly. No doubts allowed to set in, no room for error. Pete, or whoever the son of a bitch was, once she found out, wasn't going to know what hit 'em!

CHAPTER 9

Once the security company left, Cris felt the need to be productive in doing something. Anything. She went into her office and closed the door. Knowing she was the intended target, Cris needed to start thinking differently; assuming it wasn't someone trying to throw her off, like Pete for instance. She began a list of previous cases to see if anyone or anything stood out as threatening or holding a grudge. Nothing immediately jumped out, but she was happy to have the list going to come back to later. She left the list on her desk alongside all the other notes she had previously compiled on Luke's case. Once she was done, she locked the office door behind herself, knowing she wouldn't go back in until bedtime.

Cris felt like she was imprisoned to the padded cell inside her skull. She had to get out of the house. She needed to relieve some of her stress. Since she was restricted from her normal release of working out, Cris decided on the next best thing, going to the range. The benefit was twofold. The last confrontation, when she did not have time to plant her feet firmly and was grazed, had left her insecure of her abilities. She couldn't get it out of her head. That would not do. Cris needed to make sure she was still at expert level, that her stance, speed, and precision were still there.

She went into the living room where Stormy was lounging on the couch and Pete was scribbling notes by his laptop.

Stormy started her drum solo at Cris' arrival and Pete turned around and smiled as he watched her petting her girl. Cris saw it as her opportunity to break the news to him.

"I'm going to go to the range and get some practice in."

Pete sighed. "You know it's really difficult for me to ensure your safety when you keep trying to run off on me."

"I'm not exactly running off. I'm telling you where I'm going."

"I'm aware of that. My point is you keep leaving the house in one form or another. It makes my job more difficult."

"I believe your job is to solve the case that you're on. Not to be a babysitter."

"And I believe you were standing right here when Chief said I was to stay with you to ensure your safety until this is over. Now, there's no point in having a pissing match here, it doesn't solve anything. I can't have you going out there alone, but I also don't intend to try to stop you. Please let me drive you and drop you off. I think it's secure enough to leave you alone once you're on the training island."

Cris thought for a minute. She did have to get her SUV. Campbell had driven it back from Jasper while she was in the hospital. Chief had driven her home from the hospital which led to his inadvertently opening the can of worms about knowledge of her childhood, that she had always kept locked up tight. Stopping herself from going down that rabbit hole, Cris rolled her eyes at Pete and released a heavy sigh.

"How about a compromise? I do have to go to the office to get my keys from Campbell. You can bring me there and I can drive my SUV to the range from the station."

Pete's blue eyes narrowed at her for a fraction of a second. "Fair enough. I think it's sufficiently close to be safe between the two locations."

"C'mon Storm lets go out." Stormy came bounding over as Cris grabbed the leash and clipped it on her collar.

Pete glared over at her. "Damn you, Cris! What the hell is it going to take for me to get it through that thick skull of yours? You should not be out there."

"Ugh, will you stop! I will go on the left side of the house where there are neighbors and it's not secluded, okay?!" Cris didn't wait for his response but smartly turned out the door.

Cris went to the left like she said she would and thankfully Stormy was quick about it. This was hard for her since she had always felt safe in this neighborhood. She still hadn't processed how this whole nightmare happened in the preserve right next to her property line. It was surreal. It did make her realize though, Pete was right. Not that she would admit it to him, but she would try to remember it and cut him a little slack.

She walked into the living room to see him placing his laptop and all his closed files and notes into his backpack. Cris assumed he was taking no chances on her looking at his stuff. Thinking of her own locked office, she completely understood.

Pete looked back at her. "I'm going to do some work at the office since you'll be in the vicinity."

Cris was proud of herself. In her own way, she remembered to show him some mercy by keeping the bite out of her tone.

"You don't owe me an explanation of your work or time. I'm not your boss."

Walking into the kitchen, Cris grabbed Stormy a treat. She had already jumped up on the couch and was content, as Pete and Cris walked out the door. Cris was happy to successfully set the alarm remotely from her phone after they walked out. She had motion detectors installed but did not activate them now since Stormy was in there. She was confident they installed them high enough to accommodate her, but Cris did not want any interruptions from a false alarm while on the range.

They loaded up into Pete's truck. She wasn't surprised, but Cris still inwardly smiled at how neat and clean it was. As the engine and rumble of exhaust came to life so did his music. He quickly pushed at the buttons to turn it down.

Pete glanced over at her. "Sorry!"

"Seriously? Did you forget who you're talking to? My music is always blaring. This is a good song, turn it back up!"

Smiling, Pete indulged her by turning it up louder, but it wasn't until they turned out of her community before he really cranked it up. Not only was it a good song, but it was also a good excuse to not have to partake in anymore small talk. Cris was staring out her window enjoying the surrounding beauty on the short drive to the office. She always loved going over the Intracoastal Waterway bridge when she was in Luke's truck. She could see so much further out compared to her car. Being a passenger, Cris was often able to spot dolphins jumping and circling. She was getting the same satisfaction in Pete's truck. Cris realized how nice it felt to be out of the house. Traffic was good and only two songs in, they arrived at the station.

Pete got to the back door, swiped his badge and held the door open for Cris. They walked down the hall towards the chaotic hub of the office. Reed was walking towards them, heading for the breakroom. Pete stopped to talk to him just outside the breakroom door. Cris realized she had forgotten to bring her water, so she went in to grab some. She hadn't even made it to the water cooler before she saw Moretti throwing his coffee cup away. At their last encounter, Moretti was making a joke of Luke's death and Cris put him in his place, unknowingly, in front of some of their colleagues. Suffice it to say, they weren't exactly friends. Moretti turned her way and they locked eyes, glowering at each other. Cris was trying hard to keep her mouth shut. Moretti spoke, "Well, fancy seeing you here. Your arm looks like a botched suicide attempt and I heard you got yourself shot in the head up in Jasper."

Cris was pissed but still tried to bite her tongue. "Much to your dismay, pencil dick, I'm not going anywhere. I'm making it my mission to stick around and make your life miserable."

She thought she saw Pete and Reed staring at them from the doorway, but Cris didn't care and she sure as hell was not breaking eye contact with Moretti. Cris would give no signs of backing down.

"Look, Steele, can't we stop this and be civil to each other?"

Cris knew by Moretti trying to wave the white flag and call a truce, she had succeeded to hit his self-proclaimed Italian Stallion's pride where it hurt, in his pants. Cris got inches from his face and was very terse with her words. "I am being civil, you simple piece of shit! You were joking about what happened. You think it's funny? Do you know how it feels? Go fuck yourself, Moretti!"

She shoved him backward into the wall hard enough to jar his bones on impact. Reed came rushing in, grabbed Moretti and roughly sat him in a nearby chair. He walked up next to Cris and put his hand on her shoulder.

"Sorry about Moretti. He's an asshole. If it's any consolation, I don't think he saw that coming and along with "pencil dick" I think you can also call him "skid mark" now because I'm pretty sure he just shit himself."

Cris chuckled at that one. "Thanks, Reed. I'm sorry you're stuck having to work with him. You're a better man than I would be."

Reed walked her to the door where Pete was waiting, before turning back to deal with Moretti. Pete put his arm around Cris' shoulder, gave her a brief squeeze, then released her.

"Ah, Cris. What am I going to do with you?"

Cris' heart dropped to her stomach. A memory vividly crashed. Luke was saying the same exact thing when they were kids on the playground after she had just stood up for herself and her family to Raquel, the school bully. The only difference was Luke held his arm around her shoulder the whole time as he walked away with her. Cris couldn't believe the déjà vu going on right now. Then, out of nowhere, she heard Luke's voice whisper in her ear, "Everything happens for a reason, Cris."

Her mouth went dry. Cris realized she never did get the water she had gone in for, but she knew it wouldn't matter. Water, or anything else, couldn't stop what she was feeling right now. Everything was in slow motion and muffed, almost silent. Cris saw Campbell standing in front of her office area, looking their way. People passed them, talking on their phones or with each and going on with their lives, some nodding to Cris and Pete as they passed. They were walking by Chief's office and Cris looked over. She saw Chief sitting at his desk, looking towards her with disapproval. *Focus, damn it! Pull out of this! You can break down later, right now you need to pull your shit together!* Cris was so frustrated and emotionally spent, she just wanted to cry and let it out. Knowing that wasn't an option, she tried to pull away from the darkness that was close to drowning her. Everything still in slow motion, she turned to Pete. Her movement and speech felt slow and thick like she was drunk. Cris prayed it didn't appear that way to Pete.

"I'm going to talk to Bolton a minute."

Cris turned to walk towards Chief's office, she thought she heard Pete respond, but she couldn't be sure. Entering Bolton's office, he looked like he wanted to pounce on her. Cris still felt a little out of body, but she was sure she was reading his face and body language accurately. Cris said a silent prayer. *Thank you! This means I'm starting to come back around!*

"Hey, Chief."

Cris sat down in what she now considered her dreaded chair where her "interview" in Luke's investigation took place. That was the first time she had accused Pete of being Luke's murderer and the first time Chief Bolton hinted at her past. It all started to be too much again. Chief must have noticed the crack in her iron shield, because his face went from anger to concern. He went over and shut his door then knelt beside her.

"Cris, what's wrong?"

She was chastising herself for her mental weakness. Cris always kept herself together in front of anyone else. Hell, she hadn't even allowed herself to shed a tear at Luke's funeral last week. Now, she was at work having a breakdown over a simple friggin' sentence from Pete before hearing, no not hearing, *remembering*, Luke's voice. There was no way she actually heard Luke's voice. Cris shook her head, temporarily shaking the demons off.

Cris looked Bolton in the eyes. "Nothing's wrong, sir. I had another go 'round with Moretti in the break room. I'm just trying to contain myself is all."

"Bullshit, Cris. I know you too well. Well enough to know you've got your shield back up and won't tell me what's really going on."

"With all due respect, sir, we still haven't finished our ambiguous conversation. So, it should come as no surprise that my shield is back up. It still pisses me off that we even discussed my shield and possible lack of superpowers. You took advantage of my diminished mental capacities after leaving the hospital." Cris looked at him and tried to look serious but smiled.

"There's that smartass, Cris. So, since I know you are back with full body armor, I can ask, what the hell are you doing here? I will refrain from commenting on the mental capacities until you answer my question."

"Simmer down, Pollywog. I'm only here to get my keys from Campbell. I rode over with Bryan, and I'm sure you'll be elated to hear that he's doing a fantastic job of babysitting me."

Cris hadn't meant to call Chief that. It was something her dad used to say, and she couldn't believe it came out of her mouth. She hadn't heard or said it in years. *What the hell is wrong with me?*

"Well, I'm sure as hell no Pollywog, but thanks for letting me know you weren't here to work. I was not up for an argument with you today."

"Yea, me neither. Thanks, Chief. I'll talk to ya soon."

Cris stood up and headed for the door. She walked past Pete working at his desk and went to the next glorified cubicle of Kim Campbell. Cris was immediately assaulted by her pink and purple lair but was pleased to see her sitting at her desk.

Cris knocked on her cubicle wall. "Hey, Spicy Eyes."

Campbell whipped around, eyes wide, strands of long blonde hair lingering across her perfect face. "Steele, it's good to see you! You look much better than you did the last time I saw you on the floor with blood coming from your head. But, don't go telling people about that, it's embarrassing. Please keep it to yourself!"

While Cris had a minor incident with a bullet grazing her head, Kim had a slight altercation with some demonic hand sanitizer while they were up in Jasper. This resulted in her eyes being "spicy" according to her. While it was serious and Cris felt bad for Campbell, it was also one hell of a comedy show.

"Ah, no worries Campbell. That's your story to tell, not mine. Although, as a side note, you may want to keep that consideration in mind when thinking about discussing my little white bags with others. Chief told me you enlightened him about what I do for the homeless Vets when you gave him some bags for our expedition home. Anyway, food for thought and water under the bridge. I think I'll call you Spicy for short. It sounds mysterious, sultry, sassy and sexy. Right up your alley." Cris leaned in, put her hand next to her mouth and whispered, "You never know, maybe Bryan will be interested in someone named Spicy."

"Real funny, Cris."

"I'm really just here to get the keys for my Explorer."

Kim turned and grabbed them from her desk and handed them to Cris. "Here ya go."

Cris stood up, ready to end the small talk and go now that she had what she came for. "Thanks. I also signed the reports you wrote from Jasper. They looked good, and thanks for leaving out some of the information that could be considered nonessential to the investigation. Like me going in ahead of the SWAT team."

"No problem."

Now, Cris was standing just outside Kim's cubicle, which bordered Pete's. Seeing Cris standing there, Pete stood up and moved towards her. Cris looked over at him.

"I'll see you later back at home, er, my place, ugh, the house."

Cris saw the look Campbell gave them both but wasn't going to acknowledge it. She didn't know if Campbell knew Pete was ordered to stay with her and she didn't want to discuss it. They had debates about Bryan when they were in Jasper. Cris knew how Campbell felt about him, as well as her incorrect suspicions about his feelings.

Before either of them could say anything about her babbling blunder, Cris took off towards the back door to head to the range. She was thankful not to cross paths with Moretti on her way out. Reed must have put him somewhere to lick his wounds.

The gun range wasn't far from the station. Cris had to go about a quarter mile down the road, then over another bridge. It was on its own island owned by the county and that was where all of their training sectors were. Everything in tactical training happened here, away from the tourists and public. Cris already felt her neck and shoulders relax as she crossed over that bridge. *Ah, guns, ammo, and destruction, here I come!*

It was getting to be late in the afternoon and she was happy to see a training class was calling it quits for the day as they were staggering out into the parking lot. Cris knew she would most likely have the range all to herself. She started indoors, but it was weird. Her aggression was gradually lessening, but she also felt slightly creeped out, as though someone was watching her. She tried to shake it off and focus on her form and targets. After expelling several magazines, she still didn't feel satisfied. Cris decided to grab her stuff and go outside. The outdoor range had the standard stationary figures and simulated scenes of homes and yards where you would be likely to encounter suspects and return fire.

Walking out back of the indoor range, Cris still couldn't shake the feeling of having eyes following her. The hairs on the back of her neck stood up. While holding firm to her fully loaded, safety off Smith & Wesson, Cris tried to inconspicuously look around the surrounding area which was barricaded by trees. Blatantly, she held her pistol up as she racked the slide and got into stance, daring someone to mess with her right now.

Bring it on bitch, I'm ready!

CHAPTER 10

Once Cris turned to leave, Pete went back inside his cubicle office area. He shut down his laptop as he placed his notes into the folders and stuffed it all into his backpack. Pete thought he heard Campbell saying something, but he didn't listen as he rushed towards the back door. He had to come out when Cris was leaving so she wouldn't see him, and time it perfectly or he would miss her. Pete needed to follow her at a considerable distance so Cris wouldn't know, which would not be easy. He needed to be sure of where she was going. Seeing her make a left out of the parking lot, he knew Cris was really going to the range. The only thing in that direction was the bridge leading to the training island. Knowing his truck would be too obvious to her or any others that may be there, Pete jumped in his county issued SUV so he would blend in better.

Pete got there as a training class was letting out. Since they had not completed their training yet, they were still in their personal vehicles and the two trainers were in their county vehicles. Pete had to think expeditiously where he could park unobtrusively. Thankful for his meticulous thinking, he knew this was the best time. While so many vehicles were traveling around on their way out, his vehicle would easily intermingle. Pete backed in on the other side of the building, lined up against the trees in between some broken down old vehicles. Anyone seeing it would assume the back was rear-ended or it had somehow malfunctioned. Pete scooched down in his seat just enough so he could still see what was going on. He watched Cris walk into the indoor range and all the other vehicles depart without a second glance. Aside from her SUV, the parking lot was empty. *Good, she's alone, which will make this much easier!*

Watching as the last of the parade turned the corner and drove away toward the exit of the island, Pete soundlessly crept out. He instinctively reached to his weapon as he heard the first shot explode. Cris obviously wasted no time in getting started. Confident she wouldn't hear him now, Pete walked at a much quicker pace. There was a window which looked in on the lanes of the range and also had a large bush in front of it. He would have to remember later to suggest trimming it back since it can be a security and safety hazard to anyone inside. For right now and those reasons, it served his purpose perfectly. Pete squeezed between the bush and the building and sneakily glanced inside the window, still careful in case Cris unexpectedly turned around. He was happy to see she picked a middle lane. He could stand off to the side and look down the line without being directly in the window. Chances of Cris or anyone pulling in seeing him were practically nonexistent.

He watched as Cris had several magazines lined up and ready to go. She shot rapid-fire at the targets, not stopping until the magazine was expended. Before releasing the spent magazine, Cris would look at her impact points then shake her head. Knowing her, Pete could almost hear her cursing and saying "grr" or most likely much more colorful expletives. From where he was standing it looked like all of her shots were spot on, either to the head or the chest. Obviously, they weren't up to her standards of perfection. While still shaking her head and grimacing, Cris was already slamming the next clip in and getting her body into stance.

Pete wanted to rush in and hold her and tell her it was okay and understandable to be less than perfect at the moment. She would get it back, and he would be there to help her every step of the way. They could do it together. He knew Ms. Independent would not like that. Pete continued to watch helplessly. He had to admit though, he was enjoying it. Maybe a little too much judging by some stirrings going on. He watched as every muscle in her body, from her shoulders down to that tight ass, flexed with each racking of the slide. Her muscles were taut with concentration, then barely moving as she stayed rock steady through the recoil. Pete suddenly realized she was packing up already. He chided himself for becoming so engrossed in watching her. Not knowing where she was going and not wanting to get caught, Pete ran over to his Explorer and shut the door as silently as possible. A minute later Cris walked out and around the other side of the building. Pete realized she wasn't done. She was ready for more extensive and tactical training outdoors. He smiled.

He could see the whole back training area from where he parked. He didn't have to get out and risk being seen or heard yet could still watch her every move. Pete saw her stop and look around, almost like she knew someone was there. Cris held her pistol up towards the sky, taunting as she racked the slide and dug her heels in, getting firm in her stance. He could tell she was daring someone to mess with her and grinned. *That's my girl!*

Seeing the bulge of her cell phone in the pocket of her pants and knowing he would need to leave before her and get back to his truck, Pete called and asked how much longer she thought she might be. He told her he'd like to follow her home to be sure she makes it safely. He'd watch for her and could pull out behind her as she passed the office. Pete knew there was no way to leave without her hearing, but since Cris was on the backside of the building, he was sure he could pull out and be around the corner before she could run around to see the vehicle leaving. That's what he hoped at least as he disconnected the call. Pete waited a few seconds for her to start firing the next round then he started the engine and left as fast as he could while trying not to spin the tires. Pete was fairly confident he was successful as he started down the road to leave the island.

He got to the office and parked his SUV where it had been and hopped into his truck. Pete parked by the entrance of the parking lot so he could see her as she was coming, then fall in line behind her as she was expecting. He felt like he had accomplished his mission and hoped it was true. Pete had a lot of things in mind for Cris, but another argument wasn't one of them.

CHAPTER 11

Ready to leave the range, Cris was back in her Explorer with all her weapons paraphernalia. It did relieve some of her stress and aggression. It was quickly brought back with feelings of being watched though. Pete's phone call and the perfectly timed vehicle leaving right after hadn't helped. Aside from that, it did take away the insecurity of her expert level shooting abilities. Cris felt recharged and revitalized tactically, and ready to take on whoever was after her. This trip had served its purpose.

Cris decided to call Chief before she left the parking lot. While things were certainly peculiar between them, Cris felt she could trust him. He was the only one now and Cris was thankful to at least have that going for her. She was not surprised when he answered on the first ring.

"Cris, what's up?"

"Hey, Chief. I think I need to tell you something, like I need someone to know about this in case something should happen."

Chief cut in, his concern evident. "What happened? What's wrong?"

"Nothing necessarily happened. Things were just a little weird here at the range and I want you to know. So, first of all, I felt watched. Hair standing up on the back of my neck kind of watched. I trust my instincts; they don't usually steer me wrong. I know you understand that."

Chief quietly interrupted. "Yes, I do."

"I know you do. Along with that, Bryan called wondering when I was going to leave so he could watch and follow me home once I went by the office. The strange part is, right after we hung up, I heard a vehicle start and leave. Sir, I never saw another vehicle in the parking lot after the training class left. It was empty every time I looked. I know Bryan stayed at the office to work while I was here at the range, but the timing was uncanny."

Bolton's voice bordered on concern and confusion. "Bryan's been gone for a while. Hang on, I'm going out to the parking lot now. Damn it, I need to start working out again… Okay, I'm here. Hmm, his truck is there, but not his Explorer. Maybe he went to your house for something?"

Cris was quick with a comeback, while she instinctively felt at the small of her back for her weapon. "Well, I can check the alarm codes entered once we hang up, which will answer that question."

She could tell Chief was still reaching, trying to find a logical explanation. Not wanting to believe what was obvious to her about Pete. "Or, maybe he went to his place for something. Oh, wait. I see him pulling in. I'm going to stand off to the side and watch. Hopefully, he won't see me. Stand by."

Cris would like to say she waited patiently, but the thirty seconds or so that passed felt like an eternity while waiting for Bolton's report. Finally, he came back, speaking softly.

"Okay, he went right to his truck. He had a backpack on his back. It really looks like he ran to his house for something, which would make sense since he knew you were safe on our range. He's driving towards the road now. Oh, wait, he parked by the road. I assume he's waiting for you like he said he was going to."

Cris blew out. "Pfft, how convenient. I'm not buying it. I felt watched, Bryan called, and I heard a vehicle leave. Anyway, I'm not calling to make false accusations. I'm calling you with the facts of what happened while I was here. You can keep them under your proverbial hat to do with what you wish."

"I can assure you, Cris, they are duly noted. I'm not saying you're right or wrong, but I'm thankful you trusted me enough to call and tell me. I know that must not have been easy for you."

"That's a conversation for another time, Chief. One we'll have soon. I won't forget everything we need to talk about, aside from the case."

Chief chuckled. "I know you won't. You would come back from the dead and haunt me until we finished it. No misconceptions on my part. We'll talk about it once all of this is behind us. I promise."

"You're damn right, on all counts. Anyway, I'm going to head out now, so I'll talk with you later."

Chief's voice was low and compassionate. "Promise me you'll stay safe Cris. You know to contact me anytime for anything."

Cris wasn't going to acknowledge any of his comments specifically. There was no way to do it without showing emotion. That would not do.

She gave a simple reply, "Yes, sir," before disconnecting the call and pulling out.

Going over the bridge and back down the road towards the station, Cris saw Pete's truck sitting there. She didn't give any kind of wave or acknowledgment as she passed. It was a test to see how closely he was watching. Apparently, Pete was right on his babysitting A-game, as he pulled out behind her.

Cris got home, felt at the small of her back, then grabbed the rest of her gear and got out. She went in, disabled the alarm on the keypad without a problem, greeted Stormy and turned on the green light outside the front door, all before Pete made it to the porch. Dusk had set in, with full darkness soon to follow, inside and out.

Pete bounded in, obviously trying to catch up. "So, how was the range?"

Innocent or guilty, Cris was not taking the bait. "It was great, but quite honestly, I'm really tired. I think I'm going to call it a night."

"I'm glad you enjoyed your time, get some rest. I'll take Stormy out, then I'm ready to wind down myself."

Cris gave Stormy a quick pet behind the ears and kisses to her head. "Good. Night, then."

"Good night, Cris. See you in the morning."

Cris stopped petting Stormy and turned away. She was trying to feign tiredness and sleep, so she could go into her temporary chamber and be alone. Pete walked out with Stormy and Cris stole the opportunity and unlocked the office door. She heard Pete and Stormy coming back up onto the porch and quietly pulled the office door. Cris left it cracked so she wouldn't have to worry about the doorknob betraying her in a few minutes. Cris had already planned and grabbed a glass of ice water for bed. She could drink the small amount of water and still have the necessary ice without the noise of getting it. She walked to the end of the hall to her bedroom. Once it was quiet for a few minutes and she felt certain Pete was settled for the night, she softly crept into the office and locked the door. She pulled her sleeping things back out, which included her new friend, Sailor Jerry. Proud of her quick thinking with the ice and no experience in this field, she watched as that nostalgic amber liquid flowed into her glass.

Putting the glass to her lips, Cris thought of her dad. The first taste was cold on her tongue from the ice, then burned going down. Cris swore she could feel it flow from her esophagus down to her stomach. She was brought back to her dream last night. Inspired by it, she took an even longer pull on the liquid and decided to take the letter and his dog tags out of her desk drawer. Cris always kept them hidden in case of any rare company coming. If anyone saw, they might ask whose they were. Cris didn't willingly offer up personal information, and most certainly kept all those demons from her childhood locked away, buried deep in the basements of hell. Luke was the only one who knew, and he took them to the grave with him.

Already finishing her first glass, Cris decided she needed one more to get through this process. She poured in a little extra and took a sip. It wasn't the same without the ice, it was a constant burn the whole way. She wanted that initial coolness. Cris inwardly wondered, *like father, like daughter after all?*

Assuming Pete should be asleep by now, Cris was confident she could be quiet enough to go out and get more ice. She thought she turned the knob silently, but she did undeniably realize she was feeling more than a little buzzed right now. The Sailor was hitting suddenly and hard. Cris was still cognizant enough to know her senses were definitely off, although admittingly feeling drunker by the second. Tottering out of the office and past the doorway to go to the kitchen, she noticed a dim light in the living room. Out of the corner of her eye, Cris saw Stormy at the end of the couch and the shirtless figure with the carved abs at the other end reading something under the light. Cris smiled.

"Don't stay up too late Luke. You know you'll regret it when we get up at the crack of dawn."

There was a pause, then a very subdued response, "Um, okay."

The barely audible reply was his typical retort. She refreshed her ice in the now half-full glass and went back into the office. As she quietly shut the door, Cris noticed her ears were ringing from the Sailor. She had already forgotten her practically one-sided conversation.

Sitting back down on her bed-on-the-floor, she topped off her second round. Cris now fully understood how it made her dad feel and she was equally enjoying the numbness it cloaked her in. Just like she had referred to it as her dad's companion as a child, Cris was already considering it hers too. With all the recent events, and undoubtedly a little extra courage from her newfound companion, Cris decided she would start wearing his dog tags. She fleetingly thought about other people seeing them and questioning her. Taking another slug of courage, she wasn't worried about it. Everyone knew Cris was private and would most likely know better than to say anything to her. If they did and she didn't answer with anything but sarcasm, they would not be the least bit surprised and would certainly back off.

Putting the dog tags around her neck, she felt hot tears falling. It felt like he was right there with her. Cris took another big swig, squeezing the dog tags in her right hand so hard she thought they would bleed again. She looked up at the ceiling, mentally seeing beyond it. *Daddy, let these do what you hoped they would. Give me strength and courage and feel you constantly by my side. I need you now that Luke's gone. I need you both. Please help me.*

The tears were still silent but fell harder. Knowing, even in her numbness, the letter would send her completely over the edge, Cris decided to tuck it back in the drawer for now. She took a big swallow of what was left in the glass. Pouring herself another, she licked her lips with anticipation as that amber goodness swirled over the top of the still fresh ice.

CHAPTER 12

*C*ris sat catatonic against the wall, semi-watching the police do their work. She saw fuzzy movements and heard clips of conversations like bad reception on a TV, cutting in and out. Things were black and silent or were intermittently slow and fuzzy. Her sense of time was entirely lost. Cris didn't know if she had been sitting there five minutes or five hours, nor did she care. Emotionless and detached, she felt nothing but an empty black hole.

Like reception foggily cutting in, Cris heard someone, somewhere. "His grandmother came and got him after she saw all the police cars arrive. He was sitting in the back yard and wouldn't leave because Cris had told him to stay out there. He knew he couldn't go inside because she told him not to before she ran in, but he refused to leave her. The poor kid kept waiting for her to come back out."

Blackness again. At some point, Cris thought she heard her mom talking to her and trying to get her to leave the room. Cris vaguely registered it as she stared blankly at the bloody wall ahead. The fuzzy service was back again. Cris perceived a man's voice, probably a police officer, cutting in and out. "Unresponsive... Better for psyche to leave her right now... Try to pull her out... Cause a mental break..." Mom's voice cut in. "Finding her father like this... Psychological break... Never be the same... How...

Happen... Laying on him... Covered in his blood... Not blinking... Lost..."

Time passed, Cris had no idea how much. She realized her senses must be coming back to pay a visit for a little bit as the strong metallic smell hit her all over again. Her eyes blurrily came into focus and without moving her head or body, only her eyes, she looked around. The room was empty, in more ways than one. Cris remembered her dad being bagged up in slow motion. People in boots walking around, then suddenly gone. The familiar sound of a truck. Her mom talking to a man in the otherwise silent house. It sounded like they were both crying. Cris closed her eyes and put her head back against the wall. At some point, she must have fallen asleep and curled up on the floor. She vaguely heard her mom and the man talking nearby. He was insisting on "doing it for her" which Cris soon realized must've been herself, as he scooped her up off the floor and into her bed. Her mom pulled the covers up over her and they walked out shutting her bedroom door behind them. Cris happily fell back into the blackness.

Later the next day, Luke came over and knocked on the door. Cris couldn't answer. She saw the concern all over his face and his fidgeting hands as she peeked through the blinds. She still couldn't bring herself to talk to him. After waiting a few minutes, Luke shook his head and walked back next door. Cris stepped away from the blinds and realized her whole day was lost. She had no memory of anything she had done. She couldn't even remember where she just had been before Luke knocked on the door.

Seeing Luke gave her a minute of clarity. Cris felt some strength returning. She wasn't sure how long it would stay, but she was thankful for it. Seizing the moment and the strength while she still had it, Cris decided she was definitely going to school tomorrow. She was not going to show there was anything wrong with her to further warrant "Crazy Cris." She got her clothes ready and set her alarm while she was still cognizant, knowing if she inadvertently checked out for the rest of the day, she would be prepared when the alarm went off in the morning.

Cris was not happy about her recent cognitive lapses and wanted to take full advantage of her current lucid state. Knowing it might throw her back into the vegetative frame of mind, she still took a chance and walked into her father's room. Her head started getting dizzy, she felt like she might pass out. She scurried over to his nightstand and grabbed her blood-spattered letter along with the dog tags off the stand and hurried out, bringing them back to her room. She shut the door and tried to continue to stay aware and alert. Thinking back on some of the times on the playground and Luke doing deep breathing to try to keep her calm, Cris decided to try and use this tactic now. She didn't know if it was the breathing or the thought of Luke, but she was thankful either way that she was still coherent. She was more surprised at the level of her brain returning as Cris realized her mom's letter wasn't there, meaning she had already taken it.

Cris knew from experience over the past two years that they would never tell each other what their letters said. It wasn't like when dad was deployed and sending a letter to them both, plus individual letters that they enthusiastically shared. Nope. Cris knew they would never talk about him at all. They wouldn't be able to without breaking down, which was not something they did. They would both force everything down, deep inside, where it would remain forever hidden and locked away. It was its own irrational family bond. It was the Murray way.

Cris knew she was not able to read his letter right now. But she still recognized the strength and was thankful for the ability to be able to go retrieve it. She pulled out the bottom drawer of her dresser, placed the bloody envelope and dog tags underneath, then put the drawer back in place. Her essential tasks must have been completed for the day since that was the last thing she remembered.

When Cris went out to the bus stop the next morning, Luke looked at her with his crooked smiled then gave her a big hug. He sat with her on the bus as usual, but he didn't say anything to her. She realized at that moment just how well Luke really knew her. He was showing her that he was there for her, but he knew she would not want to talk about anything. Cris had a huge lump in her throat as she stared out the window the whole way.

When they got to school, Cris constantly reminded herself to try to focus on her work, keep busy and act normal. Everything was a blur; she didn't hear anything the teacher was saying. A few times Cris felt her eyes glaze over and after some time, she felt a poke from Luke that brought her out of her withdrawn state.

For once, Raquel didn't say anything directly, but Cris could hear whispers and see the averted eyes. She sat on the grass with Luke at recess. They weren't talking, but thankfully the silence wasn't awkward. Cris unintentionally kept slipping in and out of conscious thought, and time and place continued to be a blur. She heard whispers nearby from Raquel and several others. Cris couldn't make out what they were saying, but she could tell it was not the normal taunting, it was gossip. No doubt she and her family were the hottest news all over the school right now. For the first time in her life, Cris didn't care. Out of the corner of her eye, she saw Luke look over at her. Apparently, he did care and had no intentions of letting it continue in his presence. Without saying a word, Luke got up and walked over to the group hanging out close by.

"Why don't y'all try something new and show some respect? Go blabbermouth somewhere else."

There were some inaudible grumblings, but Luke pressed on. "Someday every one of you will have something happen that will shatter your sheltered diminutive lives. I can only hope when that happens and you see how it feels, you repent for your behaviors you have now."

Cris heard Raquel's familiar squeal cut in like nails on a chalkboard. "Oh, listen to you with your uneducated southern drawl trying to use an educated man's words. Go back and check your dictionary because those ain't even real words, moron."

Cris saw Luke shake his head. "Ain't real words? Okay, thanks for that educational tip, Einstein."

Cris still couldn't muster up the give a damn to get up and help Luke and that was the part that really pissed her off. Luke was too sweet, not good enough with the insults to take on the likes of them. He would get eaten alive. Cris was reluctantly getting up to go over, knowing in her state of mind it wouldn't be good. There was nothing to restrain her right now, she wouldn't care if she got expelled for breaking all their noses. She hadn't gotten very far when she saw a teacher walking over to the group. This was a first. Cris could see she was yelling at the group and not Luke. She was sticking up for him and Cris and dishing out punishments for the others.

Cris sat back down and looked up at the sky as her eyes started to get hot. "Thanks, Dad."

She knew the group would come after her and try to make her pay for them getting in trouble over her, but she didn't care. Cris could feel she was starting to come around again and knew she just needed to get through the day. After that, she would be ready for them. Luke came back over and resumed his position next to her on the grass. He was silent again.

Cris couldn't look him in the eyes, instead, she looked at the ground and started picking blades of grass. "I'm sorry I didn't answer the door yesterday. I wasn't ready to talk or see anyone. How did you do it, Luke? How do you get through it? I remember the look on your face the first day I met you and asked where your parents were. I know you know how I feel right now."

"I do know, and I won't ask you to talk about it, but you know you can if you ever decide you want to. In the beginning, I just kept putting one foot in front of the other. Then after I met you, it got easier. I had you to spend time and have fun with. It still hurts, but you make it hurt less."

Cris had tears threatening to spill, which she knew wouldn't do. Her response was almost inaudible. "Thanks, Luke."

"You're welcome, Cris."

Luke put his arm around her shoulder and pulled her towards him quickly, then released her. As close as they already were, Cris knew they now had an inseparable bond. Two broken kids against the world.

CHAPTER 13

Cris awoke to a pounding in her head. She knew it was a combination of her dream and too much of her new Sailor friend. Pissed off about both, she decided 36 hours was close enough. Her patience was gone, it was time to exercise. Like an addict, she had an itch she knew only a run on the beach would scratch right now. As she sat up on the hard floor, she felt the pain in her lower back. Cris knew she must've been knocked out and had not rotated at all. That was nothing compared to the spinning the room was currently doing. *Ugh! Damn it!* She chugged down a bottle of water she had nearby, trying to flush her companion away.

It was still early. Cris got up, grabbing onto the adjacent chair to steady her swaying head. She left her sleeping arrangements for now but locked the office door as she exited. Cris softly padded down the hall to her room and got dressed in her workout gear. She was sure to include her steel comrade Smith & Wesson in her attire. Initially hesitating as she went to put her hair up in its usual high pony, Cris decided to do it anyway. It was unlikely she would see anyone this early, and if she did and they saw her partially shaved and stapled head, she didn't care. Cris had always marched to the beat of her own drum and not given a damn about what others thought. It bothered her that she questioned it for a fraction of a second. Pulling her hair back and snapping the band in place, a sharp pain radiated from the laceration on the side of her head around the back of it. Cris could see the area still looked very red and swollen, some pus still oozing through the staples. She briefly thought of the 48-hour restriction that she was still slightly short of, then shoved it aside, like everything else in her life.

Tiptoeing out to the kitchen, Stormy lifted her head as Cris passed, but thankfully didn't move off the couch and wake up Pete. Grateful for her good vision and adaptation to the darkness, in more ways than one, Cris didn't turn on any lights as she traveled throughout the house. Grabbing her protein drink from the fridge, Cris downed it as she scribbled Pete a note in the dark letting him know where she was heading. She left it on the breakfast bar for him, so he wouldn't worry if he woke up and somehow realized she was gone. Taking her phone, Cris silently disabled the alarm. Happy with her stealthy departure, Cris smiled as she went out the French doors onto the back deck and deeply inhaled the fresh and already heavy, humid, air. Turning the knob to silently close the door before releasing it, Cris put an earbud in her right ear and fired up her playlist. The sun would be coming up within the next half an hour and she wanted to be on the beach to catch it.

Leaving her yard, then soon her little community, Cris was watchful going over the bridge where she saw the questionable stranger the previous week. There was a possibility he was from the neighboring community and completely innocent. The way he was watching her though made him wholly suspicious in her book, especially since Luke had just been murdered in the same vicinity. Not seeing anything apprehensive today, Cris began to feel more invigorated as the smell of the salt and fish from the ocean tantalized her nose. She was inspired to kick it up a notch now. At the increased exertion, the dog tags began heavily moving and clanking as she ran. Cris innately felt closer to her dad. She knew he would've felt the same thing from those same tags against his chest when he was on active duty.

She suddenly felt like he was running right beside her. Focused on her pain and longing for both him and Luke, Cris pushed herself even harder.

The morning sun began burning in the distant horizon of the sky. Cris finally stopped and collapsed on the beach, her chest heaving as she gasped for air. She could feel the pulsating headache more intensely radiating through her skull now. Looking at her hand after touching the sweaty staples, Cris saw fresh pus and blood. She knew at that point she probably should've followed the doctor's orders of the 48-hour minimum, but her give a damn was busted. She was scratching the itch that she couldn't take anymore.

Ignoring the physical and aching symptoms of her head, Cris turned and sat with her ass in the sand, legs extended out slightly with bent knees, and arms wrapped around them. She watched intently as the waves crash down and started to lose herself. Often the waves crept up and gently lapped, like kisses at her feet. Cris was overwhelmed with a feeling of humility and purity; like the waves were a symbol of being washed, cleansed, and loved by God Himself. It almost felt akin with going to confession. She was already feeling her breath getting steady and the tension easing as she leaned her head back to fully succumb to her surroundings.

In her mindfulness, she observed the pelicans diving for their breakfast and felt inspired to seek out more. Making the conscious effort to become more aware, Cris noticed a few other locals out jogging along the shore, most of them with their dogs. She noted the washed-up jellyfish, discarded horseshoe crab shells, some lines from olive snails looking for their next meal, as well as the outlines of the sand dollars waiting for the high tide to come back in. Judging by their clothing and loud conversation, there were also a few obvious tourists walking along the shoreline. Even over the crashing waves, she didn't have a choice but to overhear their banter as they were getting closer.

"I'm so glad we got up to do this and catch the sunrise. No wonder they call it Shine Island, the sun is shining all the time."

Cris rolled her eyes. In general, she avoided listening to them talk and interject their assumptions. Sometimes she didn't care so much and let them go. Most times though she was feeling hospitable and politely corrected them or gave them directions, tips, and advice. Today Cris was mixed. They were approaching from her left side, but she realized she still tipped her head further to the right. Hopefully, they wouldn't see her oozing head.

Getting closer, they slowed and acknowledged Cris with a smile. "Good morning."

Hospitality arose, whether Cris intended it to or not, and she was grateful she didn't say what she was thinking about the locals trying to enjoy the quiet time while they could. "Morning y'all. I hope you don't mind, but I couldn't help but overhear your conversation as you were walking up."

The duo stopped, looked slightly confused, but still pleasant. One of them spoke. "About what?"

"Well, I heard you joking about Shine Island being named that because of the constant sunshine. While that is true more times than not, the truth is, it got its name from moonshine."

They looked fascinated. "Really?"

"Really. Back in the day, this island used to be only accessible by boat. Due to its privacy, it was a hot place to make moonshine and do its own little internal export of shine. Of course, eventually not only did the illegal moonshining get shut down, but the bridge got built and everything changed from there. Still, that is where the origin of Shine Island comes from. Not the sun, but the moonshine."

The ladies' mouths were aghast. "Wow, that's so cool! So, you grew up here?"

Too personal, time to stop the chit chat and resume her thoughts and observations. "I didn't grow up here, but my husband was born here so I know a lot of the history. You ladies enjoy the rest of your stay."

Thankfully, they took the hint. "Thank you, I'm sure we will!"

Trying to go back to her thoughts before the interruption, Cris looked at the burning sun which was beginning to come up. The sky was turning a beautiful spectacle of red and Cris automatically thought *Red at night, Sailors delight. Red in the morning, Sailors take warning.* Cris remembered sitting by the water so many times with her mom for the sunrise and sunset. They would say that together while thinking of her dad deployed on a ship thousands of miles away, wondering what color his skies were and how his day, week, or month, was going.

Those sunrises and sunsets weren't nearly as breathtaking as the ones Cris had here now on Shine Island. It made yet another memory of her dad that was embedded in her brain come crashing down, pounding like the present waves. This had been happening way too much this past week since Luke had been gone. It used to be relatively frequent, but nothing like this. Luke was always there to get her through and ease all the thoughts, feelings and emotions that went with it. Even though Cris didn't show them, Luke always knew they were going on and exactly how to make it better, or at least effectively distract her. Cris knew it was no coincidence she was being overwhelmed and bombarded more often with these demons since he left.

Cris fought back the tears and the lump in her throat as she again remembered seeing him that last time, in his bed surrounded by his own pool of blood. She fought with every fiber in her body to gain that inner strength, to have the inside be like the iron shield she carried on the outside. Cris had been trying to do it her whole life for one reason or another. It had never worked before and she held no false delusions it would suddenly happen now.

"I remember Daddy, you're standing watch in heaven. You and Luke have both promised."

Wiping away a tear that had inescapably fallen, Cris looked back at that nice red sunrise and prayed it wasn't an omen for this Sailors daughter and she had better take warning.

CHAPTER 14

Like a voyeur, the sun began creeping around and did its best at intrusively peeking through the blinds. The rapidly brightening room woke Pete up. Looking over at the time on the cable box, Pete was shocked he slept in this late. He was usually up before the sunrise. Obviously, he needed sleep. Pete had stayed up late working on Luke's case. He had quite a bit he had wanted to get through and was behind since he chose to watch Cris at the range instead of staying at the office to work.

Stormy must have sensed Pete's awakening as she belly crawled from his feet to his face and began giving him good morning kisses. Pete smiled as he slid back and rolled onto his side making more room for her and began rubbing behind her ears. Thinking back about his late night, he remembered Cris coming out to the kitchen and calling him Luke. It was so odd. Pete was shocked but didn't want to correct or embarrass her. He hadn't known how to respond. Pete assumed his response was appropriate since she didn't say anything or realize he wasn't Luke. He was still concerned about her mental state. Was she half asleep? Pete knew she wasn't drinking. Cris rarely drank. Plus, he watched her go to bed with a glass of ice water and that was what she had come back out to the kitchen to get. Cris never showed any cracks in her armor. Pete wouldn't blame her if she did with everything she has been through, but it wasn't in her DNA to allow it. The fact a hairline crack was shown was what worried Pete now.

Those thoughts in mind, Pete realized the house was silent. Cris didn't sleep in this late and he couldn't hear the shower water running. What was she doing and more importantly, was she okay? Trying not to overreact, he stopped petting Stormy and sat up, swinging his legs onto the floor. Pete grabbed his t-shirt, pulled it down over his head and took his pistol. With Stormy by his side matching his steps, Pete walked out to the doorway where the kitchen and dining room were to the left and the hall to the rest of the house were to the right. Looking down the hall he saw her bedroom door was shut, as was, of course, the suddenly secretive office door. Pete didn't hear a thing except the birds singing outside. Habitually looking towards the windows, he saw a note on the breakfast bar. Heart rate increasing, Pete rushed over and read it. Cris couldn't resist the urge anymore, she had to go for a run. She had her weapon and was running to the beach; she would be back soon.

Pete slammed the note back down while turning on his heel to get his shoes on. Looking at the keypad for the alarm as he grabbed his shoes right below it, he realized the alarm was disabled. He had never heard the beep from it being turned off. Pete began to mentally berate himself for sleeping through it. Even in his sleep, he was always on the alert and heard everything. He realized she must have done it silently from her phone. Just as he finished tying his shoes, Stormy made a beeline for the French doors. Pete pulled his gun out as he was standing up and looking towards Stormy. Cris was just opening the door. She looked at him and put her hand to the small of her back. Realizing it was Cris, and what she was grabbing for, Pete immediately set his gun on the stand next to him.

Cris narrowed her eyes at him but still hadn't brought her arm back forward yet. "What the hell were you bringing your weapon up at me for, Bryan?"

Pete released his breath as he began to walk towards her, leaving his gun on the stand behind him. "Damn it, Cris. I saw your note and was getting ready to go look for you. I had just finished getting my shoes tied when Stormy bolted for the door. I didn't know who she was going after until you walked in."

She cut her eyes at him but brought her empty hand out from behind her back. "Well, it's just me, so at ease there cowboy."

Cris began walking into the kitchen. Pete noticed she seemed to make a point of keeping him to her left side. He knew it must be because her hair was pulled up meaning her shaved head and injury would be visible. Cris wasn't vain in the least, nor did she give a shit about what people thought about her. Pete knew it had nothing to do with aesthetics and everything to do with her protective shield.

He also noticed Cris was now sporting a ball chain necklace around her neck. The same type that was usually accompanied by military dog tags. Pete had no idea where they may have suddenly come from. One of the few things he did know about Cris was she did eight years of college, no room for a military stint in there. It was the same for Luke, they weren't his. Pete was perplexed but averted his eyes from her head and her neck. Hopefully, Cris wouldn't realize that Pete knew her as well as he did, even though she was locked up tighter than a vault. This was difficult because it only left him with looking at her from the chest down. Pete involuntarily smirked. He had no issues with that view, in fact, he rather liked it. If Cris saw him looking there she would not believe or appreciate the fact that he was trying to give her a form of privacy. He was proverbially screwed with no lube no matter what.

Before she turned around from the cupboard with her glass, he realized he was deep in thought, flustered and had to divert. He fastidiously bent down and started petting Stormy, looking at her instead. Cris turned and Pete looked up at her like he was acknowledging her for the first time.

Pete habitually rubbed his right hand over his buzzed head and stood up. "If you'll promise me you'll set the alarm, I think I'll take a shower now that you're home and safe."

"Yes, my steadfast babysitter, I'll set it. I'm going to get my sweaty, stinking ass in the shower myself."

Pete was annoyed with himself, but he couldn't hold back his grin at the sweaty and ass reference. "Gee, I'm honored you hold me in such high esteem, My Lady." He gave a slight bow.

Cris finally cracked a smile. "You're an asshole."

There's my Cris. Pete chuckled. "You're not the first one to tell me that and though I don't understand it, no doubt you won't be the last."

He walked into the living room and retrieved his pistol off the stand. Knowing Cris was telling the truth because that was the only way she rolled, Pete felt confident she would do as she said she would. A temporary load of stress off, Pete strolled into the bathroom. He took a semi-cold shower and did his best to not think about Cris directly, but instead to try and focus on the case. Pete had gone as far as he could last night. It was going to be re-interviewing from here, which he was restricted on since he had to ensure her safety. Unless she was otherwise safely occupied, he would have to stay nearby. He wasn't complaining, simply trying to make his plans accordingly.

After getting out of the shower, Pete decided to make coffee. He used his best detective skills and hoped he wasn't using coffee, or a cup, that was sacred to Cris for her own reasons and she would be upset. Since she kept everything inside it was hard to know if something shouldn't be touched. Pete had observed her long enough and knew by her facial expressions and body language that she held some things as "untouchable." Certainly, anything of Luke's would now fall into that category. Cris came out a few minutes later and did not show her telltale signs of OCD annoyance, so Pete assumed he had at least gotten one victory for the day.

"I made extra coffee if you would like some."

"Thanks. I don't need any extra dehydration right now."

Cris paused for a second. Pete sensed her desire to say something she wasn't looking forward to and waited while taking a long pull of his coffee.

"I need to get the hell out of this house today. I can't stand just sitting here, I'm going nuts. I think I'm going to go for a drive. I have no destination in mind other than to get the fuck out of Dodge for the day."

Pete was mentally composing himself. He sat at the breakfast bar and took another long, slow, sip of coffee. Knowing he was as prepared as he could be, he responded simply and matter-of-factly.

"Okay. Where are we going?"

Cris shot back with a cocked hip and eye roll. "I didn't say *we* were going anywhere. I'm quite sure I'll be safe in my car and I'm also quite sure you have work to do."

Pete remained calm. "We've had this discussion about you being alone and what I am supposed to do. No need to rehash it. To address your second objection, I stayed up late last night working. I'm in good shape for the moment and think a head clearing road trip would do me good." *Checkmate.*

He heard Cris as she mumbled under her breath. "Of course, you are. How convenient." She concurrently looked out the window, shook her head, sighed and further murmured. "Red in the morning, Sailors take warning."

Pete ignored her comments as he got up, walked over to the sink and washed out his coffee cup. He thought about the fact that Cris didn't acknowledge him being up late last night. Pete wondered if it was her typical disregarding response, so she didn't have to talk about it, or if she really didn't realize she had called him Luke last night. He knew he would probably never find out.

Perhaps it was inspired by Cris being so ready to pull her gun on him, Pete didn't know, but he did realize he was in a mood to get her goat. He turned from the sink after placing his mug in the drying rack.

"So, are we taking Stormy on our journey too?"

Cris raised her voice, the irritation palpable. "Sure, why not? I want to get the hell away, so let's all load up for the grand fucking adventure. Be ready to ride in five." She skulked down the hall towards her bedroom.

Pete smiled as his voice automatically went up an octave when he turned to Stormy. "You hear that girl? We're going for a ride!"

Stormy shot up, thumping her tail, jumping and twirling. Pete snapped her leash on to take her out before they left. They were ready and waiting in the driveway when Cris appeared.

He noticed Cris had some plastic bags in her hand and tried to covertly put them in her trunk. "I take it as you're ready?"

Pete smiled wide. "Yes, ma'am."

He walked over to the passenger door and opened it, sliding the front seat forward as Stormy anxiously jumped in. Pete put the seat back and hopped in, riding shotgun, as the trunk slammed shut. Within seconds, Cris was sliding into the driver's seat. Pete tried not to look directly as she slipped on her sunglasses, pushed in the clutch and fired up the horses. He noticed Cris was wearing a thin, nevertheless, long sleeved shirt in "feels like" temperatures of over 100 degrees. Pete knew she must be trying to hide the gash on her arm, which he knew nothing truthful about, but found extremely curious given its location. Pete also noticed Cris kept running her fingers downward through her hair only on the right side. No doubt trying to make sure her staples and shaved head wasn't visible. Instead of taking the chance of drawing attention to himself and that he noticed these things, Pete reached back and began petting Stormy who was standing in the middle of the backseat. Her paws balancing on the center console affording a front seat view.

Stormy was one happy girl, wagging her tail vigorously as she showered both Cris and Pete with kisses. Cris finished up with the music preparation, which included a seriously increased volume. She seamlessly shifted into reverse and backed out of the driveway, tires slightly spinning. Pete had ridden with her several times in her county vehicle but had never been in her personal one. No matter which mode of transportation, he knew how Cris drove. Apparently, so did Stormy as she dug in and knew exactly how to lean as Cris pushed the pedal to the floor, short shifting the gears as she left the turns within her small community. Once getting onto the main roads to leave the island the short shifts turned into fast ones, putting Pete's head back against the seat, amping up the RPM's as well as the speed. They were already doing 60 mph in second gear and in less than 5 seconds. Pete smiled to himself.

He didn't say anything as Cris drove seemingly aimlessly along. She had already said she didn't have a destination in mind. Pete didn't care where they were going. He was thankful to be along for the ride and was enjoying the beauty; in and outside of the car. Although the car rode rough, Pete didn't mind as he appreciated the sounds and power of that as well. He had no complaints as he enjoyed all the sights and music while silently taking it in.

Pete could tell Cris was trying to stay pissy, but between Stormy's kisses and his sporadically interspersed positive and happy comments, he could see her faltering. Cris turned down the music as she turned from the back road towards a city.

It appeared the head clearing she was trying to achieve began to work. "I could use some espresso. There's a nice coffee shop down the road where we can stop."

"Sounds good to me."

Cris parked at the outer end of the busy parking lot. They both agreed they could not leave Stormy in the hot car alone and decided Pete would go inside to get the drinks while Cris walked Stormy in the nearby strip of grass. While waiting in line, Pete was looking around the vicinity outside. He watched as Cris walked Stormy. Nobody else was around and all seemed well there. He observed a park directly across the street. It looked like a nice area within the city. It housed several benches, a large pond, many sections of grassy areas to play or hang out in, along with a fountain in the middle, all under the outstretched branches of live oaks with dangling Spanish moss. Pete turned and placed their order, then moved down the simulated assembly line to wait for the drinks. Again, keeping his eyes on Cris, Pete noticed she was walking back to her car and getting ready to climb in with Stormy. The sight of them made him smile, he couldn't hide it if he tried.

He went from feeling content to high alert in an instant. Pete watched as Cris cracked the windows of the car, then shut the door and locked it. She ran across the street to the park. Pete's stomach started turning, he wanted to reach across the counter and grab the barista, demanding the drinks immediately so he could run after her. Growing more impatient by the second, Pete habitually reached around and felt the steel tucked at the small of his back. He watched as Cris approached a dirty man on one of the benches. Pete began to feel enraged and needed to get out of there and see what the hell she thought she was doing. Adrenaline rushing, he was ready to bolt out the door. He heard his name called from behind the counter and tried to regain the composure he was known for as he grabbed the drinks, thanked the barista, and flew out the door.

Pete decided to go to the car first to be near Stormy. He set the drinks down by the front tire since he didn't have the keys to get into the car. By the time Pete stood up, Cris was jogging and almost back to the car. She looked at him with wide eyes. He couldn't tell if she was surprised or embarrassed.

Cris quickly recovered either way. "I'll unlock the car for you. Stormy went potty, she's good. Make yourself comfortable, I'll be back in a second."

She opened the trunk and grabbed a full white plastic bag. Cris closed the trunk and headed back across the street before he could even begin to process anything.

Pete didn't respond. Couldn't respond. He really didn't know how to. He opened the door and with his left hand, pet Stormy's head, who was presently residing in his seat. Pete stood just outside the door and watched Cris jog back across the street to the man on the bench. Pete again instinctively felt around to his concealed weapon. He watched as they exchanged a few words, Cris gave him the bag, followed by a tight, genuine hug.

Pete was perplexed. Cris never showed this type of emotion, or certainly never hugged anyone. He looked down at Stormy but was talking more to himself. "What the hell?"

Stormy thumped her tail on the seat as she was also watching and saw Cris coming back over. Pete stopped petting her since she was now excitedly moving all around in anticipation. He understood exactly how Stormy felt. Cris got closer and came clearer into view, and Pete wasn't sure how to read her. She looked both happy and sad. He was drawn again to the newly adorned dog tags bouncing on her chest and was even further confounded.

Seeing Cris was safe and wanting to hide his thoughts from her, Pete grabbed the coffee cups and hopped back into the front seat of the car. Stormy resumed her position at the middle console as Cris slid back into the cockpit. Pete handed Cris her cup and gave her a raised eyebrow. Letting her know that he saw the whole performance and wanted details. She took the cup and shot daggers back. Making it clear to forget anything he saw because she was not going to discuss it. Pete was both thankful and found it sad that they could communicate with just looks and body language. They had only been coworkers for about a year, yet they instinctively could read each other so well and had immediately clicked. He shook his head and knew he needed to keep his mouth shut about what just transpired to avoid a heated discussion.

Sailing home through the back twisty roads, pistons pumping and horses running, they continued their small talk in between enjoying the quiet moments of the music and scenery. They joked and laughed together, while also going for long periods at a time in comfortable solitude, appreciating the journey. It felt so natural.

It wasn't a spectacular day in of itself, but Pete found himself disappointed the trip was over as they pulled back into her driveway later that evening. He knew those small moments of the day were actually immeasurable.

Going back into the house, Cris appeared tired. In reality, Pete knew the outwardly mundane day was probably very draining on her with everything that she had been through in the past week, both mentally and physically. He still had some work to do for an hour or so. Therefore, he didn't question or argue when Cris seemed like she wanted to turn in for the night. Pete tried to take the lead and make it sound like he was beat from the day too, trying to make Cris feel better.

As he curled up on the couch with the lamp on low, files on the armrest and Stormy at his feet, Pete couldn't stop thinking of Cris and being in her house like this. He wondered what he was going to do, and where his life was going.

CHAPTER 15

The drive had served its purpose for the most part. Cris felt better since she had gotten out of the house for the day. The open road and music were a good diversion. The clearer her mind got though, the wilder it went. The squirrels in her brain were chasing each other around at full speed. She had a hard time focusing after giving the homeless Vet the bag of food and water. She kept jumping between thoughts. The outrage of the treatment of Veterans after returning home. That led her to think of her dad. Also tracking in the squirrel chase was that Pete had seen most of the operation go down. Cris was appreciative Pete took the hint and didn't say anything, but it still hung there, stagnant between them. The show emotions in front of someone she knew, didn't make her happy. She couldn't take it back, and given the chance, Cris would make the same choice again, helping the Vet over wielding her shield.

Even though she felt mentally better from the drive and avoidance at the house, Cris still felt awkward around Pete. She was anxious to escape the wheels spinning in her psyche at the maximum knots per second. In this spirit, Cris was mentally conspiring and convincing herself that some Sailor Jerry would make it slow down and feel better. As they got closer to her house, she became increasingly quiet and yawned more frequently, already trying to plan her bedtime escape to join her new liquid friend. Pulling into the driveway and getting out of the car, Cris added an extra-long stretch, followed by an obnoxious yawn. The yawns weren't fake, Cris was tired, but she knew her new Sailor companion would revive her through suppression.

Pete must have taken the intimation. "I'll walk Stormy. You go ahead in. We'll be there soon."

"Okay, thanks."

Cris hurried to the door, disabled the alarm from the keypad and scooted to the office door to unlock it before Pete came in. Still not hearing them come up the porch steps, she ran to her room to change into her pajamas. She threw on the first pair she grabbed and walked out and closed the door. Stormy came barreling down the hall and Pete was walking into the kitchen at the end of the hall. Cris knelt to pet Stormy and the dog tags fell out of her low-cut pajama top. She not so gracefully tucked them back in but did glance over and see Pete had his head turned, looking their way. *Whatever, it seems to be the day for this. Just going to ignore that anything happened like I always do.*

Cris stood up and began walking down the hall towards Pete, Stormy underfoot, matching her strides. She went to the cupboard and grabbed a glass, filled it with ice, then added a small amount of water. Setting the glass on the counter, Cris bent down, making sure her knees were against her chest, so her shirt stayed closed and the dog tags remained in place and as hidden as possible. She began rubbing behind Stormy's ears, telling her it's been a long day and good night. Next to them, Pete tried to stifle a yawn as he stretched, his shirt riding up showing his carved abs. Cris quickly looked back to Stormy, pretending she didn't notice.

"I guess I'm tired too. It was a long day of peaceful fun and I have a few things I need to finish up. I think it's best I get to it before I'm knocked out." Pete then called Stormy to come with him.

Cris grabbed her ice water again and began walking towards the hall. Pete stopped midway into the living room and turned around. Cris stopped too, realizing he had something he wanted to say. There was no way to expect or prepare for what came out of his mouth though.

Pete shook his head and looked very uncomfortable. "I'm sorry, Cris. I can't go to sleep without making sure you're okay? I really didn't want to say anything, but I'm concerned. I can't stop the nagging in my head about you calling me Luke last night."

The room got a slight spin to it and her mouth felt like cotton. Cris was so taken off guard and confused that she wasn't aware she had water in her hand to help with the sudden desert stretching across her tongue.

Thinking back to last night, Cris began to panic. All she remembered clearly was putting on her father's dog tags and enjoying too much of the Sailor. This made Cris wonder what was going on when she called him Luke. She wanted to do her usual and ignore it, or even deny it, but she had been drinking and Pete most likely had not. Cris was on the spot and didn't know how to respond, but knew she needed to and quick. She didn't want him to know she was drinking but depending on what they were doing, he may already know. *Damn it, think! Come up with something to buy you a few seconds!*

Shooting from the hip, Cris gave it her best shot. "What the hell are you talking about? Are you sure you weren't dreaming?"

"Um, no. I was wide awake, sitting on the couch doing some work under the lamp."

Cris felt some relief. Pete had been working, nothing more. This was the second time in a week she couldn't remember a conversation that had transpired with him. Both were after she was drinking, and it pissed her off. She wasn't a drinker and these two memory lapses were a good reason to keep it that way. Now she had to quickly counter on how to respond. Why was she with him while he was working?

"Sorry, Pete. I don't remember it. Maybe I was sleepwalking?" She released a sardonic scoff.

Pete looked even more concerned and shook his head again. "I have no experience with that, but if you were, you are damn experienced at it. You managed to walk out and get some ice water without spilling it and telling me/Luke not to stay up too late because *we* would still be getting up at the crack of dawn."

The brief and fuzzy flash of memory hit her like a brick to the head. She didn't remember the whole thing, but she did remember chunks now of refilling her ice for another drink and how Luke's brief response was typical. Cris had to think of a way to cover her drinking and mental lapse. Her mask and shield had already been cracked a little today with the homeless Vet, she couldn't let it break further. *Damn it, Cris, pull it together!*

She didn't have an appropriate response, so she tried her best at her typical blowing it off. "Look, Pete, don't worry. I was probably mostly asleep and realized the bed I just left was empty without realizing why. My mental health is fine. I'm still exhausted from my adventures up in Jasper, that's all. Sorry for concerning you. Good night."

Pete looked back at her with one eyebrow halfcocked and spoke softly. "Yea, okay. Good night, Cris."

Cris was proud of her cover up. It sounded at least semi-truthful and maybe most importantly, made it appear like she was actually sleeping in her bed. She went down the hall into her room and left the door cracked, listening as she drank the small amount of water in her glass. After just a few minutes of rustling papers, it sounded like Pete had sat down on the couch. Cris confirmed she was correct when she heard Stormy jump up onto it. She could picture Stormy settling in at his feet and fluffing her blankets to begin sucking on them and then going to sleep. Feeling brave, and being honest with herself, the pull of her new companion, Cris dared to gently creep down to the office. She silently turned the knob and held it before she went in and inaudibly released it, closing and locking the door behind her.

Knowing she would have the door locked, she never put her bedding away this morning. Cris sat down on her rough-and-ready bed. Glass in hand, she was already forgetting about her anger a few minutes ago for the drinking and memory lapses. Cris reached over and involuntarily licked her lips as she watched the amber swirl over the ice, taunting and seducing her. Feeling comfortable in her lair she began undergoing a special camaraderie with her father. Always a thinker, Cris inwardly smiled as she realized her numbness was beginning to get numb. That made her ponder the irony and craziness of it all. *It doesn't even make sense, you drink to numb your numbness.*

She kept looking at the thrown together war room area surrounding her desk for Luke's murder. Cris still wasn't sure if the letter about her being the target was true or instead was intended to throw her off to stop looking into Luke's case. Taking the last swallow from her glass, the still fresh ice clinking, her mind kept revolving in different directions. Cris decided it was time. She was going to research Luke's death a little more. She had to assume Pete was sleeping, and if he wasn't, there was still no reason for him to come and try to disturb her. From the closet in the office which held some of their extra clothing, she threw on a pair of jeans and t-shirt.

Seizing a mug from her desk sporting the American flag, she dumped the ice from her glass into it. She chased the ice down with a hearty pour of her new found companion and snapped the top on. Removing her Glock from under the pillow, she replaced it at the small of her back. She now possessed both of her companions, Smith &Wesson and Sailor Jerry. The sane part of her mind, which currently appeared to be on vacation or locked in a padded cell, knew that guns and alcohol don't mix. Her dad was her first experience with that, then life as a homicide detective kept reinforcing it. She shrugged it off acknowledging she hadn't been sane in a long time. *I'm done fucking around Luke, it's time for answers.*

Cris aggressively grabbed her phone, opened the app for the security company and silently disabled the alarm. She was satisfied again for her decision of making herself the only one with the authority to arm and disarm her passcode from a remote device. She went over to the window, opened it up and quietly popped the screen out. She reached down and let it rest on the ground then set her mug on the railing of the porch, which was right next to the office window. She dropped down to the ground. Using the porch railing like a jungle gym, Cris stealthily climbed up to close the window, leaving it open just a crack so she could push it up to get back in. She quietly replaced the screen. Nobody should notice. Cris snagged her mug. Not wanting to take any further chance of being seen in the front of the house, she crouched down and snuck around the side and back, thankful for the closed blinds.

Entering the preserve neighboring her property line, Cris began laughing to herself. She realized how slow her reflexes and thoughts were at this point and was amazed that she was able to pull this off, at least as far as she could tell. Deciding it called for a little victory drink, she took a good size swig from the mug. The sun was about ready to set and walking along the trail under the outstretched tree limbs, it was practically black. Cris didn't need the sunlight, she knew the way.

The destination was about a mile in. Cris knew she wasn't being quiet as she heard the pine straw rustling and rocks sliding underfoot, even in her drunkenly ringing ears. Cris thought she heard some crunching a few times from elsewhere and she stopped, listening. Instinctively, and with extremely slow reflexes, she placed her hand on the butt of her weapon but didn't hear it again once she stopped. Cris shrugged and drunkenly dismissed it as nervousness and alcohol. She was certainly feeling more than a nice warm tingle. A thought slithered through her brain. Maybe Luke was trying to tell her to turn back and go home? Trying to see through the tree covered canopy, she looked up at the increasingly darkening sky. *I'm sorry Steele Appeal, but hell no! I am going to get to the bottom of this and end it. I'm done with this shit! I promised you I would find this son of a bitch and I'm going to!*

Shuffling along the almost black trail, Cris took another nip from the mug and tried her best to square her shoulders. As she moved off the trail, onto the grass she got closer to the big live oak where they were having the picnic just over a week ago. Cris saw the big yellow ribbon tied around the tree into a bow. Getting up close to it, she saw it was the crime scene tape with the yellow facing out. Somebody's attempt at a yellow memorial ribbon. Cris knew right away it had to be Pete. He would've been the last one to leave the scene and been taking the tape down. Deep inside she knew Pete was the type of guy that would've wanted to put some kind of memorial in place. Thinking about the way she had been treating him, she felt like an ingrate. Cris was so conflicted. She knew him. He was a great guy; no way was he capable of this atrocity. But… Her instinct had never proved her wrong before and there were too many coincidences.

Her swirling, squirrel running on speed brain couldn't process anymore. Cris decided to silence them all for a bit, sit down and let the numbness take over. She sat at the base of the tree; in the exact spot she was sitting when that fatal shot changed everything. The bullet hole confirmed it was precise.

Resting her head back against the tree Cris looked up through the vast clearing. She was watching the sun as it now fully set, no red in sight. Cris remembered the red sky this morning and briefly thought in passing about the warning. Putting the mug back up to her lips, she smiled. Cris was ready for the warning, she was ready to end this by whatever means necessary.

Under the bright moon, hearing nothing but the mating calls of tree frogs and crickets chirping, and maybe due to the inhibitions from her new companion, she began to relax against that old tree. Cris didn't know how long she had sat there and wondered if perhaps she had even drifted off to sleep as she opened her eyes wide. She put the mug that had almost slipped from her hand to her mouth, only to find it already empty. Instinctively, her dad came to mind. Cris looked back at the yellow ribbon. She fell deep in remorse while thinking about her dad and Luke. She thought she heard a slight rustle, like a twig snap. Her nervous system instantly back to fight mode, albeit a very delayed reaction, Cris turned to look around. She didn't see anything lurking in the shadows or walking in the open.

Cris suddenly and clearly heard a male voice right near her. "I told you next time I would not miss."

Reflexes delayed, it was too late to pull her gun or stop the blow that connected hard with her stapled head.

CHAPTER 16

Cris regained consciousness and slowly opened her eyes. Disoriented, she had no idea where she was, but distinctly felt drool going across her face. Cris tried to look around and the pain shot around her entire head. It was bad enough that she was unable to pick her head up or even move it. Knowing she had a high threshold for pain, this realization terrified her. Her eyes automatically went wide, and she looked around as best she could. *Damn it, Cris, think!*

The smell of sand and soil brought her awareness to the fact that she was outside, curled up on the ground. There were trees all around as far as she could see with the nonexistent range of motion of her head. The surroundings made her remember walking into the woods and sitting by the tree. Then, hearing the twig crack followed by a male voice before being struck in the head with something big and hard. Cris also realized now, what she thought was drool across her face was most definitely blood. Testing her theory, Cris licked her lips and tasted the distinctive metallic liquid which confirmed her hypothesis. The pain in the right side of her head was excruciating, like nothing she had ever felt before. She knew the staples were probably gone and the remaining wound was now wide open.

The pain was settling in and becoming intolerable. Images were getting fuzzy and Cris felt like she was going to pass out. In the near distance, she heard a male voice talking. She couldn't be sure, but Cris thought it sounded like a one-sided conversation. It also sounded like something was being dragged across the ground, followed by the sound of digging. Beginning to panic, Cris tried with everything she had to lift her head, but the pain was just too much. For the first time in her life, tears consequentially poured out from physical pain.

Her head began to spin, her ears rang even louder, and she broke out into a sweat. Cris could tell she was close to losing consciousness again. She closed her eyes briefly. Even in the blind darkness, the stars still swirled behind her eyes. *C'mon Cris, hang on! C'mon damn it! Fight this! You are not going down like this!* The silent, involuntary tears fell faster.

Cris opened her eyes, planning to come up with a way to fight. She looked in the direction of where she last saw the figure and heard the voice. The spinning got faster, and the sweating became more profuse. Cris knew she was going to pass out at any minute. She squinted her eyes and saw a flash of something shiny in the moonlight as it moved in a shadowy hand. Fighting her best fight, she tried to process what was going on. It was crudely interrupted while Cris hypnotically watched the sliver of light go up and down in the moonlight, when she lost consciousness again.

CHAPTER 17

Like it does every day, no matter what's going on in someone's life, the sun crept up. Blinds still closed; Pete was trying to ignore the night stealing thief as he sat propped up on his pillow on the couch. He had been lazily petting Stormy for quite some time now, while he was distracted thinking about the interviews he needed to reconduct today. Knowing it was futile, he was going back over the lists in his head, which he had already tirelessly done. The mourners from the church service, all of Luke's students and parents, the soccer teams and their parents, his coworkers. Pete was reaching as he had written down people who barely qualified as suspects.

The real focus needed to be on Cris now since she was the target. Pete dreaded that even more. Her history was a mystery. He snorted at the inadvertent rhyme. Bolton had already told him not to go there, which grated his nerves even more. He had nothing to go on and his hands were tied. Yet, he was expected to solve this. Pete was going to have to look into the only thing he could, Cris' past cases. He had briefly looked at them over the past two days and so far, nothing jumped out. It was time to dig deeper. Maybe a family member of someone she had put away was holding a grudge. It wasn't unheard of.

It was not going to be a great day and Pete knew he was procrastinating to avoid getting it started. He would call

Bolton in an hour or so to see if he could come occupy Cris with something while he got the footwork done.

Suddenly sensing something wrong, Pete detached from his thoughts and realized it was after 6:00. Cris hadn't come out of the bedroom yet. She said herself she never slept in. He looked at Stormy as he gave her one last pet, then got up and put his shirt on. He knew Cris was tired when she went to bed early last night. It would make sense that she was sleeping in, but that was not what his instincts were telling him.

Pete walked towards the backside of the house, glancing at the counter and table looking for a note like she left yesterday. Once he realized there was nothing there, Pete tried not to overreact. He walked as slowly as his anxiety would allow, which was more like an addict meeting their dealer for their next fix. Pete glanced in the guest bathroom as he walked past. Empty as expected. Next to that, he opened the door going into the laundry room and garage. Dark and empty. Reaching the end of the hall and Cris' bedroom, Pete gently knocked on her door. No answer. No shower water running. Not a rustle of movement or even breathing was heard through the door. Getting more concerned, Pete knocked harder.

He spoke calmly but loudly. "Cris? Hey, you're beginning to scare me. I'm worried about you and I'm going to open the door."

No response, and still no indication of noise or movement from within. Pete counted forcefully to five, then braced his right shoulder against the door expecting resistance from the lock. He turned the knob and almost fell into the room as the unlocked door effortlessly opened. The room was empty, and he could see the bed had not been slept in. Pete walked in to look towards the master bathroom. The door was open, and the room was as vacant as a gambler's pockets after payday. He turned the light on and glanced into the shower. It was bone dry, Cris had not showered this morning. Pete was confused and extremely concerned, especially considering the cracks in her armor witnessed over the past two days.

It was uncharacteristic of him, but for the first time in his life, Pete wasn't sure what to do. He considered calling it in to dispatch, or maybe call Chief first. Then his normal cool head kicked in. Pete knew he had to clear the house before going off the rails and calling in the cavalry. Starting with a general sweep, he decided to check the workout room. Pete knew he didn't hear Cris slip in there. Still, he thought, or hoped, perhaps she was doing yoga or meditation or some crazy shit. Walking into the silent room with the door already open, Pete flicked on the light. Empty. He flipped the switch down again, returning the room to darkness as he walked back into the hallway.

He looked to the left to the only remaining room and saw Stormy sitting outside the office door staring at him, moving her front paws up and down, seemingly agitated. Pete already knew there was something going on with this room. Cris was keeping something hidden since before she left for Jasper last week. The dread was creeping in as Pete went to the closed door. Like the bedroom, but with markedly more urgency, he knocked. Nothing. Pete knocked again louder, saying almost the same thing, "Cris? Are you in there? I'm worried about you. I'm going to open the door unless I hear your voice right now."

Pete didn't bother to count to five this time. After no immediate response or noise, he eagerly turned the knob. He was shocked to realize it was locked. Pete knew what he needed to do within a fraction of a second. He realized if he was wrong, he would hear and feel Cris' wrath. Right now, he didn't care. Raw fear gripped him. Pete made up his mind as he put his right hand on the knob. He leaned to the left then quickly jolted himself right and shoved his shoulder into the door. Pete ignored the pain that radiated down his right side as the door busted from the frame. Stormy initially cowered to the side, but then promptly followed as Pete entered.

Turning on the light, the first thing he saw in the middle of the floor was the spot where Cris had set up camp. Pete tried to scan the room and take in what was important. He noticed a pillow and blankets laying neatly on the floor, surrounded by the empty glass of water she had brought in as well as a few other items. Pete also noticed a big bottle of alcohol next to it, which was half empty. This shocked him and he momentarily forgot the real reason for going in there. Pete knew she wasn't a drinker. He wondered if this was the real reason why Cris called him Luke the other night. He just couldn't believe his eyes. *When did she start drinking? Why the hell is she sleeping in the office?* Pete watched as Stormy went to Cris' sleeping area, did a little spin, then plopped down, resting her head on the pillow. Trying to refocus himself to the mystery at hand, he shook his head and attempted to close his jaw.

Looking around more fully at the hideout Cris had created, Pete saw her organizational murder chart on the wall. Captivated, he walked over to the desk area for a closer look. On the desk, Cris had a map of the crime scene and the suspected trajectory of the bullet, and therefore where the killer must have taken his shot.

A whiteboard hung on the wall just above her desk where she had listed the crime/suspects/ruled out... Under the suspect column, Pete saw his name, along with the description of some stranger she came across on a bridge. They were the only suspects. Pete was dismayed at seeing his name. It meant Cris really did question him and wasn't just throwing out accusations in the heat of the moment and frustration.

His heart was full of disappointment and sadness. Pete cared about Cris, he hated that she really questioned his trustworthiness. Trying to push his emotions aside and focus on both Luke's case and Cris, Pete began to wonder about this stranger on the bridge. *Who was he? What bridge? When was this?* Cris hadn't put down any details. This didn't surprise Pete since this was strictly her board and this man and all the details were clear in her head. *Why didn't Cris tell anyone about this encounter that made her uneasy enough to include him on her suspect list?* Pete already knew the answer, it would show a crack in her shield and possibly ruin her outward appearance. It also might end up giving light to the fact she was trying to solve this on her own. Pete didn't agree with it, but knowing Cris like he did, he understood.

Trying to look away from the mock war room area, Pete's eyes were drawn to the window at the right of the desk. It was then that Pete saw the barely cracked window and the sadness he was feeling was overtaken with cold hard fear.

CHAPTER 18

Jeff was standing at his kitchen counter pouring his second cup of joe. He winced as he slurped a sip of the too hot coffee while staring out the window. He had been up since oh-dark-thirty with an unease harboring inside him which he could neither define nor comprehend. Jeff looked out at the brightening blue sky and all its splendor as the elusive uneasiness continued to pull at him. Trying to ignore it, he began thinking of his day ahead. He would head into the office soon.

Hearing the shower water turn on, he knew his wife was up now too. He slugged back what was left in the mug, then began rinsing it in the sink. He just finished drying his hands when his cell phone came to life on the table. Jeff looked at the time and his unease intensified. He did a quick leap from the counter to the table and saw it was Bryan's number. His heart took a sudden trip south arriving at his stomach, while the acid of the morning coffee started churning northward up his esophagus. Jeff knew this couldn't be good. He had no idea just how bad it was going to be.

Knowing to trust his instincts and gut, Jeff spent no time on formalities as he hit the answer button on the phone. "Bryan, what's wrong?"

Bryan was always calm and levelheaded. Jeff could practically hear the anxiety sizzling through the earpiece of his phone as Bryan spoke. That worried him more than anything.

"Hey, Chief. I'm a little freaked out here and between you and me, I wasn't entirely sure what to do. I decided to call you first."

Bryan took a very brief pause, but Jeff heard him inhale loudly before blurting out what had him so upset.

"Cris is gone. I've searched the house, she's not here. But, here's the scary part, the window in the office is cracked open. I don't know what to make of it, but everything inside of me is screaming it is important."

Jeff's head was spinning, he couldn't have seen this coming. There had to be an explanation, he just needed to think for a second.

"Maybe Cris opened it earlier for some fresh air and forgot to shut it? And maybe she went out for a run this morning?"

"She went for a run yesterday morning and left me a note on the counter to let me know. There's no note. There's also something else I think you should know. Cris has a hideout set up in her office and has kept it locked and a secret. I had to bust the door open to get in. There are some things in there that concern me in addition to the window. I think you should take a look and see."

What the hell was he talking about and what the hell had gone on there? This was just surreal.

"Damn it, Bryan, there's gotta be something you're missing. And, you broke the door in?"

"Yes. It was locked. I cleared the rest of the house and Stormy was sitting in front of the door. Like she was trying to tell me something. When Cris didn't respond and I heard no sounds, I got worried and did what I had to do. Chief, I hope you're right. I hope I am missing something. I really hope there is a logical explanation and I am completely overreacting, and this will be a waste of company resources. But damn it, I don't think so."

Jeff understood Bryan's uncertainty of what was going on, he couldn't believe this or make sense of it himself.

"What about the doors going outside? Are they locked?"

"Yes, sir."

"What about the alarm?" More reaching for something Jeff knew he wouldn't find.

"I kind of forgot about that, let me check right now." There was a brief pause. "Shit! It's disabled."

"Are all the vehicles there?"

"Yes."

Knowing he was dry on ideas; Jeff blew out an enormous sigh. "Son of a bitch! Don't leave the house in case she comes back. I'll be right there."

Jeff promptly disconnected the call and shoved the phone in his pocket. He felt the acid stuck at the bottom of his throat and made a quick pitstop at the cupboard. He took a handful of antacids and put his cupped hand to his mouth, tossing them all in. Jeff was working on chewing the mouthful of chalk as he grabbed his keys and headed out the door.

Jumping into his county vehicle, he was already putting the key in the ignition. Jeff quickly pulled his phone from his pocket and threw it in the cup holder before buckling his seat belt. He shut the door and put the rig in reverse and realized he never told his wife goodbye. *I'll text her when I get to Cris'. Nothing she's not used to or won't understand.*

Driving there, Jeff looked at the speedometer and realized he was speeding. He didn't care, not when it came to Cris. This was an emergency. Jeff knew he could at least turn the lights on, but no need for the siren. It was still early enough, not many people were out and most would still be sleeping. He was trying to stay focused and think of a rational reason for all this, but his mind kept wandering. The backdrop of the cloudless, already bright blue sky, in combination with his blue lights reflecting off the passing signs and windows, was almost entrancing. Jeff became imprisoned in his thoughts.

He couldn't stop the feeling of déjà vu he was experiencing. Jeff went back to the similar and unbelievable conversation with Bryan regarding Cris just over a week ago. Bryan was on the phone confirming what a dispatcher had just personally relayed to him. Cris' husband was just shot in front of her. Jeff went through the same denial, disbelief and bargaining he found himself doing now. The resemblance was uncanny.

Continuing to drive on autopilot, Jeff turned where he needed to without being present in the moment or driving. The last few conversations with Cris kept replaying in his brain. She repeatedly tried to convince him of her suspicion of Bryan's involvement. Jeff had a slight nagging feeling about what she was saying. He trusted Cris and some of what she was saying could make sense, but he also still felt like she had a conspiracy theory going at the same time.

Jeff was so confounded and indecisive. He had never experienced this in either of his adult careers. Previously, and on rare occasion currently, he had to make serious, life-altering, split-second decisions, which fortunately had always been correct. As a result, he had always trusted his gut and knowledge and it had never failed him. Cris seemed to change things and be an anomaly to what he was used to or had ever experienced. Jeff's thoughts started wandering elsewhere. To another person, place and time, where he could not allow them to go and, as usual, he shut them down.

He shook his head and grasped to refocus on the present shit storm. *What the hell was going on in the office? Was it really necessary for Bryan to bust the door open? What was this hideout and why was Cris keeping it locked?* Jeff knew one of the first things he would do was see what was going on in there. He hoped it would give him the insight he needed to know what to do or where to look next.

As Jeff was getting ready to make the right into her community, he happened to look up and saw the camera on the adjacent light pole. Knowing there were no cameras in her actual community, he had forgotten about this one. Jeff knew it may become useful in seeing who had at least come and gone from here and at what times. He hoped it wouldn't be necessary to go that far. Maybe Cris had already surfaced and Bryan forgot to call him because he was reprimanding her for scaring him. *Yea, in a pig's ass.*

Pulling into her driveway, Jeff knew by the sinking feeling in his bones that Cris had not magically appeared. He tried to breathe in the strength he knew he was going to need as he shut the SUV off. Sweat was suddenly emerging on his brow. He looked at the green light bulb still burning away on the front porch as he wiped his forehead and fought back tears.

Just before getting out of his vehicle, he whispered to the lonely house solemnly looking back at him. "It's gonna be okay Cris, I promise!"

CHAPTER 19

Cris slowly pried her eyes open. The first thing she realized was the obnoxiously loud ringing in her ears. It was quickly and terrifyingly overridden by perfectly choreographed thumps. Cris was disoriented and not positive what the noise was, or for that matter, even where she was or what had happened.

She was struggling, trying to focus through the ringing ears and pounding head. Assessing whatever this situation was, she could tell her legs were bent. Cris tried to move, only to discover she couldn't. She was restrained, or more accurately, constrained, somehow. Cris had never been claustrophobic but now began to panic. *Think, damn it, what the hell happened? Focus!*

Images began to flash through her memory, quick and then fading. Cris remembered sitting against the tree thinking about the color of the sky. Next, hearing a rustle then getting smacked upside the head. Cris also thought she remembered waking up at some point, smelling the earth, not being able to move her head and watching the moonlight flash off something as it moved up and down. Then, Cris released a small moan causing the flash to stop in the distance, the moonlight shining off it as it got closer. Through the ringing in her ears, hearing something which sounded like, "Die Bitch," before the moonlit object came smashing down on her head again. Cris couldn't be sure what was real or not at this point though. Perhaps these were dreams she had while unconscious. She was pretty sure she had been slipping in and out of consciousness no matter what any other reality was.

Reaching up to feel her head, it felt like a few staples may have come loose or were gone altogether. It was hard to tell with the swelling. Cris could feel the sticky blood going down her face, ear, and neck. *How much blood have I lost? Where the hell am I?* The only answers were the continuing thumps, which only added to the confusion.

It was mostly pitch black, but when she looked upwards, she thought she could see a few slivers of faint sun. *Why can I only partially see? Please don't tell me I've lost part of my vision, anything but that!* Cris closed her eyes, not wanting to see it and think about it. Tears threatened to fall and with it came the rush to her head which intensified the pain and throbbing. She was feeling like she would lose consciousness again. *Stay awake! Focus! Think!* Still keeping her eyes closed, Cris tried to find her logical mind between the thumps to figure a way out of whatever she had inadvertently gotten into.

She thought about the slivers of sun and a part of her wondered what color the skies had been this morning. Had she really been gone all night? Cris had a slight glimmer of hope. Pete would notice she was gone and start looking. They would find her. Then Cris remembered how she kept herself locked in the office. It would be a while before he figured out she was missing. Panic set in again.

She opened her eyes to pure darkness; the slivers of light were gone. Knowing her vision must be completely lost, Cris felt like she was going to throw up. She was on her left side and tried to sit up amidst the pain screaming throughout her head. Cris hadn't raised her head very high, certainly less than six inches, before she cracked it on something solid, blocking her from going any further. The pain seared. Cris was even more confused. She also realized now that she could still hear the thumps, but they were muted, almost inaudible. She wondered if she was losing her hearing too.

Both frustrated and panicked, Cris started to feel around. The first thing she felt was a splinter as she ran her hand along the outside perimeter of her body. Fear filled her as she comprehended that she was in some type of box and the sound she had been hearing was dirt being thrown on top. Cris wasn't losing her hearing, she was being covered in her own grave. She began to scream and pound her fists against the top of the box. The only answer was the sound of the final throws of dirt, being concluded by a few pats trying to harden it down.

The awareness brought back her stubbornness and determination as her head momentarily began to clear. Cris realized the more she kept screaming and panicking the sooner she was going to run out of oxygen or die from carbon dioxide poisoning. Cris had no idea what the dimensions of the box were, but she could tell by how folded up she was that it must be extremely small. Not good!

With an average intake of .5 liters of oxygen with each breath under normal, non-panicking conditions, it meant she would have a few hours at best before suffocating to death or being overtaken by carbon dioxide poisoning. Cris had to make herself breathe slowly and calmly and think. Her muscles were already cramping. She tried to gently move to adjust, but there was no extra room. Cris was stuffed in there like a snake in the peanut can. She wondered how long she had been folded in here before he closed it up and started throwing the dirt on top? The pain in her head was radiating again, making her nauseous and begin to see stars. Cris wondered if seeing the stars behind her closed eyes meant she wasn't blind, even though she knew even blind people experience the same phosphenes as their vision fortunate counterparts.

That was her last intelligent thought before the demons of unconsciousness came in and stole her away again.

CHAPTER 20

Jeff tried to put his personal feelings aside and regain the strength and composure he was known for as he walked up the porch steps. Knowing the alarm on the house was disarmed, he didn't bother knocking. Jeff opened the door and went boldly in, trying to appear normal and establish control. He was greeted by Stormy running up to him, and hot on her tail was Bryan. Jeff leaned down to give Stormy her due while looking up at Bryan, fighting to hide the quiver in his voice.

"I'm assuming she hasn't surfaced?"

"No, sir."

"I figured. Shit!"

Jeff stood up, straightened his back and started moving forward. "From the sounds of what you have told me, I guess we better start in the office."

Leading the way, Jeff knew where the office was and didn't need to follow Bryan there. Jeff was striving to show the control he was still struggling to have. Bryan was right behind him, almost by his side. The first thing Jeff noticed as he turned the corner towards the hall was the violently broken door. He looked back at Bryan with raised eyebrows before entering.

Bryan squared his shoulders, unapologetic. "I told you, I knew something had been going on with this room, and Stormy was sitting outside of it trying to tell me something. I don't care if you believe it or not. I didn't get a response, and I was worried. I did what I felt was necessary."

While Jeff could fully understand it, he couldn't stop the hairs on the back of his neck from standing up. He didn't respond verbally but scowled before entering the room. Looking into the office, Jeff was shocked at what he saw. Giving it all a quick once over and not focusing on any one thing, he saw Cris' map board, then her sleeping arrangements on the floor and the Sailor Jerry bottle sitting next to the pillow. Jeff inwardly shuddered at the glass sitting next to the bottle.

The makeshift war room, Jeff was not entirely surprised to see. Although he understood Cris probably was not sleeping in her bed because of Luke, he questioned himself as to why she didn't have Bryan sleep somewhere else so she could sleep on the couch. Then it made sense knowing Cris like he did. She would never admit to anyone she couldn't sleep in their bed, and where else would she put Bryan anyway? No, this was typical Cris, putting others first and herself last, and of course, private. Jeff knew there was now another reason she didn't want Bryan, or anyone else, staying there.

What wasn't typical was the Sailor Jerry and corresponding glass sitting there. The meaning of that particular bottle made Jeff's heart sink all over again. It could've been anything else and he would've been okay with it, but not this! His thoughts started racing between the past and the present. The sight of that bottle possibly changed things. Jeff couldn't think about it right now, wouldn't let his mind go there. It was time to get his head in the game and find Cris.

Walking into the office, Bryan passed him and turned around, watching Jeff look around the room. Perhaps Jeff's eyes lingered longer on the bottle than he realized because Bryan had perfect timing with his first comment since entering.

Bryan pointed his finger towards the bottle. "I was really surprised to see the bottle right there. I didn't think she was much of a drinker."

He looked Jeff directly in the eyes. Jeff knew he was waiting for a response, almost like Bryan was daring him to say something which might give away a clue to her personal life. Jeff knew he had to hide his emotions from him and feign puzzlement, while also hiding that he cared so much for Cris or violate any of her privacy she clung onto so dear. Jeff was pissed at the imposed challenge, even if it was his imagination, though he didn't think it was. Either way, for Cris, Jeff had to blow it off.

"It was probably Luke's. Maybe they used to share it, or maybe Steele wanted to feel closer to him last night. She certainly did not drink all of that herself. She probably had a shot before bed to think of Luke and help her go to sleep, which is understandable."

Furrowing his eyes, Bryan did not seem content or convinced with that answer. "Well, I personally have never seen a shot glass so big, but maybe you're right. I'm not so sure though. She came out to the kitchen two nights ago and called me Luke, told me not to stay up too late. I found it bizarre and it worried me. Like she was starting to have a breakdown. Now that I've seen this room, I think there was much more going on."

Jeff needed to end this part of the conversation. "I'm not wasting any more time on this. What's important is finding her, and what's worrisome is the cracked window right there."

Ending the debate, Jeff began walking over to the window. He was truly puzzled about the open window and Cris being missing. He couldn't stop his mind from going back to previous conversations and disagreements with her. Was Cris really on to something with Bryan? Should he have listened when Cris said they were leading the lion into the den? Was Bryan covering it up by pretending he got concerned when Cris wasn't up yet? Maybe that was the real reason the office door was busted in? Bryan was looking for her for other malicious reasons and finally figured out she was in there, or knew it all along because he had been secretly watching her every move? Maybe Cris has been gone for hours and he had to bide his time to coincide with his story.

No, it was not logical, and Jeff knew he had to stop thinking this way if he had any hope of finding her. Cris would've known if he was watching her like that. She wouldn't have gone in there unless she knew he was in bed for the night. More importantly, along with Cris, Bryan was his best detective. He didn't have the dark side that Cris was trying to prove.

Jeff looked at the partially opened window. The screen was still in place outside. The weird thing was how it was cracked open at the bottom, instead of the top. That part gnawed at him. Cris would not have left it that way if she was trying to get some fresh air. She would have left it open at the top with the latches in place, making it more challenging for someone to get in. *Was she trying to open the window to jump out, but didn't get that far?* He shook his head. *Damn it, stop!*

Turning around, Jeff scanned the room again. Bryan was squatting petting Stormy, while also continuing to look around the room. Jeff looked at the map board. Cris had some really good stuff written down, although he wasn't surprised. Jeff found it interesting how Bryan had no suspects, yet Cris had two. One of which was Bryan and the other was some stranger she encountered by a bridge while running. He wondered how Bryan felt about seeing his name there, as well as who this stranger was. Jeff turned from the desk area and board to look at him.

"I'm assuming you have seen all of this?"

Bryan stood up and narrowed his eyes. "A brief scan, yes. While I'm disheartened to see my name there, I'm curious who this stranger is. There's no details to help us find him, or to know when she saw him."

"Yes. Once we find Steele, we will have to let her know she needs to have more detailed notes for us to follow next time."

Jeff didn't mean to have as much bite to his sarcasm as what came out, and in all honesty, Bryan didn't say anything he wasn't thinking too. Jeff berated himself to knock his shit off and focus on the case without letting his emotions interfere. He snorted out loud at the thought. There was minimal restraint when it came to Cris.

Bryan had no comeback, which was not a surprise. He seemed to be blessed with the good grace of being able to keep his mouth shut when there was nothing nice to say, or at least, saying it politely and mildly when he did respond.

Rationally, Jeff knew Bryan was innocent, or at least he was pretty sure. He still felt compelled to mention Cris' phone call when leaving the range the other night; mostly to see Bryan's reaction and hear his response.

"There is another concerning thing I should probably mention to you."

Bryan's face looked both concerned and worried. "What's that?"

Jeff wasn't sure what to make of his facial response. It could be read as concerned for Cris or for himself being found out.

"Well, Steele called me when she was leaving the range the other night. She wanted to give me a heads up in case something happened to her. Seems a little omniscient right now. Anyway, she felt watched the whole time there. Then she said you called and right after hanging up a vehicle started up and left but she couldn't see it."

He gave a slight pause, giving Bryan a chance to respond, but he didn't. It was clear he was waiting for Jeff to finish what he had to say.

Taking a deep, obvious inhale, Jeff continued, "I thought you had gone home to get more supplies while she was safe at the range. It was about the same time though and I watched you pull into the parking lot in your SUV and jump into your truck. I'm not sure why you didn't take your truck. Then, as per your phone conversation with Steele, you pulled to the exit of the parking lot to wait for her to appear and follow her home. I watched her drive by and you pull out right behind her. So, either you have horrible luck with your impeccable timing and we need to figure out what really went down at the range, or you have some explaining to do."

Bryan shook his head. "No need to call in the dogs on that one. I followed her there at a distance and used my SUV hoping to blend in. I went there to watch out for her since it is my job to "ensure her safety." Which, right now, appears to be my second epic fail in my career in less than a week. I digress from that. In my defense, if Steele had known I wanted to be there, or watch out for her, she would've fought me on it and maybe would not have gone. I could tell she really needed to go and get some stress out. I also think she was anxious with her shooting after what happened up in Jasper. I didn't want to be the reason she didn't go, but I also wasn't willing to leave her there alone. I was doing what I had to do to compromise so we could both get our way. I'm sorry I concerned either one of you, but I'm not sorry I did it."

Jeff wasn't sure if he believed him even though the timing and story matched, as well as Bryan's assessment and logic of the situation, which was a large part of what made him one of the best. Jeff couldn't stop Cris' voice and words that were running through his head, but he also felt like Bryan was telling the truth.

If this is true, just what the hell did go on here then?

CHAPTER 21

Jeff walked out of the office. No matter what had happened he knew they needed to get into action. He went back into the kitchen trying to put everything together and think. His mind went back to the disarmed security system. He began to wonder who disarmed it, Bryan or Cris. Jeff knew this information could be crucial in deciding on the next step. He remembered Cris had made him an authorized person on the account so he could access the records and information. It had only been a precautionary measure, Jeff never thought they would actually need it, but man was he grateful to have it right now.

He looked over at Pete. "I'm going to step outside and make a phone call. I'll be back in a few minutes."

Walking out the front door, Jeff glanced at the empty porch swing and rocking chair. They would be a great place to sit, but it felt almost sacrilegious to Cris to be sitting in them at this time. He silently said a quick prayer they would be able to sit out there and relax in the near future. Jeff knew he had to stay focused right now and get Cris home safely. He shook it off and walked down the steps to his buggy. Jeff got in the driver's seat as he pulled the number up in his phone. This was the most practical place anyway since he didn't want Bryan to hear his call to the security company.

The security company was just as they advertised to be, professional and courteous. Once Jeff verified his credentials and answered the questions and codes, they were very helpful and prompt in giving him the information he asked for.

Going back in the house, Jeff found Bryan standing at the breakfast bar, staring in the kitchen towards the counters. This was concerning. He could tell Bryan was troubled by something; the question was what? A guilty conscience? Because Cris came up missing on his watch? How to continue his cover-up? *Stop it! How about because he is worried about finding Cris?*

Bryan looked up at Jeff as he approached the kitchen, his normally bright blue eyes looked dull. "Chief, I've gotta tell you something that's been eating at me. Do I have your sagacity and confidentiality here?"

While he wouldn't have previously thought it was possible, Jeff's stomach was suddenly more turbulent. "I don't know how to answer that without knowing what you're going to tell me. I will say, as long as what you're telling me is lawful, then yes."

Bryan shifted his weight and furrowed his brows. "I'm not sure I can tell you then. What I did was innocent and for Steele, but recent events have me second guessing my judgment and decision. Damn her!"

Jeff was ready to sell his soul to the devil now. If he could get any information to help find Cris, he was dismayed to admit he would make the bargain.

"Son of a bitch, Bryan, you have my word!"

He noticed Bryan shifted his weight again as he sighed. Perhaps he was happy to be able to get it out, or maybe it was the admission of his word, which Bryan would know was as good as gold.

"The other day when Steele went up to Jasper, I came to pick up Stormy." Bryan looked down at the counter and stopped talking.

Jeff was about ready to reach across the bar and pummel him. If he had a way to extract words from his mouth, he would right now.

"And?"

Bryan looked up at him and sighed. "Long story short, I saw blood spatters on the baseboards and surrounding areas. I checked Stormy; they weren't from her. My mind started creating scenes it probably shouldn't have. Luke screwing around on her and she found out then staged the scene in the preserve, or they got in an argument and Luke hurt her, then who knows what from there. Or the violence from Luke's murderer started here and they were followed."

Trying to keep neutral facial expressions, Jeff knew he probably wasn't doing a good job while hearing this lunacy.

Continuing, Bryan shrugged his shoulders. "I knew it wasn't right and I told myself to knock it off. Neither of them are, were, like that. Anyway, I was still concerned and decided to call Steele about it. I've gotta tell ya, it had me nervous as all hell wondering what her reaction would be. She laughed it off, giving me some fabricated story of an intruder coming in and she "took care of things." I knew it wasn't true, that she was guarding the truth, but I knew, or thought I did, it was something innocent and she was okay. All I was thinking about at that moment was Steele being okay. She made a joke before hanging up about me being a dear to clean it up for her and where her bleach solution was. I knew she was just being a smart ass, but I thought it would be nice to clean it up for her to not only help her out, but more importantly, get a smile out of her with the "bill" I was going to leave for her saying "free for first time service." I convinced myself as I was cleaning it was all innocent and I wasn't interfering or covering anything up, like a crime scene. After the recent events, I'm sick to my stomach wondering if I inadvertently did just that."

Jeff didn't think he ever heard Bryan say so much at one time, or ramble like this. His anxiety and worry were obvious. Jeff had never seen this in him before, certainly not to such an extent. He remembered when they first came in the house after forensics had left on Sunday and Pete handed Cris a piece of paper from the bar, telling her she may want to throw it away. She shoved it in her pocket saying she would hold onto it. He wondered if Cris was saving it as evidence for some bizarre reason.

"Okay. My first question is, was the "bill" you left the piece of paper on the bar you handed to her to throw away on Sunday?"

Bryan looked reticent. "Yes, sir."

"That answers one of my previous curiosities then. Between the note and the office, I was really trying to figure out what the hell was going on with you two. I guess the office is partially explained now too. So, to be clear on this, you're saying this was right after she left for Jasper?"

"Well, that was when I saw it. It was the first time I had been in the house in a while though. I had to assume it was recent, otherwise, she would have cleaned it up herself, or it would have driven her to the nearest mental ward."

"Okay. Then she gave you a phony story of an intruder coming in and she took care of it, joking around?"

Bryan looked like he wanted to throw up. "Yes, sir. Steele said she took care of it and got a little scrape on her arm in the altercation. Of course, now since I'm telling you this, I realize she has the big gash on her arm. Had I known it when I was talking to her I would've taken her more seriously. Maybe they are actually related."

Jeff was trying to figure out how much he wanted to say to him. He felt like in good conscience he should provide some kind of explanation so Bryan could get rid of the guilt and doubt he was carrying. But Jeff also had his suspicions and didn't want to give too many details. Plus, there was always Cris' privacy which he had to protect. Jeff had to walk a thin line with this one.

"Let me try to put your mind at ease a little bit. I'm pretty sure I know what those blood spatters were from. It was an innocent accident and she was okay. Your instincts were right."

Bryan stood straight, crossed his arms in front of his chest, and made a sour face with narrowed eyes and tight lips. Jeff could tell he was livid and was trying to bite back both his anger and words. This anger was another thing which was abnormal of Bryan.

"So, you know what happened then? She told you and you're covering for her and don't have the decency or trust to tell me. I've done nothing but try to help her every chance I got, through all her accusations, and you still don't trust me? I'm sorry to say this Chief, but I don't know what your connection is with her, it's clearly something. You treat her differently than anyone else. I don't think anybody else notices, but I do. Don't worry, I will keep the observation to myself, like a goodhearted person would. As long as I don't find out something really did happen here, and it's being covered up intentionally."

Jeff didn't know what to say. He knew he couldn't say anything which would give away Cris. He was also taken aback with Bryan's underlying threat. Jeff understood his frustration though and he was sure he would've felt the same way had the roles been reversed. It was just so out of character for Bryan to say something like this. Jeff was also surprised to hear him say he noticed he treated Cris differently. He tried hard not to let it show, but once again, this was another reason why Bryan and Cris were the best. She had picked up on it previously and questioned him too. Jeff blew Cris off just like he had to with Bryan right now.

He put his chest out and shoulders back. "To ease your mind, she didn't tell me willingly. It was a necessity when she was in the hospital in Jasper. Otherwise, I wouldn't know either. I'm sorry if you feel I treat her differently, I certainly don't mean to. I guess I feel bad for her with losing her husband and being alone, but I didn't realize the sympathy showed. I'll be more cognizant of it, so it doesn't continue to happen."

Bryan rubbed his hand over his head, then shook it. The remaining narrowed eyes and tight lips told Jeff he wasn't buying it and he was still unhappy, but he had the good grace to say no more.

Jeff knew he had to end this conversation and get back to the emergency at hand. He was pissed they had wasted these few precious minutes on something that turned out to be so unimportant after all.

"Getting back to the urgent situation at hand. I just got off the phone with the security company. I wanted the details on the alarm getting disabled. Steele shut it off herself from the app on her phone."

"Well, this answers a few questions."

"It does, but I didn't tell you the scariest part. It was disarmed just after 8:00 last night. She's been gone almost 12 hours. If she had just gone out for a stroll, she should've been back an hour or so later."

"Well, shit! It must be why the window was left open; she must've gone out that way. I was puzzled because I never heard the door. I'm a light sleeper, even if it was late and I had been sleeping, I'm sure I would've heard it. This explains why I didn't, and I agree, this can't be good."

"There's no logical reason she would've left and not come back within a few hours. If she was going for a run, she would've left a note like she did yesterday and, also would have used the door instead of sneaking out. Why she was sneaking out is another mystery altogether."

"One I'll be very interested in hearing the answer to."

"That makes two of us."

Jeff kept chewing on the same question. Could someone have coerced her to either let them in or her to come out? This was not like Cris at all. Jeff briefly thought of Bryan again and Cris' words of leading the lion into the den. Cris had said he could be there and make it look like someone broke in and then say he came in and found her body, and if anything happened it would be on him. Her words from two days ago haunted him. *"Maybe this was his plan as a way to stay with me since he didn't get it right the first time… Bryan could have an elaborate story and set up of someone breaking in. Conveniently, he doesn't hear any of it and the perp is gone when he wakes up and finds me dead. Chief, if I'm right and he's guilty, it's leading the lion right in my den."* Jeff stopped her, told her again he didn't want to hear these accusations without evidence to back it up. He remembered her final comment after their little tete-a-tete. *"I'm warning you to remember this; this is your choice, not mine. If something happens to me while under Bryan's watch, it will be on your hands and conscience for the rest of your life."*

He visibly shook his head, took off his glasses and mopped his brow. Replacing the glasses, Jeff thought of the half empty bottle of Sailor Jerry alongside that particular glass and his thoughts went dark. Jeff couldn't stop his heart from sinking even further and he automatically wondered where her gun was.

CHAPTER 22

Chief seemed to be lost in thought momentarily as he wiped his forehead and put his glasses back on. Pete wondered just what in hell was going through his mind. He knew damn well he was snow blowing him with his bullshit response about Cris. It was more than him having sympathy for her losing her husband. That made him wonder all the more what was going on with them. He could feel the anger boiling inside and tried to tamp it down. Nothing productive would come of those thoughts and feelings. Still, he couldn't completely release them. Why did Bolton seem to care so much about Cris? If it was sexual, it was a good cover. Pete had excellent instincts and it appeared Chief's marriage was good, and he knew beyond a shadow of a doubt Cris was solid in hers. If it was sexual, it was one-sided. He *knew* Chief wasn't like that and didn't think it was the right angle. He began to reprimand himself. *What is it to you? Why should you care?* Even though he wouldn't admit it, he knew why. Pete felt like rubbing his head, but realized the impression it gave and stopped himself.

Bolton looked at him wide-eyed, like a deer in the headlights. "Do you happen to know where Steele keeps her gun?"

He was surprised by the question. "I don't. It seemed like she always had it on her."

"In some ways, we can only hope. If something did happen, she'd have a fighting chance."

Pete picked up on the wording, it was no mistake, Bolton was always careful and precise with his words. "In some ways? I can't think of a single reason not to have hope of her carrying."

Chief seemed frustrated. "There's not. I didn't mean for it to come across that way. I'm going to look in a few places for it. Could you please call forensics to get back out here?"

"Yes, sir."

Pulling his phone from his pocket, Pete made the call while remaining at the bar. They would get there soon. Holding his phone in his hand, Pete realized he never tried to call Cris. A huge lapse in his detective routine. He realized how off his game he was on this one, it was too personal with Cris. Her phone didn't ring but went straight to voicemail. Cris had either turned the phone off herself, not wanting to be bothered or located, or someone else had done it for her. Pete looked back down the hall at Chief.

From this vantage point, Pete could see every room Bolton was going into. Pete noticed he started with the bedroom. He thought it was kind of futile since they knew that Cris wasn't sleeping in there and she hadn't been in there before she made her escape out the office window.

He wanted to go back into the office and inspect it more thoroughly, not only for clues to what happened but for clues to Cris in general. Pete knew the office held the key to some of her secrets. He also knew he had missed his chance for it. Since Chief was here now, he would guard it like a sentry protecting something sacred. *Why? Why the hell is he so protective of her? She's not some fragile creature who needs protection, she is hands down, without a doubt, the strongest person I know, male or female.* Pete felt himself getting irritated again, which only added to his current frustration. He clasped his right hand over his left arm.

After a short amount of time in the bedroom and workout room, Pete watched as Bolton tried to skulk into the office. Stormy was content resting by his feet, making it easier to strain his ears and listen to every opening of a drawer or rustle of paper being moved. Pete heard a desk drawer open and what sounded like something being set down on the desktop. He heard a barely audible, but obvious emotion filled sigh, followed by "Ah, son of a bitch! Murray, I hope you're watching over and protecting her right now." After a very slight pause, and judging by the quiver in his voice a tearful one, Bolton followed it up with, "Damn it, where are you, Cris?"

Pete silently crept closer to the office door. He made it to the outer door frame without hearing any movement from Bolton's feet. He dared to peek his head around the broken door frame. Pete saw the figure of Chief hunched over at Cris' desk with a picture frame just to his right. It was a picture of a man whom Pete had never seen, but he couldn't deny the man was identical looking to Cris. He watched as Chief stood up, removed his glasses, wiped his eyes and put the glasses back on. Pete stealthily went back to the breakfast bar. He could hear Chief opening and closing drawers now, along with what sounded like the slide of the closet doors. It wasn't much longer before he came out.

"After a quick search, I didn't see it."

"It doesn't surprise me, she seemed to always carry it on her. Some of the time I wondered if it was for protection from me in her mind. I had quickly laughed it off, but after seeing my name on her board in there, maybe I wasn't so far off. I know she's hurting and confused right now, whether she'll admit it or not."

Pete added the part about her being watchful of him just to see Chief's response. He wasn't entirely disappointed. Pete noticed Bolton looked suspicious during the conversation by his narrow eyes, a quick sideways glance, then raising his eyebrows while simultaneously frowning and tightening his lips.

Faster than flipping a light switch, Bolton transitioned into attention. "Gun aside, when forensics gets here, I only want them to check the outside of the window frame for prints. I see no need for them to check inside the house or office since you were in here when this happened. I'm confident nobody got inside, there's no need to try to get new prints from inside the house. We have more productive uses of everyone's time. Also, I would like the "arrangements and conditions" of the office to remain private and between us. I know I don't need to explain how Steele would feel if any of this got out. Since you just expressed how all you've been trying to do is help her, I'm sure you'll agree with this."

Chief worded it in such a way that Pete would've felt like a total ass if he didn't agree whether he really did or not.

Pete put aside his underlying curiosity, anger, and resentment. "Yes, sir."

He watched as Bolton's eyes tracked out the side kitchen window, before turning towards the living room and front door.

"They're here."

Pete went into the living room and looked out the front window. Bolton was out there talking and pointing to the office window. Pete knew he wasn't needed out there, Chief had it under control. He figured it would be best to stay out of the way anyway after what Cris had said to them last time about reporting any findings to Chief and not himself. Pete knew forensics wouldn't be long and there was nothing else here for them. It was time to get to the office and get a plan and team together. Pete began packing his laptop and notes into his backpack.

Stormy was circling at his feet and Pete realized he hadn't taken her out yet. "Sorry girl. Let's go."

Leaving his stuff on the couch, Pete grabbed her leash and snapped it on. Seeing the crew still out front, he decided to take her out back. He needed to get and stay focused, stop worrying about what other people were saying or doing, especially Chief. Whatever his reasoning was for his thoughts and treatment of Cris was none of his business. *Then stop making it your damn business by letting it rub you raw like sand in your underwear.*

The sound of Stormy snorting at him pulled Pete out of his reflections as he looked down at her. "You reading my thoughts? I would love to hear your opinion on it, I'm not sure what your snort was trying to indicate, it could go either way. I know, it was probably more like you telling me to wake the hell up and get you back into the house, right? C'mon, we'll go in."

Stormy galloped back to the deck and bolted up the stairs two at a time. Pete unclasped her leash and walked to the front door to hang it back on the hook. Just as he got there, Chief came back in. Pete moved over to make sure he was out of the way.

"Are they done already?"

Bolton expelled a huge sigh, which already said it all. "Yea. They are going to go back and run everything through right now. This is top priority and obviously trumps everything else… These guys are damn good. Their initial belief is that the only prints there are Steele's. Which means she went out on her own, nobody was trying to come in through the window. It still leaves the question of why did she feel she had to go out the window as opposed to the door? And, of course, where was she going and why?"

Pete had always been able to rely on his instincts and he was sure Bolton was throwing an accusation his way. He reminded himself he was not going to get drawn into all the external bullshit. His only goal at the moment was to find Cris; alive and unharmed. So, he refocused his energies there, where they belonged.

"I don't know the answer to those questions any more than you do, but, I want to find them as much as you do. I don't think there's anything else here that will help us answer these questions, and most importantly, find her. It's time to get to the office and get some backup. Twelve hours of being gone is unacceptable, and we need to get every able body into action. Now." He walked over, grabbed his backpack and secured it across his back and shoulders.

Pete wasted no time, and was making it clear, it was time to go. On his way to the kitchen to get Stormy a bone, he decided to grab a pen and paper. He scribbled a quick note for Cris letting her know, should she return, that she had scared the shit out of them and now they were working on pulling out every person, tool and arsenal they had to locate her. If she should arrive home, please let him know so he could call off the dogs, literally. He grabbed Stormy's bone and called her up to the couch. She jumped up by her pile of blankets and Pete gave her the bone.

"Be a good girl. I'll be back in a while."

The lump in his throat made Pete aware he couldn't look back after he set the alarm and closed the door.

CHAPTER 23

Bryan joined Jeff in his office upon arrival. He shut the door as he came in and sat down in the chair at the front of Jeff's desk which Cris so recently sat in. Jeff wanted to tell him to get up, like the seat was sacred. He fought the irrational urge and instead reached into the drawer of his desk, grabbed a few antacids and threw them in his mouth. While chewing the chalk again, less than two hours after the last handful he had choked down, Jeff habitually looked at his watch. A few minutes before eight o'clock. Heart in his stomach, acid rising to his throat and the ill-equipped chalk shit to try and chase it all away. Again, Jeff started to revert to the time when some form of antacids were his meals. *What the fuck is wrong with you? Why do you keep trying to go back there? This is not the damn time!* Making himself refocus, he thought of the physical time, here and now. *It's been about twelve hours now.* The antacids were ineffective at the new lump rising in his throat and the hotness coming to his eyes as he fought back tears. *Damn it, Cris, where are you?*

Looking across the desk, Jeff noticed Bryan set down his backpack, pulled out a notebook and was apparently as settled as he was going to be. Jeff tried to cover his eyes which were no doubt watering and probably getting a little red. He grabbed a nearby tissue from his desk, blew his nose then removed his glasses and wiped his eyes.

"Damn reflux and allergies."

Bryan looked back at him with suspicious halfcocked eyes as he cleared his throat and leaned forward.

"Okay. So, as I already told you, I've been going back through Luke's case looking for anyone who may have been off, even a fraction of an inch. I didn't come up with anything. In light of the recent note and change of victim, I do believe if they were at the services, and they probably were, they were truly mourning since Luke wasn't the intended target. I believe we need to look at Steele's background to try to solve this, but since you've tied my hands from it, I have no information there. In doing the limited research I was authorized to do; I didn't come up with any red flags from any cases since she's joined us here on Shine Island. Previous to this she was in college so there were no cases, as I'm sure you know. Since seeing her secret burrow and war room, I didn't see any connections made to past cases as having potential enemies. We know there was some unidentified male on a bridge during a run, and me. Of course, you can do what you feel you need to do at the present moment, but my request and plea is you leave me out for the immediate time. My focus is on Steele and finding her safe. I will not waste any more time chasing empty bullshit. If we don't get any leads or find her in the next twelve hours, at most, we know it's probably too late. At which point, I say feel free to start wasting your time looking at me. Until then, I'm begging you, for Cris, to put your suspicions of me aside and pull out every fucking resource you have to find her. Sir."

Jeff had never heard Bryan cuss like that. He could sense the radiating hostility and frustration from many of Bryan's comments, and assumed the resulting frustration of those led to his abnormally long assessment of the situation. He understood Bryan's thoughts and feelings, but he also had Cris to protect.

"I agree with you on all of these points. For the record, I never said I suspected you…"

Recomposed, Bryan cut him off. "You didn't need to, sir. Your body language and cohesion with Steele was clear enough. But that's not what's important right now."

Jeff felt bad, but he still held his ground.

"I was the one defending you to her. I told her I didn't want to hear any of those accusations unless she could give me solid evidence to back it up. But you're right, it's not what's important right now. I can tell you from her employment records there's nothing in her past to waste your time on. Anything of relevance would have to be since she started working here. So, just like not spinning our wheels looking at you, we don't need to spin our wheels looking any further back on her."

Jeff hoped he was convincing and sold his story enough. He used his previous career's tactics of body language, wording, stern authoritative voice and language to try to appear convincing, in charge, and also genuine. This will get people to believe, respect, and do what you request. Jeff couldn't allow Bryan to look into Cris' past. He thought he did a decent job. Especially with his comparison of not spinning wheels on unimportant information to finding Cris. It wasn't necessarily solving the case because he still had a small suspicion of Bryan thanks to Cris, but it would hopefully hit home and look like a fair and even trade off. No looking at Pete as a suspect right now, and no looking into Cris' past before her employment here.

Bryan threw up his right hand. "So, where do we go from here?"

Sitting back slightly, Jeff crossed his arms over his chest. "Well, on the drive back here I contacted missing persons and Campbell to get them actively working on assisting us too. I also have the K-9 patrols aware and are standing by to help if needed as well as the Medivac team. As far as our investigation, let's begin by thinking about the fact she was obviously on foot. We know she wasn't exactly running away from home. If she was going a long distance, she would've risked you hearing the sound of a vehicle and driven."

Bryan leaned forward. "Which reminds me, I forgot to tell you I tried to call her cell phone and it went directly to voicemail. Either she shut the phone off herself after disabling the alarm from it, or someone else did. I'm sure missing persons will look at the cell phone towers to see where the phone was last, but I don't expect it will lead to much since it's turned off."

"Well, shit. It may not matter anyway. Unless she left and called a cab. Then we could track her wherever she was traveling, but that's not her style. Steele would fire up her car like a boss and smoke the tires on out of there. Checking the cell phone towers won't be helpful."

Bryan smiled. "You're probably right. So, logistically it leaves us looking at a radius within her house. She's very active, and I know she loves to run on the beach. I would say we probably need to consider a three-mile radius?"

Jeff was thankful Bryan seemed to be thinking clearly, because he felt like his own head was buried deep up his ass.

"I would say that's a pretty accurate range. I also doubt she ran on the beach, or why sneak out for that? I just can't imagine who in their sane mind would want to harm her."

He thought of the half empty Sailor Jerry bottle. Jeff was sure Cris consumed it herself recently, despite what he told Bryan. He worried about the combination of alcohol and her gun, knowing firsthand they don't mix. Jeff remembered asking her a few days ago if she had a death wish. Cris denied it, but he still couldn't help but worry from experience. Jeff knew he had to pretend it wasn't a reality and stop thinking about it.

"Although, if I'm wrong and she did run to the beach, and for whatever reasons didn't feel the need to tell you or leave a note, it could completely change everything. Not only would we be thinking human attack, but also natural or environmental, like a shark attack."

Bryan raised one eyebrow while lowering the other. "I agree, it could be a possibility, but for now, I think we should leave that angle out. One, I agree she would've told me or left a note. Two, there's no reason to shut her phone off for that. Three, if something like this happened, I hate to say it, but we probably wouldn't find her body. I feel we need to try and focus on more tangible outcomes in the beginning here. It wouldn't hurt to see if her phone was picked up on any other signals by the beach to help rule it out, but beyond this I would not suggest going down that rabbit hole right now. We don't have time for this kind of unlikely bullshit."

"Knowing Steele and her preference for simplicity and privacy, she probably has the locater on her phone off and does not connect to nearby wi-fi or hotspots, making the whole cell phone tracking an irrelevant point anyway."

Bryan smirked. "Agreed."

Jeff couldn't process what to do or say next before there was a tenacious knock at his door. Looking through the frosted glass he already knew who the figure on the other side was.

"Come in."

Jeff noticed Bryan rolling his eyes as he turned back around from seeing who was coming in. Campbell came swiftly prancing in, looking anxious. She looked over at Bryan as she threw her long blonde hair back over her shoulder.

"Sorry to interrupt, sir. While I was in missing persons to compare information, I just found out there was recently another missing person case from one of Steele's neighbors. It has not been 24 hours, but because of his mental disorder, they've made it a priority. I thought it would be important to mention because of the proximity to her house. Maybe Steele wasn't the only one who's come up missing and potentially had something happen."

"Damn it! Campbell, could you get me the details and address on it please?"

"Already have it, sir. Here you go." Kim handed him a piece of paper with a few meager details.

Jeff thought of the comment he'd just said about anyone in their sane mind wanting to hurt Cris and wondered if this person with a mental disorder wasn't a victim, but instead was the suspect and Luke's murderer. Chills went through him as the hair on his neck and arms stood up. Jeff would not dare to admit or say out loud, but he could also quite conceivably be Cris' killer.

CHAPTER 24

Bryan was already shoving his notebook in his backpack while jumping up from the chair. "Sounds to me like we have our first potential lead and next move to follow up on."

Jeff was hopeful this would be the break they desperately needed, but he was a little apprehensive of Bryan's enthusiasm. *Is he just happy to have the spotlight off himself for a little longer?* Jeff knew this could be a really big clue and he must stop those inner musings from arguing in his head if he was going to find Cris.

"Let's hope so." He looked from Bryan to Campbell.

"Campbell, could you please make sure they are looking at her cell phone records and towers to try to figure out its last known location? We know it is currently off. I expect Cris always has her GPS and locator off. I need to know when and where it was last picked up. Use whatever means necessary to find out. Also, check the cameras just outside her neighborhood starting at 7:30 last night."

"Yes, sir. I'll get on it right now." Kim's heels clicked out of his office as she flung her hair back over her shoulder.

Bryan was still standing, backpack slung over his right shoulder. He was ready to pounce. Jeff decided he wanted to keep him close. He would honor his request since he agreed for the most part and not interrogate him like a suspect right now. But he would be inconspicuously observing and scrutinizing his every word, breath, and movement of body language like he was meticulously looking for hymen in a whorehouse.

"Let's ride over together in my vessel. We can try to brainstorm and formulate a plan on the way."

"Okay. Works for me."

Already turning on his heel towards the door, Bryan was obviously anxious. Jeff decided to grab a few more pieces of chewable chalk from his drawer before leaving. He tried to repeatedly swallow it down as he grabbed his keys and headed for the door.

He walked out of his office not much after Bryan. Certainly, it took no more than ten seconds to grab the antacids and keys, yet, Bryan was nowhere in sight. Making the left from his office, walking down the hall past the break room, then around a corner to a short hall and back door, Jeff still didn't see him. He felt his brows furrow and told himself to relax, maybe it took him longer than he was estimating, which he knew was bullshit. Opening the back door more forcefully than he had intended, he saw Bryan standing at the passenger door of his SUV waiting for him.

Jeff clicked to unlock the doors. "Damn it, Bryan. I wasn't aware we were racing."

"Sorry, Chief. I'm just hopeful on this lead and wanted to get moving on it. Daylights burning."

Without responding, Jeff hopped behind the wheel. He crammed the key in the ignition and turned it forward, bringing the gas to the fuel injectors and the vessel to life, such as it was.

Wasting no time, Bryan had his backpack open on the floorboard and his notebook back out. He was hastily ruffling through it while scanning each page. He abruptly stopped at one of the note filled pages.

"So, I believe we have Tobias Calhoun, 19 years old, mentally disabled, as we were just told. He just graduated this year. He's employed part time at a local grocery store as a bagger/cart retriever. He wasn't a person of interest in the initial investigation because his parents said he was handicapped. They never expanded, and I never asked further. I didn't think it was necessary given the circumstances. I really hope it wasn't a mistake."

Jeff thought maybe he responded with a grunt, or maybe not. Either way, he felt the muscles in his forearms and biceps contracting as his hands squeezed the steering wheel like he was trying to choke the life out of it with a death grip. He was tiresomely replaying things in his mind to figure out what might've happened in her house last night. In spite of whether he actually responded or not, he vaguely heard Pete's voice continuing as his own mind was overtaken.

Maybe Cris snuck out the window to escape, or perhaps she really did sneak out for her own reasons, which Jeff could completely envision her hardheaded stubborn ass doing. She had disabled the alarm. It didn't seem like she would've been trying to escape from fear, or Cris would've let the alarm go off. Unless she was playing a game of cat and mouse, which Jeff could picture. Cris wouldn't want to appear weak or inferior, but instead prefer to outwit her prey.

Maybe she was in fear but not in immediate danger and that was why she snuck out? Which still didn't explain the excessively broken office door, other than a cover-up for his story. No. Cris would've called him… Unless. Perhaps she was stopped before she had the chance. Maybe Bryan heard her leave and followed her. The alarm was already deactivated by her, he was off the hook for entering his code and condemning himself. Maybe this was exactly the scenario he had been waiting for. The lion waiting patiently in the den, as Cris had said. There would be no evidence for forensics to find when they came to the house, and he would know it. His prints were expected there, and he would've kept them in the areas where he belonged. He was extremely smart and exceptional at his job. Cris was right, he would know exactly how to do it and how to cover it up.

Jeff involuntarily and violently shivered as Cris' words sliced through his thoughts again; *"I'm warning you to remember this. This is your choice, not mine. If something happens to me while under Bryan's watch, it will be on your hands and conscience for the rest of your life."*

Damn her, Cris was more right than she could've known. Or perhaps she really did know him that well. She was very observant of others. If something happened to her, his conscience would eat him alive. A part of him would die. What she couldn't possibly know, is just how large of a part. There would be nothing left. Jeff prayed she was safe because he knew, even as strong as he was mentally, he wouldn't be able to endure the loss of her.

He thought of his wife. Jeff loved her with every fiber in his being. Even though no woman he knew would have, she had stood by his side for the past 32 years. She fully understood and supported everything he had gone through, in his previous and present career and life. Which, of course, included Cris. Even so, Jeff didn't think he could live with himself if something serious or life threatening happened to Cris. It would be his final straw, too much to bear.

His conscious mind on autopilot, he was ready to pull into Cris' driveway. Bryan's prominent voice and movement of his right hand on the dashboard and left hand pointing out the windshield, pulled Jeff back to the present reality.

"This is it, right here!"

Jeff tried to remember the address written on the piece of paper Campbell initially handed him so it wouldn't be so obvious how lost in thought he was. He had never experienced this kind of checked out feeling before, and he certainly didn't like it. Jeff knew he needed to get back to the Chief being in full control; in all aspects.

"I got it."

Jerking the wheel to the left, Jeff peeled into their driveway like a virgin anxiously arriving for his promiscuous prom date. He was grateful to see Bryan unbuckling and getting ready to get out. It confirmed he had the right place. As Jeff shut the ignition off, Bryan was beginning to walk in front of the vehicle with notebook and pen in hand, heading for the front door. Jeff got out and matched his strides to the house.

He grabbed Bryan's arm to slow him down and spoke very softly. "Bryan, listen. Let's not let on why we're really here. They don't need to know we're looking for Steele or the fact she is even missing. I want to get a feel for them first, make sure they aren't going to try to cover up for their son if there is actually a reason to be."

"Agreed." Bryan turned and began walking briskly again.

A frail-looking woman opened the door before Bryan was able to knock on it. "Detective Bryan, I remember you from your visit after Mr. Steele's death. I'm surprised to see you here."

Jeff inwardly kicked himself, he hadn't thought about this. Bryan didn't miss a beat and was very convincing in his response. This made Jeff wonder again if he was capable of doing the same to him.

"Yes, ma'am, you're right. We work with other departments as well when needed and they wanted some extra help on this case. They're making it a top priority. I thought it might be easier if I came for this part since I had already spoken to you once, I was hoping that might make you feel a little more comfortable and confident. I know this must be a scary time for you right now. I hope I can help."

The words were rolling off his tongue sweeter than honey.

"Did you find that poor, dear man's killer yet? The whole thing just makes me sick."

"Me too. We haven't made any arrests yet, but I can tell you, we are very close."

"I hope so! The sweet soul deserves justice and I can't even bear to look over at his house and his poor wife left behind. It must be so hard and a loss for y'all as well."

"Yes, ma'am, it is. Mrs. Calhoun, I would like to introduce you to Chief Jeff Bolton, he is also assisting in locating your son and is here to help." Bryan turned his body, affording a full view of Jeff.

She extended her hand. "Nice to meet you, Mr. Bolton. I'm thankful for all the help we can get."

There seemed to be a good rapport going on between them, so Jeff decided to sit back to observe and analyze them both.

"Nice to meet you as well. I will be more of an observant bystander. Hopefully, I'll have a good idea of where to go to find your son by the time we leave here."

She put her hand to her heart. "That sounds glorious to me!"

Bryan broke back in. "We'll do everything we can."

Mrs. Calhoun turned to the side and held her hand out towards the living room, indicating for them to come in and sit down.

"Please, come in. I'm sorry, but my husband isn't here. He's out driving the streets, convinced he'll find Tobi himself somehow."

"He's desperate, it's normal and understandable."

They all went into the living room and sat. Jeff and Bryan on the couch and Mrs. Calhoun in a wingback chair directly across from them. Jeff watched as she meticulously tried to press nonexistent wrinkles out of her dress.

Bryan wasted no time in cutting to the chase but still kept his accomplished and compassionate tone.

"If it's permissible, I'd like to start with some important clarification. You told missing persons Tobi has a mental disability. I remember you also told me previously in passing he works at the grocery store. So, I hope you don't mind me asking, but it could be crucial information to finding your son. What is the diagnosis, or extent, of his mental disability?"

Jeff kept being reminded of why Bryan was one of the best and told himself it was to their benefit with Cris, not her detriment.

Mrs. Calhoun wrung her hands which were placed in her lap and took a moment before responding. She looked between both of them, then sighed loudly.

"I didn't want to tell you before because once people know, they treat and look at him differently."

Bryan leaned forward and placed his hand on top of hers as he tenderly interrupted. "Mrs. Calhoun, the only reason we'll look at him differently is in our professional training of how to best find your son. Different mental illnesses will have different responses by them and with accurate information, our search team will know better where to look."

She visibly softened. "I know Detective Bryan, you're only here to help us find our boy. I'm so scared for him and his future."

"We'll find him. His future will be just fine."

She noticeably shook her head then took a deep breath and lowered her shoulders. "From your mouth to God's ears! I'm not going to lie, I'm scared. Tobi has schizophrenia. I'm sorry I didn't tell you this before detective, I just didn't see its relevance to the situation you were here for at the time."

Jeff wanted to come up out of his seat, shake her and ask her what the hell was wrong with her? Did she realize what might have happened because of her stupidity? He knew it was wrong, but his emotions were high right now. He somehow managed to sit still, but Jeff knew his blood pressure must be high and his face had to be getting red. Fortunately, Bryan kept his cool and continued establishing trust.

"It's okay, thank you for sharing it with us. You're right, there really wasn't any relevance to what I was here for. It will help now though. Can you expand on why you said you are afraid for his future? Was he behaving differently recently or has the illness gotten worse?"

Looking down at the floor and taking a moment to answer the question, she was clearly hesitant.

"Well… the past year or so he has gotten noticeably worse, but only to us since we know him so well. We've had several regular appointments with the doctor in this time and have been diligently adjusting his meds along the way. Honestly, I haven't wanted to admit it, and for this reason, haven't taken him back to the doctor, but I believe Tobi has had more severe bouts with his illness of late."

Bryan softly interrupted. "Could you tell me when this increase started?"

"Well… it all kind of blurs together but it's certainly been a few weeks, maybe even a month." She looked up at them both like a light bulb went off. "I can tell you, without a doubt, he's been very shaken up and agitated since Mr. Steele was killed. Tobi was so fond of him as a teacher. With his disability, and recently increased blunted emotion, I never expected it to hit him as hard as it did. It broke our hearts. We knew then just how great of a person Mr. Steele must've been."

Bryan shifted in his seat. Jeff was sure Mrs. Calhoun didn't notice, but he sure as hell did, and he knew how to read body language well enough to know what it meant. Bryan's calm, rational, compassionate demeanor was losing its grip.

Sitting up a little straighter, Bryan was undoubtedly composing himself. "It's understandable, he was a great person. It's a huge loss to this community. I hope you don't mind me asking, but again, it is important in finding your son, possibly even more so now knowing the extent of his disability. I'm very concerned for his safety. Does he, or your husband, have a gun?"

Like the sails of a ship when the wind blows them flat against the masts and spars that support them, Mrs. Calhoun seemed dismayed by the question. "Um, my husband does. But he checked it before he left this morning and although he mumbled something about it had been moved, it was still here."

Bryan didn't miss a word she said. "Well, it's good that it's not missing. But, for clarity, you said it "was" here. Does that mean it *is* not now?"

She held her hand to her chest again. "Oh, mercy yes! It *is* still here. I meant it as past tense when he looked for it earlier."

"No problem, that's what I thought, but wanted to clarify. Since it's still here, would you happen to know where it is and be able to show it to us?"

"Of course." She cleared her throat, but it seemed more from being uncomfortable than an actual physical need, nevertheless stood up to go get it.

Jeff wanted to yell at her to not touch it, to simply show them where it was. They could merely look at it and know if it was potentially Luke's murder weapon or not. There was no need to touch it, but even if they did, they had gloves with them which they could quickly slip-on. He looked towards the ceiling and said a silent prayer as she walked out with a closed pistol case. Bryan glanced at him with halfcocked eyebrows. Jeff raised his in reply. They both understood what they were looking and praying for.

She thrust it into Bryan's hands. "Here, I don't even want to touch it. My husband has it for "home protection" but I've seen the way Tobi has always looked at it. When he was a pre-teen, before his diagnosis, my husband tried to teach him safety and how to shoot so Tobi would respect the gun and not be intrigued by it and be tempted to use it inappropriately. They had gone out several times, and apparently Tobi was a good shot. It was only a seemingly few short years later when things started to change, and we knew it was no longer safe to treat him like the average child, much less have him wielding a gun anymore." She paused as her eyes got clear. "I'm sorry, I rambled. I miss my poor boy and the gun brought back memories. It just doesn't seem fair for something like this to happen to such a sweet, innocent baby. I pray he's safe. He's probably so scared. I know I am." Tears started to fall, and she turned her back to grab a tissue from the nearby end stand.

Both of them stood up. Bryan opened the black plastic case while her back was turned. They looked from the pistol to each other, eyes wide. Jeff dared to hope, could it be? They couldn't speak since she was right there, but there was no need. It was obvious they shared the same hope. Mrs.

Calhoun turned around and Bryan closed the case, they had seen enough.

"I apologize, I didn't mean to get so emotional in front of you gentleman."

Bryan set the gun case in the chair and held up his hand to her. "No need for an apology, you're stronger than anyone else would be given the circumstances. I do have a question though; did I hear you correctly? Your husband mumbled something about the gun had been moved?"

She shook her hand downward as if blowing it off. "Oh, yes. But I didn't pay much mind to it. My husband is very OCD. I'm sure I hit it while vacuuming or cleaning at some point and moved it from its precise location of the seams in the hardwood floor. Things like this happen all the time."

For the first time today, Jeff felt his lips pull towards a smirk. It sounded just like Cris. If anything was moved a fraction of an inch in her house, vehicles or work area, she would notice. Honestly, he wasn't much different himself.

Bryan gave a fake chuckle. "I see. Well, I think I only have one more question, and this may be the most important, so take your time to think about it before answering if need be. Is there a favorite spot or place where Tobi liked to go? Think of times especially when he was upset or wanted time alone and to get away."

"That's easy. Not much thought required there. His escape has always been in the preserve at the end of the street. He would go there for hours or a whole day at a time. This is different though. He was supposed to work until closing last night. He always rode his bike to work and he never showed up. He didn't seem agitated before he left, there's no reason why he wouldn't have gone to work as scheduled unless something happened on the way."

"It sounds like you're right. I think we have all we need for right now. I want to get back out there now and find your son for you."

Jeff's mental red flag was at full staff, and he had a pretty good feeling Bryan's was too. They all began walking towards the door. She held it open for them with her left hand. Bryan went out first and nodded his head as he walked past and thanked her. As Jeff approached, she held out her right hand to shake his again.

"I can tell you are observant, and I know your wheels were spinning. Please bring my baby back to me safely."

Jeff swallowed and not allowing himself to break his code of honesty, he answered her, without expanding into detail.

"Don't worry, ma'am, we *will* find your son."

CHAPTER 25

Cris regained consciousness and opened her eyelids to the external darkness. Remembering her new visual condition and where she was, she began to panic again. The anxiety was mainly internal as the air was now as scarce as her restricted movements. She was unable to move her legs since they were numb, yet she could still feel them twitch. Even with her reduced brain activity due to low level carbon dioxide poisoning, Cris knew the muscles twitching was also a byproduct of the toxic poison setting in. She assumed a part of the loud ringing in her ears was also due to increased blood pressure for the same reason.

Being more cognizant of her body now, Cris realized how badly her fingertips hurt. She was confused and began feeling them. She could tell there were fingernails broken and some were gone altogether. She could feel the raw meat of her fingertips where the nails used to be and cringed at the pain as she brushed over them. There was a significant slimy feeling in those spots in particular, and Cris knew they were covered in blood, pus, dirt and probably some splinters mixed in. She must've been trying to scratch and claw her way out, but she had no recollection of it. She also knew this would've used a ton of precious oxygen and expelled more toxic carbon dioxide, which certainly explained the effects she was feeling now. Cris didn't know how much time had passed, but she did know there couldn't be much left.

Her fingertips were crusted over in blood and mud. Her head was oozing, and infection must have been raging throughout her entire body now. Cris' ears were ringing even louder, and the lifelong comrade shadows of her mind were chasing and taunting her. She would swear there was a figure repeatedly passing in front of her face. Of course, being shut in this tiny box, along with her loss of vision, Cris knew realistically it wasn't possible. It was obvious delirium was setting in, the end was upon her.

Innate fighting instincts kicked in and made her dig deep within herself and she started clawing at the sides and top again. Pain was ripping through her fingers and radiating up her arms that were now twitching. Tears were pouring from sadness and anger. Cris inhaled as much of a breath as she was able to and released out a frustrated scream. She knew she was going nowhere and was just using up whatever last minutes of oxygen she had even more quickly.

Cris grudgingly stopped. Instinctively, she tried to feel for the rosary she always carried in her left pocket, which was the side she was on. After much pain from the probing with twitching fingertips on her numb, juddering thigh, Cris didn't feel any of the rosary and finally remembered it was home. Broken. Just like her.

Her compacted body stuck with nothing left and she began to wonder; *Is there really hope waiting in the darkness? What the hell am I fighting for at this point? Besides Stormy, whom Pete would gladly take, and she would be happy with, I've got nothing left and nothing here to look forward to.*

Cris was momentarily brought back to her present reality by the new muscles twitching in her back. At the base of her spine, she felt an extra vibration in the tremor, like a heaviness pressing up against it. Her foggy brain finally conjured what the feeling was, her original comrade, Smith & Wesson.

She could feel the higher-level effects of carbon dioxide poisoning overpowering her. Cris knew it would be reducing the ability of her body to regulate her heartbeat at any moment if it wasn't already. It was hard to tell through all the different pain, numbness and twitching going on. Cris thought she had felt a few body parts convulsing and knew it was the last stage before the carbon dioxide finally killed her.

Trying to breathe as minimally as possible, Cris brought her awareness back to her comrade. She didn't know if her painful, bloody fingers or cramped and twitching muscles could reach back and pull it out. There was an overwhelming sense that she needed to try. *One bullet is a lifetime supply!*

Trying to reach back and slightly contort her body, which Cris discovered was not possible, she half-heartedly attempted to retrieve her weapon. After minimal effort she relented. Cris knew she didn't have it in her to go out this way.

Tears silently fell. *You taught me better daddy. You did it for us. This would not be for anyone but myself. I refuse to go out this way. You're right, when life gets tough, I'm tougher. I'm a Sailor's daughter, damn it! I will go out with honor, courage and commitment, just like you did, daddy! Hooyah!*

Her body started convulsing. Cris tried to hold on to her contained self as the bones of her body jarred against the sides of the box, and her head occasionally bounced off the top of it, shooting pain around her skull. Cris wasn't sure how much time had passed, but she had to guess it was about a minute before she got a momentary pause. The air was almost nonexistent now.

I've gotta have faith Pete or Chief will find this guy. My job here is done. It's time to go be reunited with my two favorite men.

Cris wrapped her left hand over the dog tags and placed her right hand around her left, rubbing her wedding rings as the tears finally stopped. She smiled, closing her eyes to the darkness for the last time.

CHAPTER 26

Neither one said a word, or so much as looked at each other, as they tried to hide from Mrs. Calhoun how expediently they were trying to race to the privacy and safety of Chief's vehicle. Doing their best to appear nonchalant on a leisurely stroll, they slowly got into the vehicle and closed their doors.

Chief turned to Pete as he was fumbling to turn the key in the ignition. "Holy shit! Can you believe this?"

"To tell you the truth, no, sir. I can't! I also can't believe they withheld the full truth from me in Luke's initial investigation *and* I didn't realize it and pursue it further."

Chief finally got the key in and started the vehicle. "Don't beat yourself up over it, Bryan. It's not surprising they withheld it, no doubt innocently. They never thought their son could be a murderer, even if by accident. I don't know too many detectives who would've asked for specifics on the disability, especially at the time. It wasn't what we were looking for then." Bolton's phone rang, cutting him off. "It's Campbell. Hopefully, she has some good news."

He picked up his phone and answered it. Pete vaguely heard Chief talk before he found himself lost in the maze of crevices in his brain. He was so pissed they had purposefully covered for their son saying he was disabled but making sure not to clarify it was schizophrenia. That would've changed things. Mrs. Calhoun even admitted it would have. Pete would've insisted on meeting Tobi and trying to interview him to get a better feel for him. He was also mad at himself for not being suspicious, asking more questions and talking to Tobi anyway. He had talked to all of the other students. He let this one go because of his disability. So close to Cris' home and right under his nose. Damn it, he was better than this, and now the one he had let slip could very realistically be the cause of Cris' disappearance. Pete wouldn't allow himself to think it could be worse than a disappearance, he just couldn't.

Bolton's voice broke through his reverie of thoughts. "Well, no big surprise. I'm sure you figured out from my end of the call, the last place a signal was detected on Steele's cell phone was in the preserve approximately a mile in, shortly before midnight."

Pete subtly shook his head to get himself back in the game. "I'm sorry, sir. Honestly, I was lost in my own thoughts trying to figure things out. I didn't hear a word you said on the phone. This does confirm our instincts after this interview. We need to get into the preserve, now!"

"Yep. I'm going to park in Steele's driveway for simplicity. Hopefully, Mrs. Calhoun doesn't watch us and decide to follow us or call her husband to follow us. No matter what, we've gotta move. I told Campbell I had the k-9 patrol on call and to get on the radio now and call them in. They shouldn't be too far behind us."

"Perfect. Pull all the way up. Mrs. Calhoun won't be able to see us alongside the house from there. Hopefully, she'll think we went into the house through the back door. We can enter the preserve further back behind her house. You know as well as I do where Steele was when she lost cell service… The tree where they were having the picnic when Luke was murdered."

Bolton seemed tense with his jaw and hands on the wheel clenched. "Yes, I do."

Pete wondered why Cris' phone was suddenly turned off, or more importantly, by who. He knew there was no time to waste in pondering those thoughts right now, it was time to get into action and move.

Stormy looked out the window at Pete as Bolton shut the vehicle off. Pete felt bad as he exited the vessel. Stormy didn't understand why he wasn't coming in. He wished the circumstances were different and he could at least give her a quick pet and treat, but this wasn't what life had planned. Its plans were to take it with no Vaseline and maybe even demand a smile with it. Pete remorsefully turned his back as he shut the door and led the way for Chief to follow.

Glancing at Stormy on his retreat, Pete promised, "I'll see ya soon, girl."

They ran into the woods toward the area of the fateful oak tree and Luke's murder. Pete tried his damnedest not to think about the last time he was running down this path through the woods to Cris' rescue, just over a week ago. He had to erase the vision of her sitting by that tree, looking unnerved, covered in Luke's blood.

Arriving at the tree, the first thing Pete saw was a large American Flag coffee cup. It was tipped on its side, empty on the ground. The smell of alcohol was unmistakable as they got close to it.

Pete heard Chief's almost inaudible whimper, "No, Cris. No!"

He stood up, took off his glasses, and wiped his eyes before putting the glasses back on. He pulled a bag from his pocket and knelt back down.

"I'm going to bag this up before the rest of the team gets here. No reason to take a chance of it getting anymore contaminated and no need for anyone else to know what it smells like… Damn it! Where the hell is she?"

Pete knew he was covering for Cris yet again, but at this point he had to let it go and focus on finding her, unharmed. Looking closer at the area, his heart sank.

"Chief, there's fresh blood here. I mean, not an hour fresh, but not from Luke fresh."

Placing the bagged mug back where it originally was on the ground, Chief turned to focus on the blood while Pete continued to look around the vicinity. Just to the right of the tree, Pete noticed straight lines going through the grass.

"Either someone was trying to walk or crawl, dragging their injured legs, or someone else was dragging their body. Look at this."

Pete watched Bolton's eyes follow his outstretched arm, pointing from the tree to the trail going through the grass into a nearby wooded area.

"Let's hope it was Cris taking out Luke's murderer. Maybe her battery died, and she couldn't call for backup."

Pete snorted, "We could only hope. That's not what my gut is telling me though."

Chief shook his head. "Yea. Mine either… Where the fuck are those dogs?!" Spit came flying from his mouth. Pete had never seen him like this.

"I'll call them, sir."

He was scrolling through his phone when he heard the bark of the dogs coming. By the time Pete clipped the phone back on his hip, the first dog was in sight. Immediately following was the canine's cohort, officer Brown. Not wanting to be left behind, the second dog was closing in, along with officer Reed, his human counterpart, close behind keeping up.

Chief waved his hand high to them. "Over here!"

The crew arrived, joined them at the tree and commanded the dogs to sit. Pete was appreciative as he nodded a greeting to Reed. He loved the dogs but knew what they were capable of if they didn't know you weren't a suspect.

"Thank God you guys are here! Have them smell the blood; this is what we need tracked. It looks like the trail goes into those woods from here."

He pointed from the new blood on and around the tree, to where the drag marks were going into the woods.

Officer Brown's words were terse. "Is this Steele's blood?"

"Well, it's either hers or her abductor's. I suspect it should lead us to her no matter what."

They gave each dog the command. Pete and Bolton didn't wait before moving. Without delay, they began running alongside the rub marks in the grass. The dogs flew by them barking before they had barely begun, pulling Brown and Reed directly behind them. Once they entered the wooded area, it was harder to see the marks. There were sporadic trail lines, but many places had large spots of pine straw covered over the top. Pete wondered how much time had passed to have this much of it already covered. He knew it wasn't a good sign.

Trusting the dogs' noses and instincts, they followed in the direction they were heading in. It wasn't long before they departed the woods and entered another grassy area. Pete stopped dead in his tracks. Just at the edge, where the trees and pine straw ended and the grass began, was Cris' cell phone. Bolton practically ran into him when he stopped, which was a good thing because he was close enough to stop Pete and pull him up when he bent down to reach for the phone.

"No! There could be prints on it. Don't touch it until after we bag it."

"Damn it, Chief, I know better than that. Talk about a momentary lapse of judgment. Thank you!"

Looking back at the grassy spot where the phone lay, Pete noticed the grass was matted down. He pointed his finger around the area he was talking about while trying to get the words out.

"A body was here. Look. You can almost see the outline. It was a small person, most likely in the fetal position… Shit, there's blood spatters. It looks like where the head would've been." His voice trailed off, he couldn't say any more.

Pete's stomach churned. No crime scene had ever made him sick before. Just looking at this outline and fully envisioning every muscle and contour of the body that was most likely within it seemed to be his nemesis in keeping both his head and stomach together.

The men now looked from the phone and surrounding area to each other. Their eyes mirrored the sick fear and disbelief they both harbored at this implication. It was like their brains were wired together.

Hearing a ruckus, they both looked towards the source of the sound. About 25 yards ahead and to the right the officers had stopped by their canine partners who were now fervently digging. Brown yelled over to them, but it wasn't necessary. Pete and Bolton were already running full speed their way. The dogs didn't break their concentration on digging as they thundered to a stop by the scene. Pete ended up next to Reed, not breaking eye contact with the excavating action going down.

Reed looked over at Pete. "This was freshly dug. Why not bury something in the woods instead of dragging it all the way through to bury it just outside of them? And why out in the open where it could potentially be seen?"

Still not breaking eye contact and barely blinking, Pete responded almost robotically. "Because there's too many shallow roots in the wooded area. Most likely, they wouldn't be able to dig deep enough for what they needed to achieve their goal. This is just on the other side of the woods where anyone rarely goes. It may have been a few weeks or may have gone completely unnoticed altogether. This person obviously knew it. He either did his research or really knows this area."

The memory of Mrs. Calhoun saying this was Tobi's place to escape came screaming back to him. He felt useless just standing there watching the dogs dig. *What are they digging for?* He couldn't bear to finish the thought or try to answer the question.

The dogs kept digging, and Chief issued an unearthly noise as he knelt to the ground attempting to assist and dig with them. Pete stepped in and wrapped his arms around his torso as best he could and pulled him back. Chief didn't fight him, but instead doubled over with tears falling, still reaching towards the fresh, soft earth. Pete knew this emotion was more personal than a boss and coworker relationship. If there was ever any question or hesitation, this raw emotion he was witnessing now negated all of it.

The dogs kept relentlessly digging when suddenly the sound of it changed. It was no longer the sounds of the dogs snarling and digging as the soft dirt flung back, now they were scratching at something more solid and tangible. The four humans anxiously looked towards the hole. Brown and Reed commanded the dogs to stand down. They stopped digging, stepped back and sat.

They all looked down with curious and dreading eyes. Pete wanted to throw up now, more than he did before, as he looked down at a handmade top of a very small wooden box. After the initial shock, they quickly came back to their usual logical selves.

Chief took command. "Steele could be in there. With our emotional strength right now, if we each grab a side, we should be able to pull this top off. I don't care how well it's nailed shut."

Not one person said a word but bent down, reaching for a side of the box and found where the lid met the box, grabbing as best they could. It seemed to be jerry-rigged and Pete was thankful he was able to get a decent size lip on the top to grab onto.

Chief commanded again. "Everyone, get your grip. On the count of three. One... Two… Three!"

Grunting in unison, they all pulled on the wood of the box. Pete wondered if it would actually work as his back felt like it was going to break. Could they really pull this off with their strength and emotion? Pete got encouraged by the sound of the nails squeaking as they protested coming out of the wood they were attached to. He wondered if the rest of them felt the same encouragement as they all seemed to give one big final heave to pull it off. As the top gave and came loose, they all fell backwards.

Moving forward and looking in with dread, Pete couldn't stop it this time. He turned to the side and threw up as he saw a deathly still, bloody figure, which greatly resembled Cris. Turning back after he got done heaving, trying to gain composure, Pete realized the others hadn't noticed his momentary weakness. They were still staring down in the hole, in shock. Chief's face was whiter than freshly fallen snow. Pete knew he had to pull his shit together, just like Cris would do if the roles were reversed.

Bile encroached his throat again as Pete looked in for further details and confirmation. It was definitely Cris. She was crumpled up and compacted in the small space, folded up on her left side. The side of her head was practically unrecognizable with all the dried blood, dirt, bruising, swelling and gashes. Pete looked back at the top of the box they pulled off. It was covered with blood spatters and chunks of her hair.

Looking back into the box, Pete noticed the top and sides were also covered in blood spatters and chunks of something. Some places looked like palpable claw marks. Chief's voice seemed far away as it vaguely broke through Pete's visions of disbelief.

"Someone call the fucking Medivac, now! They're waiting on standby."

Pete was still in shock. He was staring, unwilling to believe this immobile body in the ground as he heard a voice in the background. Pete knew one of them would be calling for help. Right now, he was frozen. Stuck. Never had this happen before, not even close. Pete wanted to look away but couldn't, he also wanted to throw up again. He felt the urge to grab her body and shake her back to him. What he wouldn't give to be arguing with her stubborn ass and hardheaded spirit right now. He should've kept better watch; he was supposed to keep her safe. Foggily, Pete thought he heard a louder voice.

"Bryan!"

Pete lifted his heavy head and glanced at the other three. Chief was looking at him, concerned.

"Bryan! Are you with us?"

Pete tried to shake out the cobwebs, "Yes, sir."

"Okay then. Grab her feet and ease her out with us. We have to get her out of this and assess her condition. Again, on three. One… Two… Three!"

All four of them had their designated body parts to lift out. On the ascension from the box, Pete noticed her bloody hands had been clasped around the dog tags he had caught a glimpse of yesterday morning. They pulled her wedged body out as carefully as they could and placed her supine on the grass next to her makeshift grave.

Right away Pete noticed Cris' lips were blue. Her fingertips were too crusted with blood to tell what was going on underneath. Pete also realized her missing fingernails were probably a significant part of the clumps of matter he saw by the claw marks on the inside of the wood. Her head was beyond belief. The right side, where she already had the staples, was layered with a combination of blood, dirt and fresh gashes which extended across her face. The swelling made it impossible to see the extent of the damage. Chief's voice again began to pull Pete out of his stupor.

"She's unconscious and not breathing. I can't find a pulse."

Chief wiped unashamed tears from his eyes and refocused. "Son of a bitch! Reed, how long before the damn Medivac is here?"

"They said within five minutes."

"Hell! It feels like it's been an hour already."

"Agreed, sir!"

Chief had his fingers back over Cris' wrist, searching desperately for a pulse. Pete tried to come back to reality. His anger was now rising, and he could not give up without a fight.

"I'll begin CPR, sir. You keep feeling for a pulse."

"I can't tell if I feel a faint pulse or it's my own heartbeat I'm feeling, shit!"

"Either way, she's not breathing and already blue in her lips. We need to get her air." Pete tilted her head back and began breathing in her bloody mouth.

"Keep going, Bryan. I'll do some chest compressions. You keep breathing and see if she will start on her own."

Pete watched her chest rise with each breath he breathed into her, but not once did she begin to breathe on her own. He was getting lightheaded from trying to penetrate her lungs with deep breaths. It felt like it had been hours, but realistically Pete knew it was probably no more than one to two minutes. He prayed Chief was right and they weren't making a mistake by doing the chest compressions. Pete was no doctor, he had to rely on faith which was running thin right now. He felt like he couldn't possibly get another breath out without dropping but thought of Cris and found the strength. Pete refused to give up, even as the sounds of the helicopter loomed closer. Before he knew it, the crew was there with a backboard and ready to place it under her.

Sitting back on the grass like he had been pushed aside, Pete couldn't remember how he had gotten there. He vaguely heard the crew as they shouted over the rotating blades and engine of the helicopter.

"Fading pulse… Wounds… Infection throughout bloodstream… Chances of revival slim… County hospital."

Pete watched dumbfounded as the chopper lifted into the sky and took off. The silence quickly set in and Pete looked at the empty hole and blood-spattered lid. Ire overtook him. Something fell from his lap as he stood up, he didn't care what it was. Nothing mattered anymore, except he was ready to find Tobi and kill the son of a bitch.

Completely out of his mind with rage and maybe more than a little madness, Pete took off in the direction of the next nearest adjacent woods and the way he was certain he saw some matted down grass.

CHAPTER 27

Pete went barreling into the woods after he followed the direction of the worn-down grass. There were still a few trail lines visible amongst the darkened, pine straw riddled forest floor. Pete hoped he was going in the right direction. Reed's canine flew past him, the only sound being issued was his paws slamming on the ground as he ran. Reed was hanging onto the leash, towing along behind him and Pete picked up his pace to follow.

The dog stopped at a small amateur cabin type structure and began barking and scratching at the door. Reed commanded him to stand down once more and the dog obeyed. Pete was shocked to see something like this in the middle of the preserve, albeit hidden way off the beaten trail. He refocused knowing that wasn't important right now. Finding Tobi, Cris' assumed murderer, and most likely Luke's, was priority. The cabin and the rest of it would come out during the questioning and investigation.

Pete stood to the side of the cleverly crafted door. "Tobi Calhoun, are you in there? Your mom's worried about you."

Hearing rustling from within, Pete and Reed looked at each other and drew their weapons. Very casually the door opened, and a decent sized young man stepped out, grinning. His clothes were sporting stains from dirt and dried sweat, but on top of those were the spots Pete knew all too well and made his own blood run cold. Bloodstains.

"My mom sent you? She's worried about me? She always worries about me even though I tell her not to. I know how to take care of myself."

He had lifted and turned his hands up slightly, palms out, as he spoke. Pete noticed some red spots which may have been splinters, but most definitely blisters, on his hands.

Pete could barely speak. "So, you're Tobi Calhoun then, correct?"

He proudly beamed. "Yea."

Pete was trying to play it cool but also look around him to try to see inside his little hideaway. He was almost positive he could see a shovel leaning against the wall behind him. Tobi must have noticed him looking.

"I'm sorry, would y'all like to come in? It's not much, but I'm pretty proud of how it's come out."

Reed visibly stepped back a few feet while wrapping the constantly growling dog's leash in his hand.

Pete shook his head. "Not right now, thank you. Your mom is really worried, and I'd like to bring you back to her if you don't mind. I do have a question though. Is this some kind of tool shed? Is that a shovel behind you?"

Tobi sneered. "No, it's not a tool shed. This is my getaway escape I built when I was a kid. I keep perfecting it over time. That is a shovel though. Since you are obviously with the authorities, I'll tell you, you're welcome for getting rid of the monster bitch for you. It's my community service to you."

Feeling his eye twitch, Pete knew he wouldn't hold his composure. "You mean your neighbor, Cris Steele?"

"Yea, that's the murdering bitch I'm talking about. That coward even killed her own husband when she pulled poor Mr. Steele in front of her when she heard the shot. I buried her like I watch her do to other people in her back yard. I hit her in the head a few times with that shovel there before burying her with it. Even though she was unconscious, I made sure she was still alive when I crammed her in the box I built special for her. Let that executioner suffer like she made all her victims do. I delivered the karma to her that she deserved."

Pete charged after him like a raging bull and throttled him to the ground. He could feel his temples throbbing, knew his blood pressure must be astronomical, but otherwise, he was oblivious and out of his head.

"Do you know what you've done? You have no idea what an amazing person she was! You will rot in hell you son of a bitch! I'm gonna fry your ass."

Pete's left arm was holding Tobi down and his right arm was raised, ready to throw the first of many blows to his head. Out of nowhere, Reed pulled him off before he was able to release his punch. Reed pushed Pete aside as he took over calmly holding Tobi down while holding the leash and commanding his four-legged friend to sit.

"Damn it, Bryan. You can't do anything that will get this case thrown out. I know you care about Steele but take a step back, catch your breath and find your head again."

Dumbfounded and numb, Pete sat back and watched the officers finally arrive. Reed told them to read Tobi his rights and cuff him. He had just confessed to Luke's and Cris' murder.

It was such an oxymoron how things felt like they were moving in slow motion, yet, Tobi was efficiently cuffed, Mirandized and being hauled out. The crime scene tape had been rolled out and was in place.

Pete looked around like he was just seeing things for the first time. "Where's Bolton?"

Reed furrowed his brow, "He went in the chopper with Steele."

Trying to bring his brain back to reality, Pete shook his head. "Well shit, we drove his vehicle here. Mine is back at the station."

Concern was carved on Reed's face. "He gave you his keys before he left. They were in your lap."

"Oh, yea. That's right. I know where they are then."

Pete remembered now when he had stood up to find Tobi something had fallen from his lap. He knew it must have been Chief's keys. Pete fought with everything he had to appear normal. Things had been happening to him this past week and a half which have never happened before, and worse, were totally out of his character. He knew this case was going to be hell and too personal for him, he never imagined it would get this bad. Shaking his head and standing up, he tried to camouflage his true instability, like everything was okay.

"I bet it's nice to be out without asshole Moretti."

Reed snickered. "Yep. I love the k-9 calls. It's my chance to escape and I love actively working with my boy here. I just wish it wasn't Steele we had to be called out for."

Pete willed himself to keep holding it together. "Do you know where they flew her to?"

"I overheard them talking about the Sun County Medical University. I don't know for sure that's where she went, but it's my best assumption."

Looking around, Pete was still trying to grasp what he needed to do.

"I guess I need to go through this crime scene and where Steele was buried."

He almost choked on the words but knew it was reality, especially with his job, and he needed to man up and get over it. "I also need to somehow deliver the news to Mrs. Calhoun we found her son, but he won't be coming home with a likely two counts of murder on him."

"I don't think you need to worry about that part. It sounded like they were assigning it to missing persons, which is whose job it should be. I believe Campbell is going to go with them to help if needed."

Pete didn't mean to, but he snorted. "Well, I hope so, one less thing on my plate. I've got more than enough to deal with here."

"I know you do. I already gave my statements. You need me to stick around and help you with anything else? I don't mind."

How long had he sat there after Reed pushed him off from Tobi? Everything was already in the works or done. Pete chuckled, trying to make a joke and act like he was normal, like this was just another ordinary case. Inside he was quivering. Never had he felt like this or had this kind of emotion during a case. Shit, not even on a case. Never in his life *at all*.

"No, I'm good. Really. I know you're just looking for an excuse to stay away from Moretti a little longer. Believe me, I don't blame you, but I've got it from here." Reed smiled and Pete felt a little less alone. "Thanks for all your help buddy. I think I'm going to go scope out this cabin Tobi built and hid so well that no one knew it was here for the past however many years. Feel free to work on your paperwork for a few hours, or even the rest of the day, to avoid Moretti. I got your back."

Reed laughed as he patted his furry best friend. "He doesn't faze me. I just tune his mouth out and continue with what I'm doing. Call me if you need anything. I mean it. Even if it's hanging out and venting after work, I'm here for ya man."

"Thanks, Reed. I really appreciate it and I'll keep it in mind."

Pete knew Reed meant it. For the first time in his life, he thought he might actually need that, and have to take Reed up on it. He didn't know how he was going to get through this, and the foreign concept terrified him. Pete turned to walk away and the only thing on his mind was Cris.

Pulling himself to this new reality, albeit with difficulty, Pete looked at the cabin now as he was coming back upon it slowly. He tried to absorb this structure that had remained hidden in these surroundings for God knew how long. Pete noticed an antenna placed on top of the greenhorn cabin. He was confused by the antenna with an obvious lack of electricity. Pete knew he needed to inspect this hideaway more intensely to try to get a better understanding of Tobi Calhoun.

Approaching the door of the cabin, Pete was able to look at it more meticulously this time. The craftmanship was really quite impressive, especially for a boy his age and with his disability. Tobi clearly had a knack for carpentry. Pete was careful not to touch anything with his non-gloved hands. He opened the cracked door with his covered shoulder as he entered, then held it open in place with his heel. A fellow county team member, whom Pete didn't recognize, was already in there. Pete nodded as he came inside, noticing he had already bagged the bloody shovel.

Doing a cursory scan of the cabin, Pete was amazed at the details. He saw a small TV screen propped in a corner. Taking a closer look, he realized it was battery operated. Pete knew he had to check it out and pulled some gloves out of the nearby bag of gear. He easily figured out how to turn it on. There was a weak signal. Tobi must have been able to pull in some channels, even if they were intermittently snowy.

Spinning around in the small quarters, Pete saw well executed wood seating with some small storage areas. Blankets and pillows were stacked at the end of the seating area. Completing his spin, Pete found himself facing the officer.

"Hey, I'm Detective Bryan, the lead on this case. Aside from the shovel, see anything else of interest?"

"I'm still looking and processing, but I don't think we need any more than the shovel. It has blood all over it and multiple chunks of skin and red hair. I don't think DNA or evidence is going to be an issue in this case."

He seemed so nonchalant, but Pete did everything he could not to throw up at the words and corresponding images which came to his mind. Namely, Cris' bloody, crumpled body in the tiny coffin made special for her.

"Thanks. Good to know. Since you seem to have things under control here, I'm going to move on to the burial site for now. Do me a favor please, don't leave anything unturned. I want his ass to cook for this. I'll stop back here in a little bit when I'm done."

"You got it, sir."

Pete tried to compose himself as he started through the woods towards Cris' dishonorable grave. He knew he had to find a way to get back to his normal levelheaded, naturally calm, self. If he didn't, emotionally he was not going to be able to get through his investigative job. That was not an option. Pete cleared the woods and saw the yellow crime scene taped cordoning off the area. The image brought back the last time he was in this preserve, just over a week ago. Pete was coming up on the crime scene tape just being rolled out and placed. Cris was there that day though. Alive. At least physically. She was mentally in another place, staring off and hadn't even noticed him coming. Pete shook his head. *Damn it, so much for pulling myself out of this.*

He was almost to the quarantined area. Pete reached the taped off section and ducked under. He went straight to the inept burial site and looked at the well-crafted box sitting beside it. Pete was again momentarily impressed with the carpentry craftsmanship. It was lost and forgotten as Pete looked at the evidence and details inside. It was filled with blood spatters, chunks of red hair, whole broken fingernails and deep bloody scratch marks running throughout the tiny provisional coffin.

Despite his best efforts and natural tendencies of being calm and removed, Pete dropped to his knees and doubled over at the image. He turned his head to the side and involuntarily vomited again. Tears inexplicably began to fall. It was too much. Pete never would've thought he would be subjected to something this close to home when he went into this profession. Cris held a special spot in his heart to say the least. Being honest with himself, he knew it was distorting the reality, it was much more than a special spot she held.

Police were all around the scene, including who he thought was Campbell with her long flowing blonde hair. Try as he might, Pete just couldn't bring himself to focus, look or care as he wiped his mouth on his sleeve and pulled his head closer to his knees next to the empty hole in the ground.

Still hunched over, Pete remembered telling the young rookie in the cabin he would be back before he left. He realized this was the second time in his life he was going to be breaking a promise and all in the same week. It was only a few days ago he had promised Cris' safety and see where that got him. No; his first failure was the initial investigation in Luke's case. Then falsely ensuring Cris' safety. Now being unable to return to the cabin. Pete's whole life felt like a fraud, in one single case and week. Pete knew in his heart he had solved Luke's case, and now Cris', but he still felt utterly lost and empty. *What the hell happened to me? What do I do now and where the hell do I go from here?*

CHAPTER 28

Jeff sat next to Cris in the chopper and watched helplessly as she began to seize. Her body thrashing and jolting while she was still unconscious was unbearable for him to observe. Jeff began yelling at the medic who was sitting on the other side of her and already helping as best he could.

"Do something! Help her, damn it!"

The medic loosened her straps enough to turn her onto her side while playing with the knob which controlled the oxygen mask already affixed to her nose. He remained calm as he triaged and spoke loudly to be heard over the rotating blades above.

"I'm doing everything I can, sir. It's most likely a result of the reintroduction of oxygen to her brain. I just turned it down slightly. Hopefully, she won't have any more seizures after this."

Jeff was pissed and stupefied. "What do you mean due to reintroduction? How the hell can you get too much oxygen? You should've given her less from the beginning then! Why wait for a seizure to happen?"

The medic continued to hold onto Cris even as her body stopped convulsing. "It's not that simple, sir. If we had given her too much oxygen too quickly she may have ended up with more brain damage. Put simply, if you reintroduce too much oxygen after being deprived, the brain cells are more likely to die than thrive. I already had it at lower than the normal amount, but maybe it was still too much. It is, unfortunately, a guessing game to find the "sweet spot" if you will. While it's not necessarily the response we want, the seizure is at least a positive sign of some life."

"She hasn't been conscious since we unburied her, and God only knows how long before then! Where the fuck is the sign of life?"

"This seizure is a start. It's a double-edged sword. You don't want to see a seizure, but at least it shows some form of life. If you look behind you at the monitor, you will see her heart rate is coming up, which is certainly a positive sign."

Jeff turned around at the monitor on the wall over his head. "Well, of course, her heart rate is up, she was just flopping around like a fish deprived of oxygen after being pulled out of the water."

The young-looking medic gently rolled Cris onto her back again and began retightening the straps. "Remember we could barely get a pulse when we arrived? This is at least an improvement, and in this field, we take any improvement we can get, no matter the size."

Jeff was terrified and didn't have a response for once in his life. Instead, he grabbed Cris' gauze wrapped hand and held onto it firmly. He wanted to put his hand on her head for more reassurance. To let her know she wasn't alone in case she could feel it, but it was strapped down and so covered and crusted in blood, it was basically futile.

Being honest, Jeff realized it was probably more for his own sake than hers anyway. He knew he was trying to reassure himself more than anything. Jeff had made a covert promise to himself to protect Cris years ago and the reality of what happened was excruciating. This was the final blow and he had no idea how he was going to overcome it. The thought sickened him, and he continuously swallowed down the bile which kept insisting on creeping up.

His phone vibrated in his pocket. Jeff impatiently grabbed the phone with his right while keeping his left hand over Cris'. It was a text message from Bryan. *Update: We located Tobi in a cabin in the woods not too far from where he buried Cris. He blamed her for Luke and confessed to her murder. He actually told us we were welcome for getting rid of her for us and admitted to hitting her in the head with the shovel a few times during the night before burying her with it. Please let me know how things are going there when you get a chance.*

Jeff was happy at the news but couldn't feel joy at the moment. He compulsorily texted back: *Thanks for the update. I'll call you as soon as I get a chance. Good job on locating and getting a confession out of him.*

The helicopter landed at the regional hospital. It had only been a few minutes since Cris' episode stopped. The medic opened the door on the side and the hospital crew was already encroaching to receive her body. Jeff stepped out right behind her. The noise of the chopper and the whoosh of the blades still rotating, swirling his hair every which way brought him back to his current senses and returned some strength to his mind. Jeff had to stop thinking about what happened and how he would get through it and instead focus on getting Cris the best care and answers he could. He had to be strong for her at all times and take each minute as they came and not be absorbed with the past, future or outcome right now.

After transferring her from the backboard onto the gurney, the nurses hurriedly wheeled Cris in as the chopper was lifting back into the air for the takeoff and return trip. The team onboard had already communicated all the information they knew to the hospital staff en route, their mission was now accomplished.

They were updating Cris' vitals on the short elevator ride. One person spoke as another transcribed. "Pupils have no response to light. Blood pressure is 61 over 27. Thready pulse."

The elevator came to a stop and dinged, and the door slid open. They rushed Cris down the hall and into a room they had already prepared for her arrival. The team seamlessly started an IV and began spewing out the names of medications they were hooking up to pump into her. Another nurse was at the computer typing in each name and quantity as they were rattled off. Jeff didn't know what most of the names or doses were, but he did understand the reasons he heard for what they were being used for. Anti-seizure, blood pressure, dehydration, anti-nausea, blood clots, antibiotics. A lab tech was drawing blood as a nurse was telling her to make sure the orders included the amount of oxygen in the blood and they needed all results, STAT. Another nurse was hooking Cris up to a ventilator, while one of the others gave her an injection in the abdomen.

Standing back out of their way, Jeff observed what looked like a well-controlled chaos as they hooked Cris up to all this equipment. All the while, there was Cris, unmoving on her own. The only time she moved was when one of the nurses grabbed a body part and moved it themselves. Jeff reminded himself to stay focused on the here and now and not what was to come as the nausea kept trying to rear its ugly head.

One of the nurses was wiping the blood off her face and head to try to get a better view of the wounds. Jeff was able to see the gashes and bruising underneath the swelling as each layer of blood was wiped away. He wasn't a squeamish person but seeing Cris like this made his head start to spin. He felt like he was going to pass out. Jeff quickly decided to sit in a nearby chair in the corner and put his head near his knees to keep from passing out. That wouldn't help Cris at all, especially when the ones attending to her would have to rush over to attend to him.

Still looking down at the floor, Jeff heard one of the nurses. He assumed it was the one cleaning and assessing the injuries. "We're going to need to get this head closed up. She's going to need surgery."

Another voice chimed in. "We need to get her into radiology first and see the extent of the brain injury from the head wounds and lack of oxygen before we go to the OR. I want an MRI, a CT scan and an EEG. We need to find out what's going on in her brain before we can attempt any surgery. For now, clean it up and do the best compression bandage you can on the head."

"Yes, Dr.… Um, I just pulled her hair back and her head is shaved around the wound. I think there was already an injury there and it was made worse."

Jeff raised his head and slowly stood up. The room had a few spinning stars, but he was able to stay on his feet as he walked closer to the staff and Cris' bed. The nurse turned and looked at him.

"I can answer that one, ma'am. She was shot at five days ago. The bullet grazed her skull. They had to shave and clean the area, then placed staples there to keep it closed. I just heard from the lead investigator on the way here. Apparently, she was hit in the head with a shovel several times throughout the night." Jeff stopped there, unable to say anymore without the quiver in his voice betraying him.

The nurse smiled back at him. "Thank you, sir. This information is certainly helpful. I can see marks where the staples were. Knowing what happened, we can be sure that's what the marks are, but I don't see any of the staples. I'm sure since it has only been five days they weren't already removed, correct?"

Jeff's stomach was churning again. "Yes, ma'am, that's correct. Perhaps they were dislodged when she was struck."

The nurse turned mumbling to herself, but Jeff heard her. "Let's hope it's the case and they're not pushed into her open skull."

Jeff had to sit back down and resume looking at the twelve-by-twelve white tiles on the floor while trying his damnedest to keep it together mentally and keep from throwing up physically. He had his elbows on his knees and his hands cradling his forehead as he traced the outline of grout on each tile with his eyes. Jeff was exploiting everything he had to stay together and focused.

He heard the male voice speak again. "We need to look at the area more closely. They should've fallen out with the impact. If any staples or bone fragments went into her head or brain, we might need to remove them before doing the scans. Providing they're not too deep and can be removed without having to go to the OR, which would change everything."

"I'm on it, Doctor."

Sitting up straight in the chair, Jeff took a deep breath. He watched as the team impeccably buzzed around Cris' bed. The nurse who had now been given the daunting task of figuring out where the staples had gone was further swabbing the side of her head. Once the cleaning was accomplished, she began shining a light around the shaved, swollen, and still oozing area. Jeff couldn't bear to watch, but at the same time, he couldn't look away.

He heard faded out pieces of their voices now like they were far away, instead of less than five feet. Jeff continued to trace outlines of the tiles on the floor in between glancing up.

The female voice, "No indication of the staples… Inward… Fell out as expected."

The male voice, "Good… Compression bandage… Stabilize for now… Radiology… Scheduled."

Jeff shook his head. He had to stop looking at the tiles and avoiding the situation, and instead get back into control. This was not him at all. He was always steady, cool and calm in a crisis. His mental behavior was beginning to rub him raw. Jeff sat upright in the chair and watched as they appeared to be finishing up with Cris. The staff was now putting her arms by her side and pulling the covers up over her as best they could with all the wires and tubes protruding from her body.

The male came over to him and held out his hand. Jeff stood, reached out and shook it as he spoke. "I'm Dr. Adkins. Sorry for the delayed introduction, but we needed to get Mrs.

Steele as under control as possible. I'm sure you understand."

"Chief Bolton. Yes, I do, thank you. She is my main priority and I'm more than happy to skip the formalities if it means getting her what she needs."

"Mr. Bolton, we were told you were the point of contact for her care. We have no next of kin on file. Since she's unresponsive, we have to confirm with you this is correct?"

"Yes, it's correct. She has no other next of kin. Her husband, who was her next of kin, was murdered last week. I'm the only other person to take on this responsibility," Jeff whispered, more to himself, "She's like a daughter to me."

"Well, let me officially update you with what's going on. You obviously know what happened since you were our main source of information. From our standpoint, we're listing her in critical condition. Until we have the results of the bloodwork and brain scans, we don't know the extent of the brain damage. We can't speculate if she'll come out of the coma, or even live. I'm sorry to be so blunt with you, but that is just the God's honest truth of where we are right now. Everything we have at this moment doesn't look good. She is on a ventilator for oxygen, she should be dead with her blood pressure and pulse alone, much less factoring in the infection throughout her body. Her pupils are still unreactive, and she shows no indication of coming out of the coma at this time. I will say if she somehow manages to pull through this, be prepared for extensive repercussions of brain damage from both the hypoxia, which is the deprivation of oxygen to the brain and the physical damage sustained from the blows of the shovel."

Jeff swallowed the bile that crept up, for what felt like the billionth time in the past few hours.

"Thank you. I understand and appreciate your honesty. Please keep me informed of anything you find. I'll be here. I'm not leaving her side."

"You got it. I'm assuming since you were in the chopper you don't have a change of clothes?"

Jeff looked down at himself for the first time. His clothes were a combination of dirt and blood.

"No, I don't."

"There are no bathroom's in the rooms on this unit, just a sink and toilet with a curtain because patients here typically aren't able to use one. There's a bathroom down the hall where you can at least clean up in the sink and change in a stall. I'll have a nurse bring you a pair of scrubs. We need to keep these rooms as sterile as possible."

"Thank you, I appreciate it."

Dr. Adkins gently placed his hand on Jeff's shoulder and spoke softly. "I'll also have my staff bring you a pillow and blanket to try to keep you as comfortable as possible. Please tell them of any other needs you may have, we're happy to oblige however we can."

The Dr. put his head down as he walked away. Jeff walked over to Cris' bedside. Her chest was rising and falling in rhythm with the ventilator. He lowered the bedrail, pulled a chair alongside her bed, set his glasses on the nearby stand and sat down. Jeff placed her bandaged hands together over her abdomen, then sandwiched his on top and bottom, squeezing as tight as he dared. Jeff put his forehead down on the bed by her side, the top of his head touching her waist. Just like he had last done eighteen years ago, Jeff finally gave in and bawled like a little bitch.

CHAPTER 29

Cris opened her eyes and instinctively squinted as the brightness seared through them. It physically hurt her head. Even the squinting wasn't working. She had to succumb and tightly closed her eyes. Her mouth was grimaced, cheeks were raised, and brow was furrowed intensely. Yet, Cris could still sense the brightness piercing through her clamped eyelids. She had never experienced anything so powerful before.

Instantaneously, she could sense and tell the brightness had shattered at the same moment a hand gently touched the side of her head. She heard a voice which penetrated as it whispered and glided through her brain, *"Be at peace, my child."*

Without understanding why, or being able to control it, tears fell at hearing the words intimately linger through her mind, coupled with the tender hand still lovingly touching the side of her head. Cris wept as she put her left hand over the existing one and leaned deeper into the strong, steadfast hand as she slowly unwrinkled her face and opened her eyes.

"Don't cry, baby. It's not befitting of you."

Cris opened her eyes wide now with the realization and inexplicably dropped to her knees while wrapping her arms around the torso, then waist on the descent. Tears were full force now. All the pent-up emotion and sorrow Cris had been carrying were finally released in the sobbing. She couldn't talk, only squeeze him with every muscle her upper body had.

Wordlessly, he reached his hands down and pulled Cris back up, then wrapped his arms around her neck. She pressed her head tightly against his and returned the embrace tenfold.

"Please don't walk away from me this time. I don't think I can take it again."

He tried to pull back from her to respond but Cris refused to loosen her death grip. He must have known better than to fight her. He stopped trying to pull away and instead came back in and intensified his hold as he spoke.

"Aw, baby, I'm sorry! It wasn't my choice. I was thankful to be able to see and hold you again, if only for a short time. I'm sorry it hurt you!"

Tears silently falling, Cris moved her locked arms from his neck and placed her hands firmly on his cheeks. "Steele Appeal, I wouldn't give that few minutes up for anything. Well, I would give them up for the chance to have never lost you to begin with. Since I can't change that, I'm begging you to please not leave me again. I've got nothing left; I'm done now. I'm weak."

Luke chuckled, and the crooked smile brought the butterflies back in Cris' stomach. "Cris, you never were, and never will be weak. Just the strength it takes for you to say those words shows how strong you still are. Believe in yourself like I believe in you."

She had to bow her head as the tears fell harder again. "I can't... I just can't. Especially without you. Please don't make me suffer anymore."

He slowly lifted her head up, tenderly kissed her forehead, then rested her head on his shoulder. "Let it out, baby. Please. You have kept too much buried inside for too long."

Cris couldn't have held back if she tried. For once she did what she was told, without back talk, sarcasm or an argument. Cris wrapped her arms around his ribs and squeezed tightly as the flood gates opened. With Luke's head resting on top of hers, one hand around the side of her head and the other around her waist, Luke caressed her as he slowly rocked from side to side. She hadn't cried like this in eighteen years, and never in front of anyone, not even Luke. Breaking down was something she did in silence, when she was alone, and it was always brief. She wouldn't allow herself to fully release the emotions. Cris also had to keep up her façade when she was around other people. She wouldn't show her struggles in front of anyone else.

His gentle rocking and caressing had a calming effect. To be inhaling the scent of him and hold his body against hers was a feeling Cris never wanted to let go of but felt her grip begin to loosen just by being in his presence. While she knew she hadn't released her lifetime of pent-up shit, she still felt more at peace than ever before. Cris began to calm down, but she still couldn't fully pull away and left her head on Luke's shoulder as she loudly tried to sniff up the dripping mucous from her nose before speaking.

"I have to tell you, those words you whispered when I couldn't see through the brightness *Be at peace, my child.* They were unworldly and brought me instant peace."

"Uh, Cris… There was no brightness, I never said that and there was nobody else here... It must have been Him."

Cris instinctively knew and finally pulled her head back and looked at Luke amazed. "You're right. There's no other explanation for the response and feeling it instantly evoked. Peace. It was like it wasn't really whispered but more like it just flowed into my brain. I can't explain it. It was timed perfectly too. I heard it, immediately before you touched my head, almost at the same time. Then all the painful brightness shattered, and I could see again."

"Painful brightness? It was definitely Him. Allowing you to enter would be my guess."

"Allowing me to enter? That means I'm staying then?" Cris was surprised to realize she felt relieved at the thought and meaning.

Luke shrugged his shoulders. "Honestly, I don't know what it means. You were only allowed to this point. I have no idea what's going on. I was told I could come see you. They aren't letting you in, but they aren't sending you back."

Just as confused as Luke, and more than slightly disappointed, Cris started to respond with more questions when she suddenly had a vision and involuntarily shivered. It must've been as obvious as it felt because Luke picked up on it.

"What's wrong?"

Cris shook her head, not knowing how to explain it. "I don't know. It's really weird. I just saw Chief Bolton put his hands over mine and put his head down, which touched my ribs, and cried. I didn't just see it; I could feel it. His hands clasping mine and the weight of his head pressing against my side, I can still feel the pressure of both right now. How is this possible? What's going on?"

Luke grabbed her hand and pulled her down, so they were both sitting now. He pulled Cris into him as he put his arm around her torso and held her tight. Cris instinctively rested her head on his shoulder.

"I don't know what's going on, I wish I had answers for you. Now that I think about it, that was the story of my life really. Always wishing I had answers for you or knew how to make it better. I tried my best. Maybe Chief can't tell you goodbye. I completely understand."

Cris laced both of her hands around Luke's, which were trying to rest on her abdomen, and squeezed.

"I'm sorry I always seemed so distant. It was my own shitty way of getting through. I'm sorry you didn't know the impact you had on me. I don't think I could've made it through without you. You made life not only bearable but so much better. I cannot tell you how much I have regretted not telling you that over the past 18 years."

"You didn't have to tell me. You showed me in your own sarcastic and loving way. I knew you loved me, and I've known since the first minute I spoke to you that you were true, caring and had a warm heart. While blunt and awkward, you were brutally honest with me and trying to protect me, when you still didn't even know me yet. Even at your own expense of losing a potential friend, you warned me not to be friends with you if I wanted a chance at having other friends. That was the moment you sealed the deal with my heart."

Cris remembered that day in the field like it was yesterday. She smiled and chuckled as a few silent tears escaped.

"Yea. I wanted you to have a fighting chance of making friends in a new school. You poor bastard, instead you got stuck with "Crazy Cris." You're right, I did warn you though."

"You know just as well as I do you weren't the crazy one. You were the strongest and sanest person I've ever known. You still are."

Cris snorted. "I'm glad you think so. I feel like I've gone fully off my rocker this past week and a half. Especially now that I know the truth about what happened to you. I've flat out accused Pete of murdering you several times and even hit him, despite his constant attempts of help and consolation. The same with Chief. He knows something about my past, I don't know just how much or how he knows, but I questioned why he was so nice to me and cared so much. I have these people trying to help me and I just want to push them further away and isolate myself. I don't think I could look Pete in the eyes again, better off for everyone I stay here."

"They both love and care for you, for their own individual reasons. Work on letting them in. Remember, I never said you were staying. I said I didn't know what was going on. You weren't allowed in or to be sent back."

"Please don't disillusion my happiness right now. I am assuming this is why Chief is crying at my side. Let me keep telling myself this and enjoy every second with you. Inside I'm quivering with fear you're going to walk away from me again."

"Come on." Luke moved to lie down on the ground with her, holding her tight. "No matter what happens here, I'll always be with you, watching and protecting you."

"I know, Steele Appeal, but I'm being selfish for once. I want to be wherever you are, forever."

Luke kissed her forehead and began to run his fingers through her hair. Cris was so tired and his actions and presence were intensifying it. They were looking into each other's eyes as she felt his calm, caressing hands. She looked at his brown tousled hair, realizing just how much she had missed it. Cris didn't want to close her eyes. She didn't want to ever stop looking into those soft, loving, green eyes again. Fear that they wouldn't be there when she opened hers again flooded her. As her eyes began burning, she started to blink incessantly as she fought to keep them open. Luke pulled her head forward into his chest and cradled her. She basked in his scent and buried her face as deep in his chest as she could. Letting him hold her in a protective swaddle and getting a euphoric high off his body, Cris remembered taking one last deep inhale before everything in her mind became a vastness of nothing.

CHAPTER 30

Pete walked out of the preserve in a daze. He was still cognizant enough to acknowledge the irony and feeling of déjà vu. It was just over a week ago he was walking out of these same woods in a similar trance like state. He had been thinking of nothing but Cris, even though it was Luke who was just murdered and whose scene he was leaving. Maybe he was consumed with her that day because he was trying to avoid thinking about Luke's case, which he had wanted nothing to do with. Pete grunted to himself. *Who the hell am I kidding? I was consumed with her because she was all I wanted to think about. I was hurting for her and wanted to be there and make her feel better. Okay, maybe deep down I was avoiding thinking about the case a little bit, but it was certainly not the main reason for my obsessed thoughts of the salty, fiery little redhead.*

Reaching the edge of the preserve, Pete made the mistake of looking up. The Steele house loomed in his vision. He stood frozen for a moment; his brain ostensibly unable to send the signals to his feet to move. Pete couldn't bear the thought of going into their house now. Then, he thought of Stormy inside. The poor girl was going to be even more confused. She wouldn't understand why neither one of them were coming home. Pete sighed and tried to hold his composure as he willed his legs and feet to carry on.

Reaching the stairs, Pete's eyes were inevitably drawn to the porch swing like a stripper fixated on the next dollar being slipped in her G string. Like he had a few days ago, Pete could fully envision Cris sitting there, both legs along the bench and head tipped back laughing at something Luke had just said from the rocking chair. Her throat fully exposed.

Pete swallowed hard as he turned his head and focused on the front door instead. Pulling the keys from his pocket, he already heard Stormy on the other side of the door. Pete could hear her tail smacking against either the wall, door or floor. The sound of her warmed and broke his heart. Putting his key in the lock, Pete tried to remember if he set the alarm or not upon leaving. Try as he might, there was nothing there to recollect. Since the slate in his brain seemed to be blank, he figured he would listen for the beeps and check the keypad upon entering.

Turning the knob, Stormy pawed at the door and then him, as he entered. Pete realized the alarm was set by the rhythmic chirps it was emitting and struggled to make the enthusiastic canine sit as he disabled it. Once the alarm stopped needing his attention, Pete knelt and gave it all to Stormy instead.

Without hesitation, Stormy put her paws on his shoulders and pushed him down, assaulting him with kisses. Pete laughed as he turned his head from side to side trying to break free from the love attack.

"Alright girl, alright. You got me! Let me come up for air!"

Pete grabbed her and sat up. He had his left arm around her neck, rubbing her right shoulder and his right arm over her back, holding under her belly. As he sat there petting and calming her down, he had nothing else to do besides look around the living room.

He was struck with visions from the past few days. Cris walking to the kitchen calling him Luke as she passed… Sitting out on the deck, albeit to get away from him most likely… Debating and arguing over every little thing… The extremely organized office area she had set up for him… Their car ride where she inadvertently showed her warm underbelly which Pete had known was really there anyway… Holding her while she accused and tried to hit him… The almost shoot out match as she came sneaking back from her run and they both had their hands on their guns… And of course, the first dinner where they ended up ordering the same thing. What he wouldn't give to be standing here arguing with her hardheaded stubborn ass right now.

Resting his head on top of Stormy, Pete closed his burning eyes, trying to stop the images and memories. He already felt his nose beginning to get blocked from the emotion and threatening tears. Pete released Stormy and stood up.

"Ah, shit. I guess it is time to get into some clean clothes and figure out what the hell we're going to do. I'll be right back, girl."

Pete eagerly changed out of his blood, dirt and puke ridden clothes. Next, he needed to call Chief for an update. More than anything, he really needed to get out of that house. He closed the door and took the phone off his hip. Looking at the porch swing, he knew he damn well couldn't sit there. Pete remembered only a few days ago looking at the swing and being wishful that someday he would be able to sit out there with Cris. Now the opportunity was gone, ripped away senselessly. Anger began to well up over the sadness. He realized it and shut it down. This was not his nature and he wasn't going to let this event destroy who he was. Pete knew it was going to be easier said than done. He would have to keep pulling himself back and remind himself many times and for as long as it took.

Knowing he needed to avoid looking at the porch area, Pete headed down the steps. He sat on the bottom one and pulled up his phone hitting the icon for Chief. He habitually ran his hand over his stubbled head while he waited for Bolton to answer. On the third ring he heard the familiar, yet weary, voice quietly answer.

"Hey, Bryan."

"Hi, Chief. I'm all done here and wanted to check in to see how things are going there."

"Hang on a minute. I'm going to walk out in the hall."

Pete realized he was twitching his foot. Knowing it indicated worry and anxiety, he made himself stop just before Chief's voice returned.

"There isn't much new here, but Bryan, Steele's a mess. She had a seizure on the way here. She's still in a coma and on a ventilator. Her vitals are still in the shitter and her eyes still aren't reactive. They're going to be taking her for scans anytime now to see the extent of the brain damage and will also be doing surgery to repair the lacerations to her head and face. They have her listed in critical condition and don't know yet if she'll come out of this or not, but the doctor was not giving me any false hope. He also said if she does end up coming out of it, to be prepared for extensive repercussions of brain damage from both the deprivation of oxygen to the brain and the physical damage sustained from the blows to her head. So, that's how it is here. Aren't you glad you asked? How is it there?"

He could hear the raw emotions in Chief's voice, a combination of sorrow and fear. Pete understood and wondered if Bolton heard the same thing from him echoing back as they spoke. He tried to think and respond but his head was buzzing, and his mouth felt drier than a freshly detoxed alcoholic.

"Thanks for being honest with me. I don't know how to answer how it is here. It's wrong. Being here without her is just wrong. That's all I can say. The teams are done with the sites. Just like after Luke's murder, it's like nothing ever happened. I came out of the woods into their yard and I swear it looks so lonely now. I went in to see Stormy and I could see Steele everywhere. It was unbearable. I had to come outside to call you."

"Well, I can assure you, it isn't any more bearable here. So, Tobi actually said we were welcome for her murder? How did the arrest go?"

Pete didn't know how to answer the question, but he knew it had to be with honesty. It was one of his quirks he would not compromise on.

"Well, to tell you the truth, I don't know. But I didn't notice any ruckus, so I assume it went as well as it could. Honestly, I started to go a little crazy after Tobi told me we were welcome. I charged him and had my arm back ready to land the first of many punches. Thankfully Reed pulled me off in time reminding me what was at stake and how we couldn't have any technicalities to get him off in court. I sat down and kind of checked out while Reed, then the patrol officers, took over."

"I can't believe you lost your cool. You are the most levelheaded and calmest person I know. I understand though,

I've had a few atypical moments myself. Was Tobi's family notified that he'd been found and consequently arrested for murder?"

"Yes. The missing persons team and Campbell were delivering the news, I didn't hear how it went. I would imagine not well. Me losing my cool, I know, it's not like me at all. I guess I found my breaking point. Anyway, if you could text me the room number, I'm going to head over there too."

"Don't worry about coming here. You need to be there to take care of Stormy. I'm fine and I'm not leaving her."

"It's not up for debate, sir. I'm coming. I'll bring Stormy with me and find a nearby hotel that allows dogs. I can't stay here with my thumb up my ass. I need to be there. For myself and for Steele. I promised her I'd be there for her no matter what. Look what happened while I was sleeping in the same house. I cannot forgive myself and I won't let her go without being by her side, like I promised I would be. Besides, we can take turns so we get the mental breaks we need, even though we may not want to admit we need them."

He heard Chief sigh, his lassitude even more evident. "I understand why you feel the need, but don't feel responsible for what happened. While we still don't know the details, we do know she disabled the alarm herself, and judging by the belongings around Luke's tree, I would say she willingly snuck out on her own accord to go there. You can't protect someone who is sneaking off on you."

"Thanks, Chief. I hear what you're saying, but logical or not, I can't just snap my fingers and have the guilt go away. I'm sure you'd be no different if the roles were reversed."

Bolton snorted. "You're right about that, and about the fact I won't admit a mental break is needed. You can come, I'll make the staff aware you are like family and to please let you in. Just remember you don't need to come for my sake. I'm not leaving her side and they already got a temporary replacement to cover the department. This is my only job until a final resolution and release occurs. Whatever form it may be. So, you can still come and sit with her too, but I'm not leaving the hospital grounds no matter what."

Pete wondered if Chief really had slightly suspected him before learning about Tobi and was carrying around his own set of guilt. He couldn't think about it now. In the end, it wasn't important anyway; it wouldn't change anything.

He stood up, ready to get moving. "Understood. I'm going to grab my bag and Stormy and get ready to hit the road. I'll see you in a few hours."

"Bryan, try to prepare yourself on the drive. Steele doesn't look like herself. The whole right side of her head and face are beaten in, with open wounds, swelling and bruising. She's not recognizable."

Feeling the nausea return, Pete sat back down. He would never have imagined how one woman and event could completely unravel his whole demeanor.

"Thanks for the heads up. I'll see you soon."

He hung up the phone without waiting for a response, even if there was one. Pete roughly threw it on the step and put his elbows on his knees and head into his hands as he silently cried and prayed.

CHAPTER 31

Jeff heard the disconnect from Bryan in his ear and put his phone back in his pocket. He knew Bryan had probably hung up so abruptly because he was close to breaking down. Jeff had nothing else to say anyway and was ready for the conversation to be over. He wasn't in the mood to talk. So much so, he wasn't taking calls from anyone except his wife, and Bryan. Not only because Bryan was the lead on the case, but also because he was so emotionally involved, and Jeff understood the feeling. He didn't want to admit it, but Jeff also knew a part of it was because he felt guilty for holding suspicions of him when he shouldn't have. He had defended him to Cris, but he still allowed the doubts and suspicions to creep in and he was sorry for that. Bryan was a great detective and an equally great, if not better, person. He felt horrible that he had lost sight of this for a little while.

All the rooms on the Critical Care Unit had the normal three inner walls, but the wall facing the hallway was glass, with a glass door in the center. The nurses assigned to each patient sat outside of the glass wall. Their computers were wirelessly connected to the equipment and alarms in the room. There were curtains which could be pulled for privacy if needed. While Jeff was talking on the phone, he was standing just outside of the glass wall on the opposite side of the nurses' station for Cris' room. Jeff had remained looking in through the door, which was the only part not blocked by the curtain at the moment. Cris had not moved a muscle the entire time.

Walking back in, Jeff left the curtain at the door area open so he could see anyone entering. He resumed his position at the side of Cris' bed by the outer wall, where he could continue to monitor the door. Jeff sandwiched his hands over hers again.

"I'm back Cris. Sorry about the interruption. It was Bryan calling. He is on his way here to see you too. Of course, he is also taking care of Stormy until you come home to take back over. Bryan really cares about you and feels horrible about what happened, so you had better play nice with him when you get out of here."

Jeff didn't know if Cris could hear him or not, but he wasn't willing to take any chances. He was only going to talk about positive things and assume she could hear him. He also wanted to let Cris know how important she was to him in case she could hear but didn't end up making it and hoped the positivity might help her come out of it. Jeff was scared, confused and in a dark place. It kept bringing him back to his daily life almost two decades ago. He made himself keep refocusing his thoughts, which wasn't easy. How he was going to achieve keeping the darkness at bay and remain positive was a conundrum.

He inhaled deeply then instinctively looked at the ventilator Cris was hooked up to and felt guilty for his innate ability to take his deep breath unassisted. "You know Cris, we still have a conversation to finish. If you would hurry your ass up and wake up Sleeping Beauty, we could finally have it. You have been nagging me about it in the middle of shit storms and now the timing is finally right. Both of our schedules are clear, and the major storms are over. Could you hold up your end of it now and join the discussion?"

Trying to speak in her language, Jeff was hoping to coax her out; if it was even an option in how all this worked. He realized he was looking at the dog tags resting on her chest. Dried blood was spattered across them and he wondered if it was her blood, or much older than that.

Tears threatened as his emotions went into overdrive again, as did the corresponding indigestion. Burning acid crept its way upward and Jeff remembered he never did eat today. He also realized he didn't have any antacids on him. Trying to look away from the dog tags, he made things worse by looking up at her battered face instead. As sweat beaded upon his brow, then moved down his face and neck, and he began feeling cold, he was thankful he hadn't eaten anything yet. He knew what those signs meant. While stretching to continue sandwiching her hands, Jeff instinctively pushed his chair back a little and dropped his head alongside her bed and let it hang in between his outstretched arms to keep from throwing up. His glasses began to fog as tears silently and irrepressibly fell.

Jeff prayed Cris didn't realize his lapse in strength as he squeezed her hands and silently fell apart. *I'm so sorry I wasn't there to prevent this or save you. I made a promise that day, damn it, and I failed. Please, Cris, come back to me and by some miracle be okay. I have been able to withstand everything all these years. Hell, since I was a teenager. The past few decades, in all honesty, were probably, without a doubt, because I had you to protect. While I love my amazing wife, I think you would be my breaking point. Damn it, Cris! Please!*

Jeff began to sniff as his stuffy nose threatened to drip. He picked his head up and scooched his chair forward again. Keeping his left hand on Cris', he took his right hand and reached to grab a tissue off her bedside table. He wiped his nose as best he could with one hand, then removed his glasses and tried, with even more difficulty, to clear the fogginess from them.

"Whatever. Good enough. Sorry, Cris. Something is setting off my allergies. Maybe it's all the sterility in this room."

Jeff chuckled trying to sound sincere and joking about his sincerity at the same time. Of course, if her eyes were open to see his face or body language he would be had. Cris had a special talent for seeing through a person's bullshit, which on the flip side included pretending to be nasty when they were actually a goodhearted person.

The irony of this thought came to mind. Cris could be the poster child for it. Her protective shield made her outward appearance as cold and uncaring. If she let you in and you really got to know her or were insightful like she was, you knew right away it was a fake wall. With enough patience, genuine love and persistence, it could be somewhat breached. Cris was covertly the most caring, loving and compassionate person there was. If you were a close friend, family, or someone she cared about, you better pray nobody messed with you because she would unleash like nothing you had ever seen.

He had just put his glasses back on, thrown his tissue away and was getting ready to replace his sandwiched hands as a nurse came bounding through the door. She had fresh linens on top of another type of stretcher she was wheeling in.

"Please excuse me. I have to get Mrs. Steele ready for her scans now."

Slightly surprised at her abrupt arrival, Jeff annoyingly heard a stammer in his response. "Oh, it's okay. I knew it was coming at some point, I just didn't know when."

Jeff sat back to allow her the room she needed to do her work. She began systematically, but expediently, moving tubes and wires, unhooking and re-hooking things while still talking nonstop to him. It was as though she required no train of thought to do everything she was doing. The nurse was down to the dog tags and in the process of removing them.

"She can't wear these into the scans. I'll give them to you for safekeeping."

Finishing unlinking them, she removed them from Cris' neck and handed them to Jeff in a neatly wadded up ball. He couldn't bear to look at them but quickly squeezed them in his hands as the chain slid through his fingers. Jeff felt nauseous but knew he had to stay strong while still in the company and vicinity of Cris. He stared at her swollen closed eyes.

"I'll take good care of these while you're away, and I'll be sure to put them back on you when you get back."

The nurse quietly tried to object. "The doctor has allowed them up until now, I'm not so sure he'll permit them being put back on after the scans. We still have a prognosis, plan of action, and surgery to schedule."

Chief shot her a look of condemnation then looked back at Cris. "Don't worry Cris. I'll make sure you have them on at all times, except when it's absolutely necessary to have them off for a short period."

Even though Jeff knew the nurse understood what he was trying to do, she still pursed her lips whether she realized it or not.

"They'll change the bedding while she's out. This particular stretcher is relatively new and geared for radiology testing, making it easier to move the patient or to keep them on it through some of the tests. It will probably take a few hours to complete all the tests they need to do. They want to get them all done at once while she is not moving to create an artifact. Then, they'll have the most accurate information to come up with the most educated outcome and prognosis. Feel free to go get some food from the cafeteria, go outside for a walk, to a restaurant, stay in the room, outside of the radiology area or whatever you need in the meantime. We'll let you know when it's done."

She hit a button on the wall and another nurse came hustling in. Each taking a side, the two of them lifted the sheet that was already under Cris and fluidly transferred her onto the new, temporary, bed. They nodded to Jeff as they departed the room with her.

Jeff sat in the empty and deathly quiet room. It lasted a fraction of a second before deciding he needed to get out of there for a few minutes. He stood up and placed the dog tags gently in his pocket. Jeff chose to take the time to use the bathroom, then went to get antacids from the store in the basement of the hospital while she was away. Knowing he needed nourishment, Jeff picked up a bag of nuts and some crackers in case his stomach settled enough to try to eat them. Feeling physically and mentally drained from the day, Jeff felt he needed a caffeine kick, or more appropriately, an IV drip of espresso. Knowing in reality he needed hydration, Jeff opted for a bottle of water to complete his purchase.

He went back to the room and sat in the chair, staring at the empty bed. The memories of Cris haunting him. Memories which may have been happy or at least pleasant for her. Now, they were slowly being consumed in black, like a thin line of fire licking then devouring a piece of paper. Despite his best efforts, darkness was trying to overtake him again.

CHAPTER 32

She opened her eyes and realized Luke wasn't there. Her heart sank and she wondered if it had all been just a dream, which seemed to be the running theme in her life. It felt real though. Cris could still smell him and feel his hands running through her hair. She felt her face buried in his chest.

Disoriented, heart struck and discouraged, she began to stand up as the panic and anxiety burned through her veins like heroin. Cris looked around and realized she had no sense of where to go or what to do. Her stupefied and confused thinking was quickly interrupted with Chief's voice in her head, as clear as fly strips in a whorehouse. To make it even more unnerving, she could even envision him sitting by her side next to her bed. Just like before, she could feel the weight of his hands enveloping over the top and bottom of hers.

Between her current reality along with the uncanny visions, Cris' head began to swim and feel lost. She mechanically sat back down in confusion. It was like she had watched a movie and was remembering clips from it.

"You know Cris, we still have a conversation to finish up. If you would hurry your ass up and wake up Sleeping Beauty, we could finally have it. You have been nagging me about it in the middle of shit storms and now the timing is finally right. Both of our schedules are clear, and the major storms

are over. Could you hold up your end of it now and join the discussion?"

It felt so real, and at the same time, Cris could sense his emotions. His joking was trying to cover his fear, worry, and sadness.

Cris remembered their ride back from the Jasper Hospital after she had woken up from a nap. Chief cryptically brought up the fact he knew about her past, but not specifically what. Besides worrying she might have a death wish, and how he had "pulled strings" to get her the job, then her resulting confusion. They had run out of time to finish it and for Cris to get the answers she so desperately sought. She had reminded him about it every chance she got, which was several times over a 24-hour period. Now, here he was reminding her. It all seemed dreamlike.

Only a short time later, Cris felt her dog tags come off and could see them in Chief's hand. She felt her heart rate increase to match her anger. Bringing her right hand to her chest, she felt the tags still there. She exasperated a relieved sigh as Chief's face and voice cut in.

"I'll take good care of these while you're away and I'll be sure to put them back on you when you get back."

Chief shot a look of condemnation at someone over Cris' shoulder, then looked back at her. *"Don't worry Cris. I will make sure you have them on at all times, except when it's absolutely necessary to have them off for a short period."*

The images and sensations were cut off and Cris felt like a lead weight dropped into her stomach. While she hadn't actually accused him of Luke's murder, she had questioned him on why he cared so much. Here he was again, by her side, sacrificing his own family time to sit by her bedside and protect her. Cris felt complete and utter remorse for her previous words and actions.

What the hell is wrong with me? I can't show real emotion, I have to hide behind my sarcastic mouth and sharp tongue. Then when strangers, who eventually become as close of friends as I'll allow, genuinely care about me, I have to question why and what their motives are. Poor Luke probably won't come back this time even though he says he knows how much I loved him, how I showed it in my own special way. How can I really know it's true? I certainly never said the right words to him. Eighteen fucking years! I think the old adage of actions speak louder than words is probably bullshit in this extreme.

Cris suddenly had a sense of Pete entering a room and briefly talking to Chief. As per her usual, she cut her eyes.

Really? I'm already feeling lower than a damn snake in the grass and now you have Pete appear? This is just like my regular life where you want me to keep taking the pounding with no lubrication. I'm sorry, but you already know my thoughts, and this is how it feels to me. Pete has been nothing but helpful, kind and supportive. In return, I've been nothing but accusatory, suspicious, and sometimes even abusive! Am I actually in the Garden of Eden to serve eternity as the snake? Is this what's really going on here? Is this why Luke said I'm not allowed in but I'm not being sent back? I have to say, that's how this is beginning to feel! No wonder Luke isn't allowed or coming back. That poor, beautiful soul doesn't belong anywhere near this serpent.

She had no idea what to think of all of these visions, or whatever they should be called, that seemed so real. Worse than those, Cris was more confused and concerned about her present reality. She was accustomed to bad dreams; this was a whole new level of anxiety and confusion. Digging down and pulling up the strength she had used as a shield for the better part of 28 years, Cris convinced herself if she was damned to be the serpent for eternity, she was sure as hell going to use all the strength she had to fight it and instead do good by it. Pissed off and focused, she had her head bowed as she squeezed her hands into balls and stood up. There was no reason for things to be any different now than they had been her whole life, she was not going to be condemned to her own personal hell without a fight.

Cris raised her head and opened her eyes and saw a familiar walk and signature crooked smile coming towards her. Those damn butterflies in her stomach took flight again, which she found both ridiculous and amazing after all these years. All of her strength and fight left her as she loosened up and walked towards him feeling the relief fill her body, overpowering the anxiety.

They clashed into a hug. Luke whispered, "I'm here, baby," as he grabbed her biceps, pulled her back, and forcefully kissed her forehead.

At the same instant, she was struck with another vision. This time it was Pete.

She heard his voice whisper, "I'm here, Cris," as he kissed her forehead in the same spot and with the same force.

Cris pulled back, shook up like she had been struck by lightning. She had seen and felt them both at the same exact time. Luke raised an eyebrow at her.

She tried to put her armor back on and pull herself together, but Luke knew her too well and would see through anything. "I'm sorry, Steele Appeal. That was bizarre to the extreme."

He kept his eyebrow cocked. "What was? My kiss was really that powerful?" Luke chuckled.

"You're funny. I don't know how to explain it, but I've been having these "visions" for lack of a better word. You of all people know better than to call me crazy, but I'm starting to lean towards that diagnosis myself. The same time you spoke and kissed me on the forehead, I "saw" and "felt" Pete doing the same thing. It was simultaneous, uncanny and downright freaky."

Luke brought back his crooked smile. "Ah, I see. No worries, I won't call you crazy. I actually think I get it. You're just as normal as you ever were. Take that how you want."

Cris had to smile even though she was even more confused now. "How can you get it? I've been out of my mind trying to understand what's going on. How do you think you know what's going on and how can this make any sense to you?"

Luke pulled her in and held her in a hug, resting his head on top of hers. "I don't think it's necessarily meant for you to understand. It's the whole limbo thing. But listen to me. Pete is a good guy with a pure heart. We have tried to show you this before, but your hardhead doesn't want to see things."

"We? Do you mean you and my dad the other day with the cardinals outside the French doors? I was upset, screaming in my head to both of you how alone I was now with no one to talk to. The cardinals appeared at the window as if in response, followed by Pete at my back. I got mad at you guys for your sick sense of humor."

She knew Luke must have smiled and gave a little laugh as she felt the blow of his breath through her hair. "So, your thick head did understand the message? Good. We were wondering with your sarcastic words if you really did pick up on it, or your normal walls were blocking the obvious."

"I'd have to say both. Internally I recognized it, but I wouldn't admit it to myself. Which is why I was yelling at you guys in my head how you had a sick sense of humor, and basically to screw off."

"Yep. Exactly as we expected. We know you way too well."

Cris cut him off. "I know."

"Which brings me to my next thing. The reason I was away while you were enjoying your beauty rest was because I was asking about your dad being able to come see you. Would you like to see him?"

Cris pulled back from him and her heart leapt. She was excited and felt strong, yet, her eyes betrayed her with silent tears. She was anxiously swaying her body and smiling. The most Cris could do at this point was nod her head up and down.

"I got permission for you to see him too. I'm still just as confused and don't know what it all means, but I'm happy to be allowed to give you this blessing."

For the first time in her life that she could remember, Cris was giddy and maybe even a little nervous, which she found ridiculous. She hadn't seen her superhero in 18 years!

"Yes! Please, yes!!"

Luke smiled. "I thought as much. Wait here. I promise I'll be right back with your dad by my side."

Luke kissed her on the lips quick and hard before he spun to walk away. Her hands fell from his head to her side as he turned his back to her. Cris stood there feeling lonely and desperate with anticipation. The realistic part of her feared she would not see either one of them reappear, the snake image ever-present and slithering through her mind. Cris feared that instead, she would wake up from the dream feeling empty, angry and hopelessly alone again, as was the usual.

Even so, Cris remained vigil, refusing to leave and hanging on to a doubtful strand of hope as she watched Luke disappear out of sight with no indication of looming figures in return.

CHAPTER 33

Pete fed Stormy and left her in the hotel room located right next to the hospital. Closing the door behind himself, he was surprised to see how dark the sky was already. He crossed the parking lot, walking as fast as was socially acceptable to get to her. Arriving at her wing, the staff was very helpful and understanding.

Approaching her room, Pete could see around the curtain covering the one side before the door. There sat Chief beside an empty bed, staring at it without blinking. Pete's stomach clenched again. *Where's Cris? Please don't tell me I'm too late?*

The glass door was open, and Pete quietly entered the room. Chief blinked his eyes and looked up as he entered. Pete walked towards him as Chief removed his glasses and rubbed his eyes before putting them back on.

"Hey, Bryan. It's good to see you."

Pete cut him off with a quiver he couldn't hide. "Where is she?"

"They took her to get the imaging done. I expect them back any time now."

Pete put his hands on his thighs and hunched over. "Oh, thank God!"

Chief came alongside him and smacked him on the shoulder blade a few times. "Yea, I'm with ya there man. Listen, before she comes back, I want to talk to you."

Pete involuntarily furrowed his brow. "Okay?"

"I'm not sure if she can hear us or not. I've heard stories about people in coma's being able to hear or feel the people in the room. I don't know. I do know, I'm not willing to play Russian Roulette though. I'm basing everything on the assumption she can hear me. I want to keep things positive and only talk about hopeful things she would like to hear or current stuff going on."

"Understood. I agree. We want her to fight to come out of this, not succumb due to a depressed bunch of people."

"Did you bring Stormy?"

"Of course. I checked into a hotel right next door. She's as content as she can be in there right now…."

They were interrupted by the sound of wheels coming and they looked towards the door. Sure enough, there was Cris, or at least a partial resemblance of her, being wheeled back in. Chief looked at the nurse.

"How did she do?"

The nurse pulled the stretcher next to Cris' bed and locked the wheels. "She didn't move a muscle."

"Well, that's good for the imaging part at least."

"Yes, it is."

Pete was having a hard time not dry heaving. He would throw up if he had anything left in his system to come out. Chief had tried to tell him, but there could be no preparing for this. Pete tried to watch the nurse instead of Cris as she had begun switching all the tubes, wires and IV stand back over to the normal hospital bed. The other nurse came around the side of the bed and they both lifted Cris' tiny, fragile body onto the bed. Pete noticed how her head just rolled to the side. The nurse positioned her head and tried to fluff and move the pillows around it.

Pete turned to Chief. "Did you need to go get some air or anything while I'm here?"

"Not really. I ran to the head and pantry when they first took her for the tests. I'll go call my wife in a few minutes though after the nurses leave."

"Okay. Do what you've gotta do, I'm here."

"Yea. Thanks."

Pete knew he wouldn't go very far and certainly wouldn't leave the property, but he wanted to put the offer out there. He selfishly wanted some time alone with Cris too. The nurse finished tucking the blankets around Cris and turned towards the door.

"Y'all holler if you need anything. We're all happy to help. I'll be leaving for the day now, but I will brief the incoming nurse on everything. Expect people to be coming in every few hours for blood work and other reflex and cognition checks. I'll see you in the morning, try to get some rest."

Chief thanked her and Pete nodded. The nurses walked out and slid the door closed behind them. Wasting no more time, Pete hustled over to Cris. He mustered up every ounce of strength he had so she wouldn't hear the tremble in his voice.

When he got close, Pete spoke softly, "I'm here, Cris."

Pete leaned down, placed his hands on her biceps and forcefully kissed her swollen forehead. He slowly stood up and looked down on her. Lost within himself, he almost jumped when Chief came over and set his hand on his shoulder.

"I'm going to go outside and make my phone call. Give you some time with Steele. I just need to do something first. I promised her." He sounded emotional.

Stepping back, Pete watched as Chief pulled something out of his pocket and leaned over Cris. Pete noticed he raised her head up a little bit, then repositioned it as he fidgeted with something. Chief was smoothing out the top of the gown as he began to stand up and step back.

"There. She's complete now. I'll be back in a few minutes." Chief squeezed her shoulder before turning his back towards her.

"All right. You know I'll be here."

Chief grabbed his phone off the stand and walked out. Pete looked down by the top of Cris' gown to try to see what he had promised to do for her. He noticed the familiar ball chain necklace right away. Pete desperately wanted to look at them to see the name inscribed, but he knew this was not the time, place or circumstance. More than this though, he would never break her privacy like that. He hoped he would get the chance to find out the proper way one of these days. The swing on her front porch flashed into his brain, and he quickly stood a little taller and tossed it from his mind.

The more Pete thought about it, the more it began to nag at him how Chief had it and promised to put it back on her. He knew he must've known about it and its importance. The same old confusion and questions of why and how swirled through his brain. He felt the anger trying to surface and refocused his thoughts. *This is not what you're here for. You are here for Cris. Now be here for her!*

He pulled the chair up next to her bed and placed his hand over her forearm. Pete began to dig deep for his strength again so he could attempt to sound normal. He tried to smile while he talked, hoping it would come through in his words and voice.

"Hey, Cris. Like a bad penny you just can't get rid of, I'm here. Guess who else is here? Stormy! Well, okay, she's not actually here in the room. But she is next door, and I'm hoping I can butter up the staff enough to let me bring her in to see you. I know it would make you feel better! She's a little preoccupied in the room right now sucking on her blankets."

He made the mistake of looking more intently at her face and wounds, then her chest rising and falling with the sound of the ventilator. He looked at her mouth, her lips dry and cracked already around the intrusive tube. Pete remembered having his lips over hers, trying to breathe life into her. He longed to put his lips back on hers again. His heart ached like nothing he had felt before. Pete hung his head down by his shoulders and put his hands over Cris'. He was filled with so many emotions. Anger. Sorrow. But most of all, guilt.

Pete was infuriated at the unfairness to her. First, she witnesses her husband murder. Next, she gets sent up to Jasper, where despite all of this, she still completes her job and finds the killer, only to get shot in the process. Then she has some sick, twisted, bastard beat her with a shovel and bury her alive.

He thought of her face and her vibrant and loving soul, despite her best attempts to keep it hidden. If Cris somehow managed to survive, all of it would be changed from this one act. Even with the best plastic surgeons, her face would never be exactly the same. Her psyche even more so. What would this do to her already armored identity? Pete had a pretty good idea and it made his eyes burn and water.

The guilt followed. How had he let this happen while he was right there? He could've prevented all this. How would she ever forgive him? Conversely, how would he ever forgive himself, no matter the outcome? Had he heard her leaving and stopped her, they could be at her house right now, arguing about some now mundane subject. Instead, here they were, where they should never be. Especially while he was on watch.

Tears escaped as he lifted his head and looked at her. "Aw, Cris. I'm so sorry I failed you and didn't protect you. I promised I'd keep you safe. I followed you everywhere, except the most important place. I can never forgive myself for not hearing you leave. I always hear everything. Why didn't I hear this? I'm so, so sorry!"

His voice started cracking as his cheeks got wetter. Pete knew Cris would hear the emotion if he didn't shut the hell up and pull himself together. The realization brought awareness to his words not staying positive. He criticized himself for failing her yet again. He looked up towards the ceiling for guidance, reminding himself he had to dig deep and watch his words.

Taking a deep breath, Pete hoped he had gained enough composure for a cover. "I think Stormy is really excited to see you. I asked her if she wanted to come see Mommy and she started prancing her paws and doing circles. You know, no matter what you guys need, I'll always be there for you two. I already told you, if you need a sitter for her, help around the house or yard, someone to vent to, scream at, or beat on, I'll be there, and I promise I'll keep coming back for more of whatever it is. You and Stormy both mean a lot to me, Cris, and I want to be there for you."

Pete heard shuffling of feet and snapped his head around. Chief had walked back in the door and was closing it behind himself.

"Any changes or updates?"

Pete shook his head. "No. But you do realize you weren't gone very long, right?"

"Yes, I know. It was long enough though."

Pete stayed at the bedside while Chief walked over and pulled out the padded chair from the corner. He reclined it back, set a pillow up towards the top and began unfolding the blankets that were sitting there.

Hearing the door opening and seeing a pair of doctors entering, Pete stood up. Chief was immediately by his side.

"Good evening, gentleman. I am Dr. Stevens, and this is Resident Miller. We have the results of Mrs. Steele's imaging and we're here to update you with our findings and course of action. Her imaging indicated minor brain damage and cell death from hypoxia. We believe you found her just in time. Had you been even a minute or two later, she might not be here at all. We already knew before the scans there was a depressed skull fracture, just not the full extent. This created a contusion and cerebral swelling. There also seems to be some minor bruising on the left side of the brain, which is suspected to have happened when the head was struck. The quick, hard impact probably moved the brain to the left side with its force, which made the brain hit the side of the skull causing some bruising. There's also indication of some minor atrophy as a result of the seizures from the lack of oxygen. We're going to be taking her to the OR to fix any brain bleeds and relieve any intracranial pressure. We'll take any of the pieces of bone that were pressed inwards and return them to their correct position using either metal wire or mesh to reconnect the pieces of the skull and fix the deformity as best we can. I know this is a lot of information to process all at once, but do you have any questions for us before we take her?"

Pete didn't know if he wanted to laugh or cry. Any questions? His head was spinning from the auctioneer sounding commentary the doctor had just spewed out.

Chief crossed his arms over his chest. "How long will this take and what is the prognosis for all of this once she comes out of it?"

Resident Miller broke in. "The surgery will depend on what we find once we get in there, but a good estimation should be around 3 to 5 hours. Then, of course, time in the recovery room before being brought back in here. One of the nurses will come in and keep you updated on the progress. We should be able to answer the prognosis more accurately after the surgery."

He was barely done speaking and the nurses were coming in to get Cris ready to go. Pete took his hands off of hers and stepped back to give them room, his head still spinning. Unexpectedly, Chief cut in front of Pete, almost knocking aside one of the nurses who was coming around the bed.

"Here, I'll take this and hold on to it."

Pete watched as Chief did movements similar to those just a few minutes ago. Pete was certain he knew what Chief was doing. Sure enough, right after he backed away, Pete noticed the ball chain necklace was gone.

The doctor had just walked out of the door and the resident looked over at them. "Which one of you is Mr. Bolton?"

Chief stepped towards the end of the bed, "I am."

"Would you mind stepping into the hallway with me, please? I have the authorization forms for you to sign since Mrs. Steele is not able."

"Of course."

Pete was annoyed Chief had that kind of power. Why was one coworker allowed over another coworker? Because he was her boss? Because he was here with her upon arrival? *Well, I was preoccupied with an equally important job, finding her damn killer!*

He knew he had to let the jealousy go. It was arbitrary and served no productive purpose. Noticing they were getting ready to wheel Cris out, Pete hopped over to the bed and grabbed her hand.

"Hang in there, Cris. I'll see you in a little bit when you come back!"

He leaned down and kissed her forehead as they unlocked the wheels. Pete knew his time was up. He stepped back and watched her go with a sinking stomach and lump in his throat.

Chief finished signing the computer screens and came back in. "Do you believe that crazy ass whirlwind?"

"No, sir. Not really. My head's still trying to process the doctor's loquacious tongue, much less how quickly she was swept out the door."

"No shit! Well listen, nothing else can be done right now. It's going to be many hours between surgery and recovery. I have all my supplies here and I'm as set as I can be for the night. Go comfort Stormy and try to get some sleep so you can be semi-refreshed and ready for the morning. I'll call you as soon as she is out of recovery and coming back in."

"Please let me know how everything goes."

"You got it, Bryan. Try to get some rest."

Pete meandered back to the hotel in a daze. He came out of it once he opened the door and Stormy greeted him with her excited love attack. Pete walked her outside, then crawled into bed, calling her up to the pillow next to him. He rolled on his side and put his arm over her, happy to have her as a distraction. It was almost like having a small part of Cris there with him.

Knowing sleep would most likely elude him, Pete still closed his eyes and tried to clear his mind. Images of Cris from the box in the ground to her current battered state haunted both his awake hours and his dreams. Everything was blood, hair, broken nails, matter, dirt, the shovel, the swollen, bruised and broken face, all swirling around his psyche, as he kept waking, drenched in sweat.

CHAPTER 34

Cris was standing watch, ever vigilant, looking for the figures to be coming her way. Thinking about it, Cris realized she had no recollection of how long she had been standing there, or even if she had been standing there the whole time. For all Cris knew she could have taken a nap at some point. It was weird, like time didn't exist, like it had no meaning or purpose here. It could have been minutes, hours, or even days since Luke had walked away to supposedly get her father. Cris had no sense either way.

Out of nowhere, Cris had a vision again. Luke seemed to understand them, but she sure as hell didn't. Cris heard Chief say, *"I promised her."* Then, she felt him put her dog tags back on, and even though Cris knew after the last time she was wearing them all along, she somehow felt more complete now.

It wasn't much later when Pete appeared again. He was trying to joke with her about not being able to get rid of him and then was talking about Stormy. *"Hey, Cris. Like a bad penny you just can't get rid of, I'm here. Guess who else is here? Stormy! Well, okay, she's not actually here in the room. But she is next door, and I'm hoping I can butter up the staff enough to let me bring her in to see you. I know it would make you feel better! She's a little preoccupied in the room right now sucking on her blankets."*

The thought of Stormy, especially sucking on her blankets, made Cris smile. She felt some of the weight beginning to lift. Stormy would be just fine with Pete. She was comfortable with him and had been with him more in the past two weeks than she had been with her. It sounded like Stormy was, and would be, adjusting just fine. Not that Cris was surprised.

She could now sense Pete's emotion, stronger than ever. He put his hands over hers then hung his head. It seemed like a short time after when Cris saw tears moving down his cheeks as Pete lifted his head and looked at her.

"Aw, Cris. I'm so sorry I failed you and didn't protect you. I promised I'd keep you safe. I followed you everywhere, except the most important place. I can never forgive myself for not hearing you leave. I always hear everything. Why didn't I hear this? I'm so, so sorry!"

Cris felt horrible. Pete was beating himself up and would carry this for the rest of his life. There's no way he could've prevented it. She snuck out and made damn sure he wouldn't hear her. This was one hundred percent on her.

She watched him raise his head, trying to look through the ceiling and up to the sky. Wrapping her arms around her torso and, while not allowing herself to cry, she looked down. "I'm so sorry Pete! I hope I can find a way to show you this is not your fault, to give yourself grace, and how eternally thankful I am for you taking care of my girl. Once I figure out how all this works, I promise you I'll find a way to show you."

Pete looked back down from the ceiling at her. He genuinely seemed to be more composed as he spoke to her again.

"I think Stormy is really excited to see you. I asked her if she wanted to come see Mommy and she started prancing her paws and doing circles. You know, no matter what you guys need, I'll always be there for you two. I already told you, if you need a sitter for her, help around the house or yard, someone to vent to, scream at, or beat on, I'll be there, and I promise I'll keep coming back for more of whatever it is. You and Stormy both mean a lot to me, Cris, and I want to be there for you."

Cris sat down and thought about all the accusations she threw at Pete the past two weeks. She fought with him when he was just trying to protect her. He wasn't getting paid to stay with her or take care of Stormy. Pete was giving of himself and his own free time because he authentically cared. What the hell was wrong with her to ever suspect him to begin with? Maybe Raquel and all the other kids were right. Maybe she really was crazy. Maybe Luke was sent to cover for her and make Cris stay deluded in thinking she was sane. Once he was taken away, the crazy train went off the rails and couldn't be stopped.

Adrift in her thoughts, Cris had lost all sense of time again. She heard Pete's voice cut in as he grabbed her hand and kissed her forehead again. *"Hang in there Cris. I'll see you in a little bit when you come back!"*

She saw, what appeared to be Chief in the background and doctors and nurses nearby. The images vanished, and Cris sat continuing to wallow in her guilt and question her sanity. She was sitting Indian style, looking towards her feet when she heard the most glorious sound behind her.

"Cris Murray! What the hell are you doing sitting there sulking?"

It had been eighteen years, but it could have been one hundred. Like Luke's crooked smile, Cris would *never* forget this blissful voice. She was already tearing up before she was able to get to her feet. Cris shrieked as she turned and jumped into his arms like a child, wrapping her legs around his torso.

"Daddy!!"

She squeezed him with every muscle in her body. He returned the hard embrace while twisting her back and forth. Tears of sorrow and joy trickled down her face. Not letting up on the grip, Cris opened her eyes, and through her blurry vision, she saw Luke standing just to the side, his smile more crooked than she had ever seen it. Her cheeks got wetter. Cris couldn't be happier than she was at this moment with her two most favorite people in the whole world.

When her dad finally set her down, wiping his eyes, Luke came over and stood next to them. His crooked smile gone, Cris cocked her eyebrow at him. Luke knew her well enough to realize his face was giving him away.

"I knew you guys looked alike, but seeing you side by side like this, as adults… this is… crazy. Sorry, Cris."

"No worries. I was just having an argument with myself in my head about me possibly being crazy all these years, and in true crazy fashion, not realizing it."

Her dad pushed her hair back behind her ear. "Is that what you were thinking about when you were sitting there in your own world?"

"Well, not at that moment. I had thought it a little bit before. I just had a vision with Pete and was feeling pretty shitty about the way things had gone down the past two weeks. But none of it matters anymore!"

"It does matter. You need to be nice and open up to him more."

Luke came alongside her and intertwined his fingers with hers. "Yes, Cris. You can trust him. Pete will be there for you. He has been showing you this, but you refused to see it. Listen to us."

"I'm not listening to this. It doesn't matter now. If it makes you feel any better though, I did just tell him I would figure out how all this works and find a way to show him this wasn't his fault, it was all mine. I would find a way to show him how appreciative I am for taking care of our girl. Although it's not like he heard me. You guys will have to show me how you did it. You know, how you made me aware of your message after the two cardinals flew in front of my face."

Her dad chuckled. "Perfectly timed with Pete arriving at your back. We knew you would get it. Your responding thoughts to us pretty much confirmed it. Ah, that was kind of fun in a sick way."

Luke smirked as he shook his head. "Yea, it was. Listen, Cris. I already told you, we don't know what's going on. You can't come in, but you're also not being sent back. We really don't understand."

"I understand. I'm home."

Luke squeezed her hand a little tighter. "I don't think your stubbornness will have any affect here. I'm sorry."

"I can't go back. I've made a mess of things. I can't face Pete after how I've treated him and the things I've said. He was nothing but nice, helpful and supportive and I was nothing but suspicious and torn in return. Don't even say it, I'm not ready to lower my shield for him or anybody else. How can I move on from this? Chief knows about my childhood somehow. I would rather do like I always do and ignore it and not have to face him either."

Her dad looked her hard in the eyes. "Speaking of which, you need to be nicer to Bolton too. You have no idea how much he cares for you. He is waiting for you to come back to him so you can have the conversation you kept badgering him about."

Cris felt tears welling up. "I don't care what he knows or how anymore. I want to sail away into the darkness with you, Daddy."

He sighed. "No, Pumpkin. There is no more darkness for me. It's all beauty and light now. The most wonderful thing is watching you in the midst of all the beauty. I see how you take in everything around you and appreciate the magnificence in everything your eyes see. You take nothing for granted. This was my prayer for you when I left. There is no greater joy for me than getting to witness it every day. I don't think it would've been the case if I had stayed. You would have been drowned by my darkness and illness instead."

Cris let go of Luke's hand, dug her feet in and violently shook her head in disagreement. "I don't believe it. I could've helped you. Helped you get better and see the beauty again yourself. Do you really think I'm without darkness because you left? It's practically drowning me every minute of my life. I feel like I'm constantly being pulled under by it and fighting every second just to keep my head above the water."

"I do know it, and I'm so sorry. But I can assure you, if I stayed it would've been worse. When I had a flashback, I was completely out of my mind and could have seriously hurt you physically, just as much as I was hurting you mentally. I really hope you understand I did it to make things better for you and your mom. I could've lived with my life as it was. But it wasn't fair to you guys to keep continuing life like that. I knew you would be better off with not having to carry my burden anymore. I know I was right because I have been watching you grow stronger every single day. I'm so proud of you." He grabbed Cris and hugged her, burying her face in his chest.

"You ended your pain and suffering that day, not mine! I ache beyond belief every day from missing you so much. I should've stayed inside and been there for you that day. I should have known what the sudden clarity in your eyes meant after our conversation. I've never forgiven myself for walking out the door that morning. I should have known. I should have stayed. I could've saved you."

Luke walked up and stood beside her, putting his hand at the small of her back. "I'm sorry Cris. I could never forget that day either, but I had no idea all this time you blamed yourself. I wish we never had the idea to build a cabin that day."

Her dad broke in. "Stop it you two. It was nobody's fault and it would've happened no matter what. Everything happens for a reason, remember?"

Cris pulled back and looked him in the eyes. "Damn you."

Of course, they remembered. Luke and herself both believed it. It was what got them through all the shit in their lives.

Luke took a few steps back so he could talk to them both. "You're right. It wouldn't have mattered what we did or didn't do that day. It still would've happened. Everything happened just as it was supposed to." He looked directly at Cris. "Which also includes what happened to my parents to bring me to you, and what happened to your dad when he was in the military to bring him to do what he did. It was all determined way before we were even born. The guilt trip needs to stop. There was nothing either of us could've done to change what happened to us. We ended up exactly where we were meant to be."

"Damn you too, Steele Appeal. You know I understand it, but I don't want to hear it. Why the hell am I cursed then? Why does everyone I love, which is very few, have to leave me? Why am I destined to loss and misery?"

Her dad looked back at her. "You're not. I wish you could see yourself as I've seen you your whole life, but especially the past eighteen years since I've been gone. You are the strongest person I know. Most people would've caved under these losses. Not you. You dig in and continue on. Most importantly, you still see the beauty in everything. More than people who have not had these traumatic experiences. These struggles are why you take nothing for granted. You do your best to help others, especially those who truly need it. Without all of this happening, do you think you would be trying to help and giving so much hope to homeless Veterans? Don't bother trying to answer. You wouldn't. Between your job and passion outside of work, think of how many lives you have impacted and even saved. I'm sorry you have suffered, but your suffering is what is driving you to make it so others don't. You were destined for greatness and you're doing it! I'm so damn proud of you, my sweet girl!"

For once, Cris was at a loss for words, she didn't know how to respond to what he said. She looked between the two of them. That was when she saw it. They gave each other a knowing look. While it warmed her heart to see how much they have bonded, she had no idea what the mutual look meant. She was out of their loop and didn't like it one bit.

"What the hell was that look about?"

They both eyeballed each other, clearly not sure the best way to answer. Finally, Luke spoke up.

"It's different here. You don't necessarily have to see, to hear. We both got the message though."

Cris mumbled. "Blessed are those who have not seen and yet believe."

Luke chortled. "John 20:29. There's my girl."

"Yea, whatever. Stop avoiding the question and tell me what the hell it means! You both got what message?"

Luke grabbed her hand again. "I want you to know, we're fighting for you. We've been telling them to send you back and ease up, give you a break. You have more than earned it and deserve it."

"Thank you, but no. I don't want to go back. I want to stay here, with my two-favorite people. There's nothing else for me anymore. Pete's taking care of Stormy, it'll all be okay."

Her dad put a hand on each side of her head and Luke let go of her hand to let him have this time. "Stop being so hardheaded. Damn it! You are me and for sure a Sailor's daughter, in so many ways! I am so damn proud of you baby! Keep carrying on my caring, fighting, spirit. Also, keep watching those red sunrises and sunsets and thinking of me and all the Sailor's still watching the sky morning and night. Maybe most importantly, make it top priority to have an open and candid conversation with Bolton. Oh yes, forgive yourself and let down your shield when appropriate. And one last time, stop cuttin' those damn eyes. I love you more than life, Pumpkin." He kissed her on the cheek and pulled her in for an intense hug before releasing her and backing away.

Luke grabbed her hand again and pulled her into him. "Be more open with others, especially Pete and perhaps even Tobi. Be understanding of his illness and how nothing happens by coincidence. You need to move on with your life. You're still young and can't waste it alone. Since being here, I've learned what my purpose was. I was put there to get you through your childhood and adolescence and get settled with the house and career you were meant to have. You would never have gone to the island if I hadn't come along. My job is done. You're exactly where you're supposed to be. Surrounded by the people you're supposed to be with. Don't make my life and death a waste by throwing all this away. Live out your destiny as it's supposed to be. Everything happens for a reason baby. Never forget it and do you and me, or your dad and I, a disservice. We'll always be watching over you and fighting for you. I love you so much! Now go thrive, damn it!"

Luke kissed her with more force than she had ever felt. He was smiling when he pulled back from her. Cris realized what it all meant, and the message they received. She was going to live, and they were saying goodbye for the last time.

Cris started screaming hysterically at the top of her lungs. She didn't even recognize her own voice; she had never heard it like this before. Cris couldn't lose them both again. She didn't want to leave them. She didn't want to go back home or move on. Luke was wrong, this was not his purpose, their story was not over.

"No! No! No!"

Tears started to fall through her crackling screams. She dropped to her knees continuing to scream and cry as they both walked away without looking back.

CHAPTER 35

Jeff picked up his bedding area and placed it in the tall, narrow, corner closet. He didn't know why he even bothered to make up the reclining lounge chair. Jeff was awake all night, as he knew he would be. The doctor had come in a few minutes ago and told him the surgery was done, along with a paltry update. In a nutshell, or he felt a nut sack was more appropriate in his current mood, Cris should heal back up nicely, all things considered. She would most likely be in the recovery room for another hour or two. He would give him a better update upon her return to the room. Jeff wanted to grab the doctor and demand more details, but he told himself to be patient and wait for the more detailed update.

Knowing he still had time, Jeff went down to the pantry and got thick, strong, coffee. He slowly wandered through the halls while sipping his hot cup of joe. Jeff knew he was slightly procrastinating going back to the empty room and his own unhealthy thoughts; thoughts of past and present jumbling together. None of it could be changed, nor did it matter right now. The less time he spent in the room alone, the better.

Dragging his feet on returning, Jeff decided to go to the first level and look outside to try to ground himself. The sun was making its way over the horizon in a spectacular display of orange. Jeff hoped it was a good omen since it was orange and not red this morning. He would grasp at whatever signs he could get.

Suddenly feeling mildly inspired, Jeff figured he should call his wife while he had the opportunity. Who knew what the day would hold and when he might get the chance to call again. Jeff had no intentions of leaving the room once Cris was back, whether Bryan was there or not. It was a quick check in. Since she was slightly further east than him, she did catch the beautiful sunrise, of which he was now enjoying. She told him to get back up to the room, so he didn't miss Cris in case she came back earlier than expected. Jeff agreed, told her he loved her, and they terminated the call until next time; whenever that would be.

On his trek back up to the Critical Care Unit, Jeff thought about how blessed he was to have her for a wife. She stood by him for decades, knew everything, and fully understood and supported both him and his obsession with Cris. Jeff knew not many would be so understanding of another woman and was grateful for at least the millionth time.

Feeling optimistic from both his wife and the orange sunrise, Jeff felt better as he entered Cris' room. Looking in as he went through the open glass door, he realized the room wasn't empty. Jeff snapped back to reality as he saw Bryan pacing by her empty bed.

Bryan looked up as he entered. "Oh, hey, Chief. I tried to call you, but it went straight to voicemail."

"I probably had no service in the basement. I went down to get coffee."

"I figured you were in an area out of service range, so I didn't bother to leave a message. I knew if anything had happened you would've contacted me, and you were out because there was no news yet."

He said it as a statement, but Jeff heard the questioning in his voice.

"Yes, you figured right. Steele is in recovery now. The doctor came in, but there is minimal information as of yet. He said we would know more once she gets out of recovery. I'm surprised to see you here so early."

Bryan ran his hand over his stubbled head. "Yea. I'm going to be honest with you, I didn't exactly get much sleep last night. I tried my best to clear my mind, I've never had a problem with that. But I couldn't stop seeing images of her. From the box in the ground to her current battered state, it haunted me both while I was awake and when I fell asleep. Everything was blood, hair, broken nails, matter, dirt, the shovel, the swollen, bruised and broken face. It all swirled around my mind. When I was sleeping, I kept waking up, drenched in sweat from the memories."

Jeff shook his head as he thought about Cris' accusations and his own resulting suspicions. "Bryan, you've always been honest with me, no reason to feel bad or stop now. I didn't get any sleep last night myself. I waited, very impatiently, for an update on her surgery. I'm not going to break character and lie either. When I got the uninformative report I did, I wasn't happy. I decided to get some caffeine in my sleep deprived system. After being alive to see another sunrise and talking to my wife, I am trying to be more positive and optimistic. Having said that, right now I am grateful for the news that she made it through surgery and from an appearance standpoint should heal up nicely."

Bryan shook his head, almost sorrowfully. "I agree, sir. It is good news. I will say, I'm thankful I had Stormy to keep me company. While my thoughts were not pleasant, being able to keep an arm over her and have her snuggling close, was pleasant. It was not only a great distraction to an extent, but it also made me feel like a small part of Steele was there with me."

He snickered. "I get it. You are fortunate to have her as both a distraction and a memento of Steele."

Bryan looked down at the floor for a minute, almost awkward, then looked back up. "I know you didn't have the chance to grab clean clothes, although those scrubs do look pretty comfy. If you at least want to take a shower, you are more than welcome to go over to my hotel room and use mine. Just say hi to Stormy and give her some love on your way through."

"I don't think I would be able to stop myself from loving on her if I tried. Thanks for the offer Bryan, maybe I'll take you up on it later. Right now, I want to stick around and wait for Steele's arrival."

Both of their heads and bodies snapped towards the door upon hearing a commotion coming from that direction. Jeff mumbled under his breath as they were wheeling Cris in.

"Well, speak of the angel." Jeff knew it must have been louder than he had intended when Bryan looked at him and smirked.

They both backed up towards the window so the nurses could do what they needed to do unobstructed.

"Well, this is certainly a welcome sight!"

The nurse nearest the door glanced up at them cursorily as she continued her work. "Yes, it is. She actually did very well in the recovery room and was able to be brought back faster than initially anticipated. Her oxygen level has gotten significantly better in the past hour, enough so, that we are going to keep her off the ventilator now."

Jeff released his breath. "This is fantastic news."

"Yes. While she's still not alert, this is a step in the right direction."

She removed the tube from Cris' mouth and placed a cannula in her nose. Even from a few feet away, Jeff could see her mouth looked swollen.

"Is it just me, or are her lips really red and swollen?"

"Yes, they are. It is from the tube. We will be putting medicated ointment on it until it heals up. Also, her throat will be very sore and gravely if she comes out if this enough to talk. It will all get better over time though, don't be alarmed."

Bryan cut in. "I'm just focusing on the positive. She made it through surgery fine and is breathing mostly on her own now. I'll take that."

"You guys both have the right attitude, which is good. She's all set now. We'll be monitoring her very closely for the next few hours. Hopefully, she remains stable and begins to improve so we won't have to put the breathing tube back in."

The nurses wheeled the empty bed out and slid the door closed behind themselves. Jeff felt a lump in his throat. There was still a long way to go, but this was the best news he'd had in days, shit, maybe even weeks. He noticed Bryan had goosebumps on his arms. He knew they must be feeling the same way.

Jeff began walking towards her, pulling the dog tags out of his pocket along the way. He leaned over her bed again and gingerly put them back around her neck. He spoke softly as he finished it, "There ya go, Cris. You're complete again."

Standing back up, he noticed Bryan had come alongside the bed. His brow was furrowed, and lips were slightly pursed. He clearly wanted to know the meaning and purpose of the dog tags. Jeff simply shook his head once and held up his hand.

"Now is not the time. Besides that, it's not my story to tell."

Bryan rolled his eyes but thankfully didn't say any more about it.

They were standing next to her bed and seemed to be in sync with their thoughts otherwise. Knowing Cris couldn't see them, they were gawking at her bandaged head, along with her swollen, bruised face and newly red swollen lips, when the doctor quietly appeared.

"Good morning, gentleman."

"Good morning, sir"

"Good morning, doctor."

He came over and stood on her left side of the bed. "It's good to see her without that tube in her mouth. Progress."

Jeff smiled. "Yes, we're very happy about it."

"So, as I told you earlier, Mr. Bolton, the surgery went well, and I expect the area will heal up quite nicely. We reconstructed the skull using titanium mesh. I know it's not pretty right now, but I assure you, once the hair grows back it won't be noticeable. Perhaps slightly so if she pulls it back."

Bryan held up his pointer finger. "Titanium mesh. So, what are the potential effects down the road from this?"

"Minimal to none. Titanium is a generally safe metal to implant and because of its location, we do not have to worry about frictional wear. It's extremely rare, but it has happened in a few cases where there could be mildly elevated levels of titanium in the lungs or regional lymph nodes. But again, I cannot stress enough how low of a risk this is. Nevertheless, I'll make sure she is tested regularly over the next few years. Providing we get the opportunity."

"What about things like imaging, or security metal detectors?"

"Titanium has non-magnetic properties. A security metal detector with imaging may pick it up. It will be obvious what it is on the image and all she will need to do is lift and part her hair to show them the scar. From an imaging and quality standpoint, titanium also has the least amount of artifact and there is no deflection or temperature changes. There should be no effects from this on all aspects."

"That's good. Thank you."

The doctor leaned across her bed to the right side of her face and pointed along the upper part of her cheekbone line.

"Coming into her face area here will have some significant scarring, there are some hairline fractures but the bone structure itself is intact. A plastic surgeon will be able to help reduce the scarring."

Jeff inadvertently snorted. "I don't see her agreeing to plastic surgery, that might be interesting."

"Well, it would be unfortunate, but it is her choice. So, as far as the injuries to the brain itself, we will need to do more imaging after the swelling goes down, which should be happening much quicker now since the surgery. I do not expect any issues from the depressed fracture repair itself. I was able to remove all of the bone fragments and reconstruct it successfully. The main concerns right now are any brain damage we couldn't see from the depressed fracture, the bruising from the sloshing after the impacts, and the atrophy as a result of the seizures. We will also double check the damage from the lack of oxygen, but it appeared to be minor previously, so it's not as much of a concern. In general, the antibiotics will take care of all of the infection. The fact her oxygen level has gotten better since the surgery, in conjunction with relieving the pressure in her head, I'm hopeful we will begin to see improvements in all of her vitals, and cognizance. Until this starts to happen, and we can get a reaction from her eyes, we are still keeping her listed as critical condition."

Jeff interrupted when he took a breath. "But you do expect her to come out of this?"

"I cannot say with certainty right now. The increased breathing on her own is a very hopeful sign. But, until I can get some reactions out of her, I will not stand here and make guesses. I've seen too many cases where they don't come out of it, and we don't always understand why. Again, I remain hopeful. Do you have any other questions at this time?"

They both shook their heads.

"Okay then. I am going to brief Dr. Adkins on the surgery and test results. If you remember, he was the doctor in charge when she was brought in yesterday, so he is already familiar with her case. Thank you both for your patience in waiting for the results. We'll keep you updated."

"Thank you, doctor."

He nodded his head before turning on his heels to walk out.

Bryan crossed his arms over his chest. "Well, that was hopeful and despairing all at the same time. There's still so many damn uncertainties."

"No shit. I always feel like my head is spinning and I have more questions than answers after they leave the room and my head comes to a stop."

"Well, all we can do is go by what we are seeing. Right now, I am seeing oxygen in a normal nose tube instead of the ventilator breathing through a big tube in her mouth. I see progress and I see her getting out of that bed and home soon."

"I agree. She's too stubborn to keep down anyways. The doctors don't know that, so they're at a disadvantage."

"In all seriousness, I have been thinking a lot about Stormy. I'm really not sure what would be better for her after this. To stay in her house for a little bit, or just take her right to my place. I'm not sure I can stay in the house without Steele there. I had a hard-enough time just getting Stormy and my few belongings before coming here. It's so empty, and just wrong without her."

Jeff didn't know how to answer, he had no advice. But he did tip his head towards Cris and kept nodding it in her direction as he raised his eyebrows and shot Bryan a look.

"Steele will be there, so you don't have to worry about it. You may need to help with Stormy for a little bit, but the house certainly won't be empty."

Jeff was trying to give him a clear hint with a silent reminder to keep it positive. The conversation was turning in the wrong direction and they needed to straighten the ship back out.

He turned and looked at Cris' face. Jeff was shocked to see tears running down her cheeks. His stomach felt sick realizing she must be crying from the pain, even in her unresponsive form she must still feel it. Jeff knew it must be bad.

"Bryan, go get the nurse, please! I think she's in pain."

Bryan looked at the tears falling, and his eyes got wide. He turned and rushed to her nurse outside the door.

Jeff grabbed a tissue and wiped her face where the tears ran down. "It'll be okay, Cris. I'm here and fighting for you. The nurse will be right here."

The nurse came into the room, with Bryan on her ass. "What's wrong?"

"I think she's in pain, she's crying. Is she on any pain medicine after the surgery?"

"Yes, sir. She is on a heavy dose of pain meds and I know it is disturbing, but I assure you, she's not crying or in pain. She's still incoherent; she can't feel anything. It's probably the oxygen. It can be very drying to the eyes and make them water. I'll put in for some eye drops, which will help stop the watering."

Jeff scowled but tried to remain professional. He needed them on his, and therefore, Cris' side.

"Thank you, ma'am."

"No problem." She turned and went back to her station just outside the door. Jeff assumed the nurse was being true to her word and putting in the request for eye drops.

Bryan stood on the opposite side of the bed. "Hopefully she is right."

Jeff didn't believe it. While partially ignoring Bryan, he answered him indirectly as he turned his attention back to Cris, setting his hand on top of hers.

"Don't worry, I know she's full of shit and it's not from the oxygen. I just don't want to piss them off. We need them to be fighting for you too. I know you're crying; I just don't know why. Are you up there watching and sad at what has happened? Are you really in pain? Can you actually feel it? Was it the mention of Stormy? I'm sorry, I'm trying very hard to understand and figure it out so I can help you."

He felt her hand faintly twitch under his, he would swear to it. Jeff swiftly looked up to her face. Nothing had changed. It was still unmoving. Eyes still closed and no facial movements what so ever. Bryan also showed no indication of seeing anything.

Jeff didn't care what the nurse said. He knew it wasn't from dry eyes, Cris was crying for some reason. When he thought about it, as much as he hated to see her tears, he was thrilled. Jeff was convinced it was another sign and response from her, and as he grabbed another tissue and wiped the tears from her cheeks again, he knew he wasn't going to let anyone influence him otherwise.

CHAPTER 36

Cris was still hunched on her knees, tears streaming down her cheeks. Both men were long out of sight now, but she was refusing to leave. She didn't know how long she'd been sitting there staring into the empty space, and she really didn't care. What snapped her to some form of reality was a sudden, unearthly force, pushing her in the opposite direction of where she had watched her men, and her whole life, walk away to. Cris stood up and dug her heels in, fighting the driving force. She wasn't leaving, and it was going to take a hell of a lot more than this to make her. Eventually, the pushing feeling stopped, and Cris started to feel victorious, knowing her stubbornness had paid off. That was when the bright light came blinding back. It was instantly followed by an even brighter flash. The flash was as quick as a lightning strike before she was submerged in a black void. The whole transition must have taken less than ten seconds.

Cris sat down hoping she was still oriented correctly, facing the direction they had gone, as she dried her tears, straightened her back and gritted her teeth. She knew that if she waited long enough, they would come back and rescue her. Besides, darkness was her best friend, it wasn't going to scare her off. Cris was ready to shake hands with her demons again.

Time was certainly different here and she had no concept of the real amount of time passing. But Cris knew by the fragments of her own encounters, along with the images she had been seeing, time was moving much faster and she was only experiencing things in slow, disjointed snippets.

Disrupted from her time lapse thoughts, Cris suddenly felt violated. She felt something go into her nose, followed by an initial throat tickle, which quickly turned to a burn and then a pain. It felt like something ripping through her throat. Cris instinctively put her hands up to her throat as she heard a woman talking about her breathing better on her own. She heard Chief and this woman talking about her lips and mouth being swollen. It was so surreal. She felt like her lips hurt, but when she put her hand to her mouth, everything felt normal, just like her throat had when she touched it. Cris felt like she had finally lost what little was left of her mind.

Next, Cris saw and felt Chief put the dog tags back on her. Like before, even though they had been on all along, she still felt more complete somehow. Which was bizarre. She heard Chief tell Pete it wasn't the time or his story to tell. Cris had to assume there was an exchange between them of some sort over the dog tags and she was thankful for Chief's response, as well as, Pete's apparent acceptance of the answer.

Feeling herself starting to go soft thinking about their love and kindness for her, Cris quickly snapped herself back in line. This was her place now, not there. Any minute, one, or both, of her men would be appearing, grabbing her hand through the darkness to pull her out of it.

The anchor was aweigh on her hand holding illusion as she heard another unfamiliar voice. A male this time. Cris now saw the man in a white coat come in and stand next to her.

He talked about her and her head, face, and brain. She heard Pete and Chief cutting in asking questions. While Cris understood what was being said, as far as she was concerned, it was a bunch of mumbo jumbo which she tried to tune out. Cris didn't want to hear it. She wasn't going back, so it didn't matter. The doctor suddenly reached across her face and touched her cheek. She actually felt it and didn't like it one bit. Cris was pissed off even more because she couldn't stop these useless images from coming. They were taking away from what she really wanted to see; her dad and Luke. She glared into the black nothingness, snarling her lips and squinting her eyes defiantly.

"Stop with the bullshit and show me what's important!"

Staring rebelliously into the dark, Cris was answered by another flash. The images started up again as real as the darkness currently shrouding her, which lit her fuse even more. She had no choice but to watch and listen as Pete stood there, with his arms across his chest. He told Chief he didn't know what would be better for Stormy, to stay in the house with her for a little bit or take her to his place. He wasn't sure he could stay there without her. He had a hard time getting Stormy and his belongings without her being there. *Get used to it because that's your future with Stormy.*

Cris felt further justified in staying since she had more confirmation Pete was going to take care of Stormy. Just like she knew he would when she was dying in that box, and like she had told her dad and Luke. There was absolutely no reason for her to go back.

She heard Chief say something about how stubborn she was, and she couldn't be kept down. *That's right, I am stubborn, and I won't be leaving here.* She thought of Stormy, Luke, and her dad. As hard as she tried to hold it back and keep the fighting spirit, she started silently crying again.

Cris felt something which was more than a tear touch her face. It was proceeded by seeing Chief wiping the tears from her cheek.

"Don't worry, I know she's full of shit and it's not from the oxygen. I just don't want to piss them off. We need them to be fighting for you too. I know you're crying; I just don't know why. Are you up there watching and sad at what has happened? Are you really in pain? Can you actually feel it? Was it the mention of Stormy? I'm sorry, I'm trying very hard to understand and figure it out, so I can help you."

Chief rested his hand on top of hers, and while still crying and annoyed at everything, Cris lifted her hand up as if she could shoo his away. She curled up in the darkness continuing to cry as her dad and Luke continued to not come back to her.

"Why aren't you coming back? Stop it! This isn't funny, I'm getting really pissed! I'm not going back, so get your asses back here!" Her voice quieted as tears fell harder and she desperately began to plead. "Please… Please."

She finally closed her eyes as the tears continued to fall from them. The images in her mind stopped at some point, and Cris welcomed the same darkness inside that cloaked her on the outside. Opening her eyes, Cris realized she must've cried herself to sleep. She again had no idea how long it had been, but it didn't matter. Her mission was still the same. Sit and wait for them to come and get her. Tears dried and newly refocused, Cris peeled her lips back, smiling in the darkness. She sat there motionless, staring into the dark nothingness for what felt like minutes, but somehow, innately, she knew it must have been hours.

Cris suddenly felt Pete's hand over hers and she lowered her right eyebrow, as she raised her left. What the hell was he doing?

"Leave me alone, damn it!" Cris felt silly as she pulled her hand back, knowing it was only a vision.

Then, Cris heard him tell her they got her neighbor, Tobi. Even knowing it was blackness, instinctively, Cris' eyes went wide. She remembered Luke saying to move on and maybe even forgive Tobi. Cris had no idea who he was talking about. She didn't care then because she wasn't going home so it didn't matter. While Cris was still dead set she wasn't going back, she was also shocked to find out this is who Tobi was. Did Luke really expect her to forgive this piece of shit? She was in complete and utter shock. Cris heard Pete say something else, but it was all a fuzzy blur.

Cris felt him touch the chain around her neck at some point. She furrowed her brows. How dare he touch it? Cris reached up and felt them around her neck herself and realized it wasn't real. She was here, with the dog tags around her neck.

"Damn you, Luke! Why aren't you here explaining these things, since you said you think you understand? Enlighten me. Please!"

She found herself getting more aggravated that they weren't coming as she stared into the un-answering, seemingly condescending abyss. Trying to calm and refocus herself and her anger, Cris closed her eyes. She kept hearing conversations with both Pete and Chief intermittently. She was blowing them off and trying her best to tune them out.

Cris couldn't block out Chief talking about a red sky sunset. Her eyes got wide as her anger got even hotter. How could he possibly know she watched the color of the skies at night and morning, shit, since she was a child?! Who the hell did he think he was talking so openly about something so personal and emotional to her?

Cris shook her head. It didn't matter anymore. Nothing did. She wasn't going back so there were no more cares, worries or anxieties about what he knows, how he knows it, or even who he tells.

"Not my problem."

Cris continued her watch in the black hole. The anger was subsiding some but was being replaced with something worse. As she stared into the silent, black abyss Cris felt herself falling into a deeper depression and obvious madness the longer it took waiting for them to come back for her.

She thought perhaps she had fallen asleep again. She really couldn't tell. It was all black either way. Cris kept hearing Pete and Chief talking but continued to do her best to pay no attention. She couldn't tell if she was dreaming about them or having the visions. It felt a little different this time because she was mostly just hearing them in the darkness, an occasional glimpse, but not like the visions had been before. Whatever it was really didn't matter. It was all dark and she felt her inside growing even darker than the vast blackness she was physically shrouded in. With time awareness being off, Cris didn't know how long it had been since her men walked away. She did know they hadn't returned, and her madness was probably as high as it could go and would not be undone. Her thought was affirmed when she suddenly saw Stormy appear. Cris knew she had reached the point of no return but welcomed it with Stormy by her side.

She finally fully succumbed to the demons she had been fighting off all these years and entered willingly into the darkness as she felt Stormy licking her hand. Cris couldn't hold back her smile. Her heart warmed as Stormy came clearly into her vision. She was really there. Her throat hurt like hell and was gravelly as she smiled wider and spoke.

"Hey, baby."

CHAPTER 37

Pete returned to the hospital at the butt crack of dawn after another restless night's sleep. Last night's no sleep feature presentation alternated between how Cris was, how they found her and how she is presently. The glass door to enter her room was shut, but the curtain was open, so he could still see in. Chief had his chair pulled up next to her bed. His head was resting on the edge of it. He looked like he was sleeping, but Pete had a feeling he was categorically awake and desperately trying to catch some sleep.

His presumption was affirmed when he silently opened the door and Chief's head immediately snapped up at attention. He grabbed his glasses off the end of her bed and put them on. He looked at Pete then back to the window behind him.

"Shit, Bryan. It isn't even daylight yet."

"Does it matter? When you can't shut your mind off day or night is of little significance."

"Aye." Chief straightened and shook his head. "You have a point there, and I can't disagree."

"Anything new since I left last night?"

"Nothing obvious. I will say though, call me crazy, but I'm convinced she flinched or moved a few times last night."

Pete felt his heart rate increase and heat come to his face. "Really?"

"Yea. I told the night nurse when he came in for his checks every few hours. He just made a *hmm* type sound and didn't say anything. I'm not sure if he didn't believe me, or he did but didn't want to give false hope or wrong information. Either way, I'm positive of what I saw, unless I'm losing my mind and don't realize it, which I won't entirely rule out. No matter what, I'm taking it as a positive sign, holding onto it and watching for more, for dear life."

"You're not losing it. I agree it's gotta be a good thing. How about the tears? Anymore since they put the drops in her eyes last night?"

"Since they put the drops in her eyes? Yes. But for the past 6 or so hours? No. Which to me just confirms my initial assumption or start of the neurosis, she was actually crying for some reason. It wasn't dry eyes from the oxygen, she was crying. I don't know why it stopped. Maybe the pain medicine kicked in, maybe whatever was initially making her cry was no longer an issue. I don't know. I do know, I didn't bother to say anything about it. I need to be smart about what I do, and don't say."

"Agreed."

Impulsively, Pete smacked Chief's arm and pointed to Cris as her mouth looked like it was sneering. His eyes were fixated and unblinking.

He whispered. "You mean like that?"

Chief seemed to be in the same unblinking state of mind. "Yep. Like that."

"Damn, that smile almost looks like she's defiant, like she's being stubborn about something. If you can imagine that." Pete chuckled, knowing it was pretty much the only way she rolled.

"Yea. It screams not only defiance but also an unspoken power to something. My worry is, what?"

Pete agreed with the assessment but didn't want to start thinking about it. It could be so many different things with Cris, and he was really trying to stay positive, at least around her. Shit, it was hard.

"Let's be thankful we are seeing facial expressions. It's more than we had yesterday."

"Yes, it is."

Chief got up and began cleaning up his useless sleeping accessories. He placed his pillow and folded blankets in the tall corner cupboard, then moved his chair into the corner, nearby the bed. Pete snickered to himself as he returned to the side of the bed and thought *his chores are done for the day*.

"I'm going down to the pantry and grab some shitty coffee. Care for a cup?"

Pete chortled. "Yea, why not? Make it black with some sugar, please. Thanks."

"Okay. I'll be back in a few minutes."

"Take your time, get some air if you need it. I'll be here."

"Thanks, Bryan. I'll see you in a few."

Pete mumbled under his breath as he watched Chief open and close the door, nodding to the nurse sitting there before he turned away. "I have no doubt you will."

He looked back to Cris, as he pulled a chair up next to her bed. His heart hurt for her. Cris still had the demented smile on her face and he wondered what was going on in her incomprehensible mind. As he remained focused on her face, he gently placed his right hand over hers which was currently by her side. Pete watched in amazement as she put her left eyebrow up and held it there for more than a few seconds. The next thing he knew, she pulled her hand out from under his, from resting on the bed by her side, to on top of her abdomen.

Pete about dropped his jaw. He would swear Cris moved her hand away because he put his there. The timing was too uncanny. Now he felt like the defiance in her smile was towards him. Did Cris still think he was the killer? She must know who it was. She must have seen him. But… What if she didn't? The thought began to crush him. Pete knew he couldn't go down that road, he had to stay positive around her. He had to think of what to say to make her understand, but yet be positive. It seemed impossible.

He reached over and gently brushed his thumb over her left cheek. "Hey, Cris. You know we got him, right? Your neighbor, Tobi? I found him in the woods nearby. He confessed, and I promise you, he'll pay for what he did to you and Luke."

Pete stopped talking as he was suddenly so shocked, he almost fell out of his chair when Cris opened her eyes. He somehow remained calm as he stood up and leaned over her.

"Hi, Cris. I'm right here. You're not alone."

She glanced at him, but there was not an ounce of recognition coming from her eyes. Her head rolled side to side for a few seconds before she closed her eyes another time. Her facial expression was blank again. No more sneering or defiance in it. Pete knew he had lost her.

His heart was still racing as he stood there not knowing what to do. Pete wanted to rush out and tell the nurse but remembering what Chief just told him along with the nurses' responses, he thought better of it. He tried to think of what else he could say or do to bring her back again. Nothing was coming to mind, it felt like a blank slate. Yet another new uncharacteristic experience to add to his list since this all began less than two weeks ago.

He looked at the ball chain around her neck, with the important end disappearing underneath her robe. Pete touched the chain draped over her collar bone, watching it rise and fall with her breathing. *I wish you would realize it's okay to open up. I wish I knew why you can't. I wish you would trust me. Did Chief find out things when he hired you and it's how he knows whatever he does? I have no idea what happened to you, but I'm so sorry! No one should ever have to feel so guarded.*

Pete looked up and saw her brow was creased. He fleetingly wondered how long it had been like that. Then, he really didn't care. It was more movement and response. As much as he hurt for her, he couldn't hold back his smile. He stayed focused on her face as he removed his hand. He was not disappointed. Just like he theorized, Cris' brow became relaxed again. He was so focused on her face, he never heard Chief come back in. Another new anomalous attribute as of late.

"Everything okay, Bryan?"

Pete looked up, slightly embarrassed about being so off his game. "Yea. I think it's going to be okay."

"Really? You seem so sure, but the way you are hovering over her makes me wonder otherwise."

"We had a few exchanges. Well, it was only partially reciprocated. She seemed to have no idea she was participating, or even here."

Looking concerned, or perhaps confused, Chief walked over to the side of the bed and handed Pete his coffee. "What the fuck are you talking about?"

Feeling the anxiety rise, another nuance, Pete slurped a sip of the steaming black swill. "Well, it started when I put my hand over the top of hers. She made a face and then pulled her hand away. I began to wonder if she still blamed me and thought I was really the killer. I didn't believe it but trying to engage her and stay positive, I told her we found the killer and that Tobi confessed. Here's where it gets really good. Somehow, I managed to stay calm. She opened her eyes and looked at me."

Chief cut him off. "She opened her eyes?!"

"Yes! But I will say, there was no recognition. She looked right at me, but clearly had no idea who I was, or that she even knew me at all. She fell right back to sleep. The previous blank face resumed. Then I touched her chain…"

Chief's neck got red. "You did what?"

"I touched her chain. Here, by her collar bone. I didn't move it, just touched it with my fingertips. Anyway, the blank face was taken over by the usual furrowed brow. Just to see what would happen, I moved my hand and watched her face. She relaxed again. She can feel us, which means I'm sure she can hear us too. She may not be coherent yet, but these are all great signs as far as I'm concerned."

Pete felt he rambled on forever. He was not normally much of a talker. He also wasn't sure what to think as Chief stood there stoically, holding his coffee, looking at Cris. Was he still upset because he touched her chain? If so, why? He didn't violate her or her privacy in any way. Was he shocked at what had happened while he was gone the short time? Perhaps upset with himself for missing it?

Chief finally shifted his coffee cup from his right hand to his left and then squeezed her right forearm in his right hand.

"Good morning, Cris."

They both watched as her head moved, almost imperceptibly, towards him. Chief looked at him and they both grinned. Pete knew they had both witnessed the slight movement.

Chief turned his attention back to Cris and continued. "It's supposed to be another beautiful day on the island today. It would be a great one for a run on the beach, especially tonight for the sunset as the temperatures cool down."

Pete knew what Chief was doing. Talking about things Cris loved, staying positive. He didn't think Cris realized she wasn't home on the island right now, so that part was of little importance in the grand scheme of things.

Chief kept talking, slowly, patiently. "I bet it will be a red sunset tonight. I just have a feeling."

Without moving any part of her body, Cris again opened her eyes. If they hadn't already been looking at her face for reactions, they quite possibly would have missed it. She looked at Chief this time. Pete noticed there was still no recognition in her eyes. Cris looked briefly around the room with those empty, haunted eyes. Pete would still guess she wasn't actually seeing anything in this room. Just like his experience a short time ago, it was short lived as Cris just as quickly closed her eyes again.

Pete looked at Chief, who seemed beside himself. He understood exactly how he was feeling right now. He had just been there too. Trying not to say too much with Cris right there, but wanting to confirm his own suspicions, he thought of what to say.

He tipped his head towards Cris. "Nobody home, right?"

Chief shook his head in agreement as he took off his glasses and wiped his eyes and forehead.

Pete nodded. "It's just like it was before. Like I said though, it's all good."

Chief replaced his glasses. "Yes, it is."

Pete kept coming back to his recurring thoughts of Stormy. Something inside of him told him the time was now.

"Ever since I hit the road to drive up here, I've been thinking."

"I'm sure you have."

"Well, yea, but specifically, I've been thinking about Stormy and how I really think she might be beneficial to Cris coming out of this."

"Good luck with that."

"Seriously. I think if Stormy gave her some kisses, especially since she can obviously feel us, it might really help."

"Look, Bryan, I'm not disagreeing with you. On the contrary, I think it's a great idea and worth the try. I'm just saying good luck getting the hospital staff to allow it."

Pete looked out the door. Cris' nurse was sitting at her station and there was one other nurse at the unit's nurses' station.

"Well, no time like the present. Wish me luck."

"Good luck; you're gonna need it."

Pete opened the door and being unsure of Cris' nurse, he decided to start with the one at the main nurses' station. He knew he had to try to use some charm, but it was so out of his character, he had no idea how to actually do it. He almost wished he paid more attention to Campbell with her constant flirting.

He leaned over and tried to make his eyes soft. He figured he probably looked more like an injured animal than anything cute and charming. Pete was appreciative when she smiled at him and at least looked sympathetic.

"Is there something I can help you with, honey?"

Pete leaned closer and spoke low. "Well, I hope so. I have an idea I think, no, I know deep down, will really be beneficial to Mrs. Steele."

He proceeded to tell her about Stormy being next door and he knew if anything could help bring Cris around, it would be her. The nurse sat listening and appeared to be interested at least. He suddenly felt an arm touch his and he looked over to see Cris' nurse had come along to join the discussion. He was afraid she would shut him down. Now, he had to convince two of them and he didn't know how to schmooze one of them, much less two.

"Sorry, I couldn't help but overhear. Okay, so I was eavesdropping since you were talking about my patient. I fully believe in the power of healing through dogs. Many hospitals have comfort dogs come to patient's rooms now for just this reason. Research on this subject has been very positive thus far."

Pete let out a breath and smiled at her. "I completely agree, thank you!"

The other nurse spoke up. "Well, dogs aren't allowed in this hospital yet."

Pete's heart dropped. The nurse he thought would be the more open one was pushing a brick wall in front of him. He saw her raise one side of her lip into a smile.

"It's a good thing her room is right across from the stairwell."

Pete felt his eyes go soft naturally this time as his heart melted. He smiled between both of them as they began formulating the plan.

"From 2:00-3:00 is the best time when there are the least amount of people milling around here."

"There's cameras, but they only go back and look at them if there's a reason. Nobody actually monitors them all day."

They looked directly at him now, then Cris' nurse spoke, "You'll have to bring her up through the back door, up the stairwell and across the hall into Mrs. Steele's room. When I give the "all clear" signal, you run over with her."

Pete felt his eyes get watery as he smiled at them. "I cannot thank you guys enough!"

They batted their eyes back at him as they finished the details. They scheduled to meet him at the bottom floor and use the employee entrance and stairways. It could only be for a few minutes and Stormy would have to go back.

He walked back in to let Chief know. Pete saw him standing there smiling and shaking his head.

"I saw you batting your blue eyes at the nurses. You know, you might just go to hell for that."

Pete chuckled. "If this works, it will be worth going to hell for."

They stood around for the next few hours making small talk among themselves and one-sided to Cris. She had a few more episodes of facial expressions or movements, faintly squeezing a hand, opening her eyes, and looking around blankly a little bit.

When it got close to 2:00, Pete nodded to the nurses as he left. He walked back to the hotel as fast as he reasonably could without drawing attention. He grabbed Stormy quickly, let her go to the bathroom and made a beeline for the back entrance of the hospital. His heart was racing with adrenaline, hoping not to get caught and sent away and also hoping this would work like his gut was telling him it would.

He was thankful to see the nurse standing outside the door as planned. Once they went through it, Pete picked Stormy up and carried her so her claws wouldn't make noise on the stairs. He wasn't so sure he wouldn't be panting before they reached the top, she was a solid dog. The nurse quietly led the way up the staircase, listening with each step. They reached their level without any obstacles. She turned around and raised her finger, indicating for him to wait. She cracked the door and the other nurse standing there gave a thumbs up indicating it was all clear. The nurse opened the door all the way and Pete rushed across the hall and through the open door. The nurse came in right behind him and before he had Stormy on the floor, she had already shut the door to the room and closed the curtains. She stood off to the side by the door listening for cues from the other nurse indicating they might get busted.

Stormy put her ears back and tail between her legs as she looked around. Chief gave her a quick and excited pet. Pete caught his breath and called her to the bed. Stormy's nose was twitching, she smelled her mama. She gently put her front paws on the side of the bed and sniffed even more. Then she put her nose on Cris' hand and licked it.

Cris smiled then opened her eyes. She looked right at Stormy. Pete could see the clarity in them this time and the lump in his throat was almost impossible to keep down.

Cris spoke with an almost inaudible, gravelly voice, "Hey, baby."

She still had a smile on her face as she closed her eyes again. Chief pulled Stormy down and began hugging her.

"You're a good girl, Stormy!"

Pete saw a wet line run down Chief's face and felt the same one on his own cheek. He looked over at the nurse, still standing guard as she wiped her eyes.

Pete mouthed to her, "Thank you!"

She nodded her head in response. It seemed none of them were capable of talking right now. He knew his plan was complete, it had served the purpose to the extent that it was going to.

"C'mon, Stormy. Let's go back to the room, girl. We'll take a little walk first, then I'll spend more time with you and get you some food and some extra treats. You've been alone in there way too long."

Chief gave her another pat. "See ya later, Stormy. You're such a good girl!"

Pete grabbed her leash. "I'll be back in a bit after I've spent some quality time with her. Please call me if anything changes here in the meantime."

"You know I will. Good job with this Bryan, although I'm not surprised."

"Thanks, sir."

Knowing Chief would call him if anything changed with Cris, Pete was focused on spoiling Stormy for a bit. She may have just been the hero of the day and with the vision of Cris and hearing her rough voice speak those two words, Pete was on cloud nine.

CHAPTER 38

Her eyes lazily began letting in some light as they slowly opened. Cris felt the brightness pierce through her eyes and her head. She ignored it as she tried to figure out where she was. Flashes of Luke and her dad came slicing through her mind, but she didn't see them anywhere in this room. She struggled to see through eyes which felt like they were slits. Her right eye felt like her vision was occluded. Cris felt like a newborn baby looking around the unfamiliar room. The light and disorientation physically hurt her head, she wanted to close her eyes again. Until. Cris saw a man standing next to her bed. He appeared to know her. She felt her eyes get a little wider and her body began to sweat. Who was this stranger and what did he want with her?

"Hey, Cris. It's okay, you're going to be okay. I'll be right here; I'm not leaving you."

He knew her name. Something about him was familiar. Was it his face or his voice? What it was, was all too much. Cris left the thoughts unfinished as she drifted back into the comforts of darkness.

Flashes came back again. This time Cris knew all the characters. Her dad coming off the ship for the last time. Meeting Luke and his crooked smile in the field. Defending them on the playground. Dodging the flying objects which became projectiles at loud noises or flashing lights. Escaping the realities of their lives with Luke all day. Hopping the trains. Sitting on her dad's lap. Watching him drink his Sailor companion as he spoke, saying goodbye, she again wished she had known it at the time. Building the first and last cabin in her backyard. She heard a loud shot and in a dual image saw both her dad and Luke's bloody heads. Cris felt her body jump as her eyes flew open.

There was that man again in this foreign room, rubbing the top of her head. "It's okay Cris. I think you just had a bad dream."

Cris cocked her head and looked at him confused. More recent images came to mind. Their wedding, buying the house, her job. She spoke slowly and lazily, her mouth like cotton. It felt like she was drugged. Her throat burned and felt raw as she tried to speak. Cris barely heard the words come out they were so quiet. The pain in her throat and mouth were so bad she brought her hand up to it and fought back tears as she slurred her thick words.

"You're my boss. Sorry. I feel like I can only remember fragments of things right now. The traumatic shit seems to be fully intact."

Cris thought she saw and heard her boss saying something, but she was too tired and unable to fight it. She let her head fall to the side and her eyes close. Cris watched as she was taking Luke to the river for the first time. His eyes were wide hopping over the shit stream. Then, he slipped going down the hill covered with black shards from river worn rocks and taking her out with him. He was mortified but she thought it was hilarious. They skipped rocks and played in the caves. It was also the first day he met her dad. She remembered trying to save him on the first day of school and told him to ignore her, so he could have a chance to make some friends.

He responded by pushing her aside with his little hips, so he could sit with her on the bus. Luke trying to stand up to the bullies by Cris' side, his poor gentle soul. Then, pulling Cris off every time she finished the job. Sitting in the grass, trying to calm her and get her to breathe slowly. Not moving from her back yard when she ran inside after hearing the gunshot. His grandmother having to come and drag him away. Luke coming every day trying to get her to come to the door so he could help her. Two lost old souls getting through the world with each other.

When she woke up again, Cris saw her boss still standing next to her. She remembered his name this time. Chief Bolton. She still didn't know where she was or why, but this time she felt weighed down or restrained. Cris desperately tried to stay awake, to get a grasp on what was going on. Cris felt like it was too much brain activity. She had to close her eyes to all the lights and stimulus assaulting her. Still fighting to stay awake even though her eyes were closed, Cris did hear Chief talking to someone about her.

"She's opened her eyes a few times, has looked around some. She spoke once, it was rough, I could barely hear her. She remembered I'm her boss, but I don't believe she remembers my name. It is very short each time before falling back to sleep, but it is happening more often, so it's good. I think you're fine to keep spoiling her for a while, I just wanted to keep you updated and I will let you know if anything else changes or happens...."

As much as Cris tried to stay awake and listen to make sense of the conversation, she fell back asleep. Cris watched as her mom walked in with the mail. Letters from her dad! Her mom crying tears of joy because her letter said he was not re-enlisting. The next time he came home, it would be for good. They had packed and prepared for their final move.

Dad's ship came in, the last time they would see him lined by the rail as they pulled into port. He dropped his sea bag and scooped her up. He said, "See ya soon," to lots of his shipmates before leaving. Soon after, they moved and bought a house where Dad had some other shipmates to be nearby. There were get-togethers and Cris enjoyed playing with the other kids, even though they weren't her age. She noticed her dad drinking Sailor Jerry a lot, but thought it was funny because it was a Sailor. Besides that, she was just happy to go play. He stopped hanging out with his friends and instead stayed home all day since nobody would hire him. His only other hangout was the bar not far from the house. Many nights, after a call from the bartender Joe, a friend of his with a distinctive truck exhaust would bring dad home. The fourth of July was a drinking celebration during the day and a war zone in their house at dark when the fireworks started. Flashing Christmas lights, thunder, or any loud noises resulted in shouting and any objects in reach being thrown at unseen enemies. The same truck exhaust coming to the rescue. A few years in, her dad having her sit on his lap to give her an odd early morning pep talk, with his amber companion by his side. His eyes as clear as she had seen them in years as he told her he loved her as she was walking out the door. The resounding sound of the fateful shot soon after. The blood trailing into the house from her thumb she had just smashed as she ran in. The metallic smell that filled her nostrils and she could never forget. The letters on the end stand, with his dog tags draped over hers, spattered in blood. Screaming, crying, throwing herself on top of him. Covered in his blood. Sitting in his room out of her mind, staring at the empty bed. The man with the truck, carrying her into bed that night. Her mom getting ready to throw his glass across the room and Cris standing in front of her, ready to take the blow if necessary and begging her not to break it. Her mom thrusting it roughly into her hand. Then, finally reading his letter to her - "Anchors Aweigh, baby."

"Fair winds and following seas, Daddy."

Cris startled herself awake when she felt the burn in her throat as she was actually saying the words aloud. She remembered enough now to feel embarrassed to have said it in front of Chief. She looked at him and saw tears in his eyes. She wondered if she had said more. Those words alone should not be enough to evoke this kind of emotion from him.

Some clarity was beginning to come to her. Cris looked around again and realized she was in a hospital bed, confined by wires running to machines. She remembered what happened to Luke, going to Jasper with Campbell, all the accusations in between, and then for the most part what happened to her. Although the details were still spotty, Cris got the gist of why she was here. She found the button to adjust her bed and weakly pushed it, so she was sitting more upright. Sharp pain seared through her head, but she had to make herself stay awake longer and think. Figure things out and get out of here. Cris grit her teeth through the pain in her head and throat and the emotions in her soul.

"I think I'm going to take the leave you were suggesting before. I'm going to go up to Virginia and visit my dad."

He sniffed. "Cris, this is the most I've heard your voice in days. Don't worry about that right now. Rest, get better."

"Thank you, sir. I will, but right now I'm having a moment of clarity, and I'm not sure if it will be staying this time or leaving me again. I need to get this out while I have it."

"I can tell you're back. Out of nowhere, here you are! My strong, stubborn, fighting girl. If you're not confident how long your clarity will last, then let me tell you, bring some Sailor Jerry to share with your dad."

Cris felt disoriented again. She couldn't imagine how he would know about the Sailor Jerry. Then she remembered she had bought the bottle and had left it, half empty, in her office when she snuck out that night. No doubt they had gotten in there and searched the room and come across it. Once she thought a little harder about it though, she connected how the meaning of his comment was in relation to her dad, not her. Immediately, another inconceivable thought hit her like a freight train. She suddenly went from feeling confused and drugged to feeling stone cold sober. Her eyes got wide and glassy with tears at the realization and instantly it all began to come together.

Like before, she was trying to put the puzzle pieces together. The difference was, now they were beginning to fit. She thought about some of the things Chief had said recently, and their conversation he had promised they would finish up to answer those questions.

"Let's just say I have some knowledge about your childhood and leave it at that. I have compassion for you, I can't help that. I feel the need to protect you, whether you need it or not."

"I'm worried about you Steele, I cannot lose you."

"I need you to promise me you don't have a death wish."

"I don't get any personal background information from your file, I'm not privy to that. My knowledge does not come from your records, Cris. But, I have to admit, you're right, maybe a small part of my concern over a death wish does."

"You've been through a lot in just the past week alone."

"I knew you were finishing up with grad school and were almost ready to graduate. What I didn't know, but was secretly elated when I found out, was that you would apply for a job on Shine Island, come back to Luke's hometown. When I saw your name with all the other applicants... Well, let's just say you don't know the strings I had to pull to get you hired over those other, even more, well-qualified applicants."

Her head was spinning, her legs, which she couldn't feel previously, were beginning to shake. Though Cris tried to keep her protective shield up, tears fell without her control or being able to stop them. She thought she showed no other physical signs of being upset. Questions were swarming through her head. Cris had to know.

Meekly, Cris dared to ask. "Did you know Joe from the bar? Did you know my dad, Patrick? Did Joe used to call you to come pick him up?"

 If this wasn't true, Chief would have no idea who Joe was, her dad or why he would be picking him up.

His eyes welled up. "Your father would be so proud of you. You are your father's daughter through and through, right down to your red headed stubbornness."

Tears of what Cris could tell was pride and sorrow were now running down Jeff's cheeks, his glasses fogging up. All this time of keeping it bottled in and keeping watch over Cris, and she certainly hadn't made it easy the past few weeks, must've been emotionally exhausting. Now, finally, a release with the truth.

Chief leaned in and hugged her, an unbelievable squeeze, tears still silently falling. "God, Cris. I can't even look at you without seeing your father. You are his carbon copy in so many ways. Another reason you worry me so much."

Even though his hug racked her body with pain, Cris was both stunned and relieved and returned the strength of his hug to the best of her ability.

"No worries. As much as I wish I could just give up sometimes, it really isn't in my blood. It wasn't a gene that daddy carried to be handed down, it was a sickness he got cursed with that nobody understood or wanted to acknowledge back then. People called his type crazy and pushed them under the rug. *'Keep your kids and family away from that lunatic,'* they'd say." Cris silently cried harder again at the memories.

"When you get back, we'll sit and reminisce about your dad. I've been keeping tabs on your mom too, making sure she's okay. She never fully recovered either, but, like you, she is surviving, and she does have some help. Also, not like you would blab anything, but I think it would be a good idea to still keep this private. If people knew I was your surrogate father, they might take issue and cry I was playing a favoritism card."

Cris was still trying to process it all in her slow brain. "You know I wouldn't say anything."

Chief stared and shook his head. "Ah, it feels so good to be able to tell you about this. He was my best friend. I was more on the computer and electronics side of things, where your dad was more on the weapons and front line. A cannon cocker." Chief chuckled deeply.

"Ah, he had it harder than me as far as what he had to see and do. We were together since the beginning. I'm talking boot camp. Same division, everything. We became fast friends and somehow managed to stay together the whole time. Fate, I guess. It was all meant to be before we even signed our names to enlist, no doubt. Anyway, I wanted to make a career out of the Navy and get at least 20 years in, as did your dad initially. When he decided to get out after twelve years, I knew I had to be there for him. The signs were already there, which was a big reason he got out then instead of sticking it out for eight more years. Shit, I gave up my retirement and I still couldn't save him. Don't get me wrong, I don't regret I did it, not one second. What I do regret was I didn't save him like I was supposed to. I should've been there for him more. In so many ways, I still blame myself to this day."

Cris was dumbfounded. Now she knew, not only was he the saving grace to her family so many times all those years ago, but he actually blamed himself. She saw him as a saint and he was struggling to live with himself all this time.

She again thought back. "You were there after it happened, weren't you? You were the one there with my mom who came and carried me out of my dad's bloody room and put me in my own bed."

Chief cried as he shook his head. "Yes. You were lost to us, so out of your mind. I didn't think you even realized it."

"I don't think I did at the time either, but it's still buried with all the rest of the shit inside me and resurfaces on occasion. You were just a figure though, a distant voice and familiar rumble of truck exhaust. I never once could recall an image of your face."

"It's funny how the mind works. What it shows us, sometimes continuously even though we don't want it to, and also what it hides from us, even though we try so hard to see it. You know, after it happened, I made a promise to myself and your dad I would watch over you and protect you. It has consumed me since he left and has become my main objective in life. I couldn't save him directly, but I can still save him through you."

Cris had no idea how she would ever repay him for everything he had done for her dad and her family for all of his adult life, ever since he was barely an adult himself. It was beyond comprehension how your life mission could be to help a friend and his family and claim them as his own. She was really at a loss for words.

"I guess you are the true meaning of faithful to the bitter end."

Jeff looked at her and smiled, obviously knowing the true Sailor origin of the term.

"Hooyah."

Cris smiled as her eyes closed. The adrenaline rush she had been riding was gone. It was too much stimulation and she was struggling to stay awake and keep her eyes open. They had rolled shut a few times during their conversation and Cris fought to keep them opened and focus. She was fighting to open them again but there was no energy left. Hearing loud noises in the hall she told herself she should really look at see what the ruckus was. It sounded like Chief had gotten up from her bedside.

"What the hell is going on? Oh shit, I need to close the curtains!" His voice became frantic.

Cris willed her eyes open to look towards the door at Chief. Her vision was jumping as her eyes rolled trying to close again. Slow motion and dreamlike, Cris watched as bullets came through her door, shattering the glass. Chief fell, blood and bullets flew. Cris gave up and closed her eyes as she welcomed herself back home to the comforts of demons and darkness.

Get ready for the next book in the Steele series:

Remembering Steele